He'd seen her drawings and ~~~~~~~~~~~~~~~ walked into a big, airy room and ha~~~~~~~~ because he was surrounded by the most beautiful things he'd ever seen in his life. He'd simply stood stock-still and gaped, mouth open like some raw recruit watching SEALs in training.

And then Lauren had walked into the room and even her gorgeous paintings and drawings vanished from his head like smoke.

And when she spoke Jacko didn't hear a word she said.

His head was buzzing too loud.

She tried twice. He got that much. He saw her full mouth open and close and all he could think about was that mouth on his while his entire body buzzed and he got the first of many, many hard-ons that sprouted whenever he was around her.

At the third try, he tried very hard to focus and managed to grasp that she was asking him a question. *Morton, right?* He simply stared at her. *Suzanne said she'd send someone called Morton?* And at the end there was this little inflection, making it a question. And fuck him if he didn't forget his own name was Morton.

It was only when he saw the first glimmerings of fear in her eyes and she took a quick instinctive step back that he pulled his head out of his ass. And felt ashamed. Having a 240-pound thug who lifted weights daily, had a pierced nose and pierced ears, barbed wire tats around his wrists, tribal tats on a shoulder, and had spent the past fifteen years training to kill people stare at you was not a good thing. Particularly if you were a beautiful woman with a slender build alone in a space with the thug.

So he'd used every single ounce of self discipline the navy and particularly SEALs training had beaten into him and nodded and said, "Yes, Morton's my name, most folks call me Jacko, how do you do, Suzanne Huntington sent me to pick you up."

She'd just stood there, staring at him. Well, he could do something about her unease. He tapped his cell and called Midnight's wife, Suzanne. When she answered he simply handed the phone to Lauren and watched as some color came back into her face.

And when he complimented her on some of the paintings she actually blushed.

And Jacko was lost.

MIDNIGHT VENGEANCE

LISA MARIE RICE

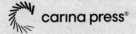
carina press®

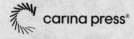

ISBN-13: 978-0-373-00288-7

Midnight Vengeance

Copyright © 2014 by Lisa Marie Rice

All rights reserved. Except for use in any review, the reproduction or utilization of this work in whole or in part in any form by any electronic, mechanical or other means, now known or hereinafter invented, including xerography, photocopying and recording, or in any information storage or retrieval system, is forbidden without the written permission of the publisher, Harlequin Enterprises Limited, 225 Duncan Mill Road, Don Mills, Ontario M3B 3K9, Canada.

This is a work of fiction. Names, characters, places and incidents are either the product of the author's imagination or are used fictitiously, and any resemblance to actual persons, living or dead, business establishments, events or locales is entirely coincidental.

This edition published by arrangement with Harlequin Books S.A.

® and ™ are trademarks of the publisher. Trademarks indicated with ® are registered in the United States Patent and Trademark Office, the Canadian Intellectual Property Office and in other countries.

www.CarinaPress.com

Printed in U.S.A.

Recycling programs for this product may not exist in your area.

Many thanks to my agent, Christine Witthohn,
and my editor, Angela James.
Fantastic professionals, both.

MIDNIGHT VENGEANCE

As the song goes,
this is dedicated to the ones I love:
Alfredo and David

ONE

Portland, Oregon
January 15
"Inside/Out" Exhibit of Suzanne Huntington's
interior designs

"GIRLFRIEND ON YOUR SIX."

A hard elbow jabbed into Morton "Jacko" Jackman's hard side. It would have knocked a lesser man down. Former senior chief Douglas Kowalski wasn't known for his gentleness or delicate touch. But then neither was Jacko. He was a former Navy SEAL too, just like Senior. But both of them were out of the service and working in the same company, Alpha Security International, so Jacko could knock Senior on his ass and not be court-martialed.

Except, well, Senior was a good guy.

Senior's elbow couldn't knock Jacko down, but his knees nearly buckled at the thought of the woman behind him.

"Not my girlfriend," he mumbled, hoping the tan he'd gotten over his dark skin this past week teaching Mexican *federales* in Baja the fine art of fucking with the enemy hid his red face.

Senior shifted his eyes sideways, a hint of a smile on his big ugly mug. "No?" He shook his head and jabbed him again. "So why the chubby every time you lay eyes on her?"

Fuck. Busted. Jacko pulled his tuxedo jacket lower. He'd learned to control his dick at fourteen. What was he—back in high school? Why couldn't he be in jeans, like he was most times he saw her? Tight stiff ones that kept the hard-on down because it didn't have anywhere to go.

Except you don't wear jeans to a fancy art exhibit. Particularly not when your boss's wife's works were on show.

"Bravo red, moving fast," the chief murmured. Anyone farther than a foot from them wouldn't have heard a word and wouldn't have understood anyway. The orientation clock. "Bravo red" meant she was moving behind him to his right. Man.

Lauren Dare.

Oh. God.

Jacko thought he could smell her but that was crazy. Still, why not imagine he could smell her, because she drove him crazy in every other way? Though smelling Lauren in a room full of hundreds of people, every single one—man, woman and other—wearing perfume or cologne, with caterers walking around with hot food on platters and glasses of wine everywhere…well, that stretched even Jacko's sense of his own craziness.

He wasn't known for this. He wasn't what Suzanne Huntington, the big boss's wife and the star of the show, would call a fanciful man. He was known for being hardheaded and hard-hearted and hard-bodied. He was a roughneck from Texas who'd be in jail if he hadn't signed up for the Navy. They'd pounded self-discipline and a sniper's focus plus a dozen lethal martial arts into him. He could handle any type of weaponry, explosives, hand-to-hand combat.

Not one ounce of his very extensive and very expensive training gave him a clue about how to handle Lauren Dare.

There she was! Alone and lost-looking against the wall across the room to his right. For such a beautiful woman, she was doing her best not to attract attention, though for Jacko that didn't work. Couldn't. It was like the roof opened up and the sun shot a beam straight down onto her like a spotlight. Jacko was surprised people weren't gasping and turning to watch her.

She was doing everything possible to keep a low profile. She didn't even want her name on the program, though all of the works on the wall were hers. Suzanne insisted she take the credit for them, but Lauren had insisted right back. Very few people knew this entire show was all hers. He had no idea why she didn't want credit. Most people were happy to receive it for things they didn't do; few refused it. But who knew why women wanted anything, anyway? Lauren didn't want anyone to know, and for him, that was that.

Lauren was moving through the crowd like a ghost, nodding and smiling and never stopping to talk to anyone. Jacko couldn't understand how the men managed to avoid staring at her, but then he'd always known deep down that most men were assholes. You'd have to be an asshole and blind to boot not to realize that Lauren was the most beautiful woman in a room full of them.

Two of the beauties were married to his employers, John Huntington and Senior.

Lauren moved gracefully, not speaking a word to anyone, accompanied by notes from heaven. It took Jacko a full minute to realize that angels weren't sending down a sound track for Lauren Dare to move to. It was Allegra Kowalski, up on a dais, playing her harp. The notes morphed into a recognizable tune he'd heard Senior's wife play a million times.

Senior's wife was a talented musician—a harpist and singer. Jacko remembered the first time he'd met her, sent to be a bodyguard while Senior hunted down the fuckhead who'd attacked Allegra and blinded her. She'd had to have tricky experimental surgery to get her sight back, which had added years to Senior's life. Jacko would have done his duty, even lain down his life, for a snaggle-toothed banshee girlfriend of Senior but as it happened, Allegra Kowalski was beautiful and sweet and had played her harp for Jacko for a couple of hours while he sat in a chair facing the door, .22 on his lap, finger along the trigger guard.

Allegra's music had fucked heavily with his head and changed him forever.

But Lauren was the one who messed with him the most. Those long, white delicate hands of hers created things he couldn't even begin to imagine existed and yet became stone hard reality for him the instant he saw them.

He'd seen her drawings and paintings first. Suzanne, the wife of his other boss, John Huntington, aka Midnight Man, designed places where you walked in and felt like you were in some kind of stylish fairyland. Suzanne had sent him to pick Lauren up in her workshop to talk about creating images of Suzanne's designs. Jacko had walked into a big airy room and had frozen because he was surrounded by the most beautiful things he'd ever seen in his life. He'd simply stood stock still and gaped, mouth open like some raw recruit watching SEALs in training.

And then Lauren had walked into the room and even

her gorgeous watercolors and drawings vanished from his head like smoke.

Suzanne and Allegra were beautiful women. They were known for being beautiful, though they never used those coy tricks most good-looking women did. But Lauren—it was like she was another species. A cloud of shiny dark hair surrounding a heart-shaped face with silver-gray eyes on top of a body to make men weep. It had been a hot late summer day and she'd worn a sundress that showed delicate pale shoulders, slender arms and a tiny waist, and when she spoke Jacko didn't hear a word she said.

His head was buzzing too loud.

She tried twice. He got that much. He saw her full mouth open and close and all he could think about was that mouth on his while his entire body buzzed and he got the first of many, many hard-ons that sprouted whenever he was around her.

At the third try, he tried hard to focus and managed to grasp that she was asking him a question. *Morton, right?* He simply stared at her. *Suzanne said she'd send someone called Morton?* And at the end there was this little inflection, making it a question. And fuck him if he didn't forget his own name was Morton.

He was an asshole and blown away by her, but in his defense was the fact that only the Navy ever called him Morton, and that was only on official occasions or when he was being chewed out. He'd been Jacko forever.

It was only when he saw the first glimmerings of fear in her eyes and she took a quick instinctive step back that he pulled his head out of his ass. And felt ashamed. Having a 240-pound thug who lifted weights daily and had spent the last fifteen years training to kill people stare at you was probably not a good thing. Particularly if you were a beautiful woman with a slender build, alone in a space with the thug.

So he'd used every single ounce of self-discipline the Navy and particularly SEAL training had beaten into him and nodded and said—*Yes, Morton's my name— most folks call me Jacko. Suzanne Huntington sent me to pick you up.*

She'd just stood there, staring at him. Well, he could do something about her unease. He'd tapped his cell and called Suzanne. When she answered he simply handed the phone to Lauren and watched as some color came back into her face.

And when he complimented her on some of the art-works she actually blushed.

And Jacko was lost.

He drove her to Suzanne's office in Pearl, which was also the headquarters of Alpha Security International, where Jacko worked. He thought driving under eighty miles per hour was for dead men but he kept it at a steady forty and would have driven at twenty miles an hour if he could, just to stay in the vehicle with her. He waited for her as she and Suzanne talked, then drove her back. At thirty miles per hour. When he dropped her off at her house, he drove around the block and stopped the car and waited for his hands to stop shaking.

When he found out that Lauren taught drawing at a community center, he enrolled immediately and got another huge whack to his system. He was *good* at it. Damned good.

The past four months of his life had been work, think-ing of Lauren, attending her classes, sitting in his empty apartment drawing maps and drawing Lauren. There hadn't been room for much of anything else. No cycling out to the boonies and letting his Kawasaki Vulcan Voyager motorcycle rip. Megadeth, his favorite band, came through Portland, one night only, and he didn't go. It was a Tuesday and Lauren taught on Tuesday evenings. So no Megadeth.

No fucking, either.

That was a shocker. He didn't even realize he'd stopped fucking chicks until three weeks after meeting Lauren. It hadn't even occurred to him. When it did, he made a point of going out that evening to his usual hole, The Spike, and picking someone up because Jacko Jackman didn't do abstinence. Nope.

A couple of chicks he'd hooked up with before stopped by and made interested noises and to his enormous surprise, his dick said no. Fuck no.

As a matter of fact it felt like his balls tried to crawl up into his body.

He never tried that again and so he might as well have been a tattooed and pierced monk these past four months for all the tail he got.

And the reason was right in this room.

Jacko tracked Lauren as she made the rounds, speaking briefly with a few people when they spoke to her, then moving on. In the room full of trendy women dressed in bright peacock colors tottering on stiletto heels, she was low key in a midnight-blue dress with ballerina slippers. Jacko couldn't even see the other women while she was in the room.

They all seemed overblown and shrill. Sharp laughing voices crackling. Lauren's voice was never sharp. It was soft, with an underlying tone like music, only not.

She was sweeping the room with her eyes and Jacko

felt a change in the air when she saw him. Her face went from slightly sad to joyous in one second, and his heart nearly exploded out of his chest when she veered course immediately, making a beeline for him. He could feel himself stiffening in every sense.

"Incoming," Senior muttered. "You're on your own here, son. I'm going to my own woman."

Palm Beach, Florida

"Go on in," the muscle said, waving toward the door with his .44, a weapon that probably cost more than he did.

Frederick Rydell stifled a sigh. The quality of Guttierez goonhood had declined sadly since the death two years ago of that thuggish, though stylish, mobster Alfonso Guttierez. The organization had fallen to his moron nephew, Jorge Guttierez. Alfonso had had discreet, well-dressed security at the gate. Frederick passed through a metal detector and that had been that.

Jorge's muscle had actually frisked him, rumpling Frederick's Hugo Boss jacket, and had taken entirely too much pleasure in touching his private parts and between his buttocks.

Really.

Alfonso would never have hired this outlandish man-child with a backward baseball cap and oversized jeans with the dropped crotch.

Morgan, Alfonso's personal bodyguard, had always been impeccably dressed, able to serve tea or shoot you between the eyes without breaking a sweat. This goon looked incapable of thought, let alone style.

Frederick opened the door to the suite of rooms Alfonso had used as a study and had to work hard to hide his shock. The two rooms were high ceilinged and elegantly decorated. Alfonso's late wife had been a bitch of the highest order but a bitch with exquisite taste. And Alfonso himself was a thug with social ambitions. It didn't really make any difference in Floridian high society if you made your money running drugs and arms and trafficking in humans. As long as you made a lot of it, you were in. Alfonso had had a lot of it and Chantal, the new wife, knew how to spend it.

Alfonso's study wouldn't have been out of place in a lord's palace. It had been filled with superb antiques, exquisite rugs, decent art on the walls. And Chantal managed the staff like a general. Frederick had never seen the mansion less than perfect. Never even a fallen petal from the numerous floral arrangements.

Now it looked like pigs had rooted through the rooms, followed by the Huns.

After the deaths of Alfonso and Chantal, the staff had kept things going but Jorge had let the staff go, one by one, replacing the maids with the girls he fucked and who had no desire to pick up after themselves.

Frederick stopped on the threshold, willing his stomach not to rise. This was the worst he'd seen the rooms, a physical manifestation of the disintegration of Jorge's personality.

The rooms smelled of sex, expensive whiskey and overwhelming perfume. Someone had vomited and someone had shat and not flushed, so there was an overlay of that coupled with disgusting smells of fast food. The French chef had been the first member of the staff to go.

Two of the sofas had been pulled askew, cushions on the ground. Pizza and takeout boxes littered the marble floor. One of the antique mirrors—fashioned by the same craftsmen who'd made the mirrors in Versailles, Chantal had told him—was cracked.

Frederick schooled his face to blandness but his mind was racing as he crossed the room. He stepped on a used condom and his throat quivered as his stomach shot up his gullet.

Jorge was sitting with his back to the huge two-inch-thick bullet-resistant windows that gave out on to a flagstone terrace that ran the width of the mansion.

"Party last night?" Frederick asked, keeping his tone light.

Jorge grunted. He was sitting in Alfonso's chair, forearms on the surface of the Chippendale table that had served Alfonso as his main desk. A satchel sat next to Jorge's right hand. As Frederick walked closer he could see that Jorge was keeping himself upright by his arms on the table. Frederick checked Jorge's eyes, overly bright with pinpoint pupils. Christ, the man was wasted.

Jorge was going to talk business stoned out of his mind.

With an inner sigh, Frederick felt a pang of pity for himself pulse through his system. He'd earned a lot of money off the Guttierrez machine and now it was coming to a close. Like most good things, he supposed.

"So," Frederick said, sitting down on one of Chantal's antique chairs, noting with a repressed shudder that the seat cushion was stained. He couldn't bear to think of what might have caused the stain. "Here I am for my monthly report."

He'd had a not-unpleasant monthly appointment with Alfonso, to deliver ongoing reports. Frederick was the Guttierrez family's computer expert and the confidential conduit for communication with the various international…dealers Alfonso had business with. Alfonso owned two hotels, three nightclubs and four restaurants in Florida, which, being Alfonso, were exceedingly well run and turned a tidy profit.

But they were fronts for what earned Alfonso the real money—drugs, prostitution, people trafficking. All activities Alfonso managed at a remove with Frederick's help. He never got his hands dirty, directing everything via secure computer, which was Frederick's lookout. Vast amounts of money exchanged hands via bitcoins on the darknet, and every month Frederick visited Alfonso, he was treated to a superb brandy while delivering his report, and watched as 25K was deposited in his account in the Caymans.

Everyone was happy.

Since Alfonso's death, the businesses, legal and otherwise, had been going to hell. Very quickly. Frederick would have left long ago if it weren't for the fact that Jorge was desperately looking for Anne Lowell, Chantal's daughter, Alfonso's stepdaughter. Right after Chantal and Alfonso's wedding, Anne had fled from her family, disliking everything about her mother's new household. Anne had come from an upper crust family in Boston and hadn't mixed well, to put it mildly.

She'd been gone years before Frederick's association with Alfonso, and no one would have given Anne Lowell a moment's thought if it weren't for the fact that Chantal had died an hour after Alfonso, as his main heir. And then Anne had been Chantal's main heir.

So she had inherited most of the estate, the above-ground one anyway, and Jorge had gone wild. Alfonso's brother had sent his only son up to Miami to learn the business, and Jorge thought he had it made for life.

But Alfonso soon understood his nephew's weaknesses and had made sure to leave everything to Chantal. Who would probably have wisely put Frederick in charge.

Alfonso had never said a word to Frederick about his succession. Alfonso had been a very healthy self-disciplined fifty-year-old and Frederick had looked forward to many more years of happy association with an empire efficiently run by Alfonso. But that happy scenario had come to a crashing halt when a drugged-up teen slammed straight into Alfonso's Porsche.

Frederick often wondered whether the teen had been hopped up on Alfonso's product. Alfonso had had a great sense of irony and would have appreciated it.

Frederick had been sorry for Alfonso but above all, sorry for himself. Alfonso's death had put a serious crimp in Frederick's plan to sock away five million in the Caymans before forty.

"Give me your report," Jorge said sullenly, slurring the words. With a sigh, Frederick complied, knowing that Jorge understood one word in ten. Concepts such as bitcoins, Tor, arbitrage, currency conversion flew right over his head.

Only one thing mattered to Jorge—Anne Lowell.

Jorge had somehow got it into his head that if Anne Lowell died, everything would become his. Magical thinking, of course. Anne Lowell would certainly never leave anything to Jorge in a will. Jorge had no concept of the legal issues pertaining to estates and succession. Somewhere in his drug-addled mind, a dead Anne Lowell equaled a magical return to prosperity.

Frederick did nothing to disabuse him of the notion. An obsessed Jorge was going to pay the monthly retainer forever, though he had no clue how to do that online. It was strictly cash, in a satchel. Frederick had upped his price to 50K a month and had stopped looking very hard. He'd found Anne Lowell. Twice. It wasn't his fault Jorge was an idiot.

In college, majoring in computer programming, Frederick had had to take a course in creative writing and had been unexpectedly good at it. He loved movies and often thought he had the makings of a decent scriptwriter in him. Lately he'd been observing Jorge and his antics, thinking he could turn the situation into one of those tragicomic TV series everyone loved so much, like *Breaking Bad.*

Jorge and his minions trying to be crime lords, but fucking everything up. Frederick even had a title for the series. *Code Name: Moron.*

It was so annoying, being paid in cash. The bills were probably all laced with cocaine. Jorge pushed the satchel of cash over to him and then fixed baleful bloodshot eyes on Frederick. "You find the bitch yet?"

"I've found her twice for you," Frederick said, as he'd said many times before. "And both times your goons botched it."

Either she was very, very clever or very, very lucky. Twice they'd killed the wrong girl. Now she'd completely disappeared.

And he'd stopped prioritizing her. Let Jorge stew in his juices.

Jorge pounded a fist on the desktop. He was sweating like a pig. The side of his fist left a sweatprint. "Find that bitch! Find her now!" Jorge's attempt at being tough was beyond pitiful. "I'll give you a bonus if you find her before May 1."

Yeah, right.

Still, something was very wrong. Frederick had heard rumors that Jorge was deep in the hole with some very bad guys. Alfonso had left some well-run businesses but Jorge was crapping all over everything around him. He couldn't get it out of his head that finding Anne Lowell and killing her would—poof!—make all his troubles disappear.

Jorge was a cretin who wanted to run with the big boys and was in way over his head. Not that Frederick gave a fuck. He planned on cashing in 50K a month until someone smoked Jorge.

A dead Anne Lowell was not going to solve any of Jorge's problems. But Frederick wasn't about to say that.

Frederick would find Anne Lowell again, sooner or later, though he wasn't putting any effort into it. Who cared? As long as he was being paid, Frederick would keep at it on a low-level priority basis. Nobody could hide forever in a country with fifty million surveillance cameras.

Pity. Anne Lowell was, by all accounts, a charming, kind young woman who didn't deserve getting whacked by a lowlife like Jorge.

But hey.

TWO

Portland

THIS IS A big mistake, Lauren Dare thought. A huge, potentially disastrous mistake.

The show was as terrifying as she'd thought it would be. Why oh *why* had she accepted Suzanne's invitation?

Lauren sighed. She knew why. Because Suzanne had insisted so strongly and just wouldn't take no for an answer. Because Suzanne had threatened to simply cancel the show if Lauren wouldn't at least show up. No matter that the show was important to Suzanne's career.

The drawings, pastels, gouaches and watercolors up on the walls were Lauren's. She'd illustrated Suzanne's brilliant interior designs, that was all. Lauren didn't want—couldn't have—her name on the program in any way and had made that abundantly clear, without explaining why. Suzanne had reluctantly accepted. But Suzanne had been adamant—if Lauren's name couldn't be on the program at least she'd attend the opening.

Suzanne was across the room, signaling her to come over, but Lauren didn't dare. Suzanne had a gleam in her eye and there was no guarantee she wouldn't let slip who had actually made the illustrations to someone she thought might be important to Lauren's career. Suzanne was almost visibly vibrating with the need to praise Lauren in public.

She didn't understand that Lauren didn't have a career. *Couldn't* have a career.

Bless her. Suzanne meant well but it could cost Lauren her life.

She shouldn't be here at all. Being here was insane, a gesture crazy beyond belief. She was still alive at twenty-eight against all the odds because she didn't *do* things like this. Hadn't put herself in the public eye in any way in two long, dangerous years. She'd stayed alive for the past two years by being invisible. And her Portland life for the past year was supposed to be all about keeping her head down.

So *why* was she here?

Affection, that was why. Her downfall. She had simply been embraced by Suzanne...

Glorious harp music began playing, notes beamed straight down from heaven.

...and Allegra. Both charming, lovely, talented women who hadn't taken no for an answer when it came to becoming her friends. A stone heart would have crumbled and Lauren's heart wasn't made of stone. Oh no.

Her life would have been immensely easier if it were.

And it wasn't just Suzanne and Allegra who had bound her in silken ropes of affection. No, there was also Claire Morrison, their friend and the wife of a homicide cop. She'd horned in too. Friendly and smart like the others, warmhearted and funny. Simply irresistible.

And Lauren hadn't resisted much, had she?

It was unforgivable. Lauren was alive because she kept her head low; she didn't make friends; she wasn't noticed in any way.

So she shouldn't be here, at a big social and media event. It was insane, and dangerous.

A trick to not making an impact, to not being noticed, was to keep moving. She'd arrived deliberately late by taxi, rebuffing offers of all three women to pick her up, and slipped in unnoticed, dressed in a dark, simple gown she could move easily in and ballerina slippers, no heels.

Because you never knew when you might have to run.

And that's when she met his eyes and broke out in a smile because she simply couldn't help it. Another reason she'd stayed on in Portland way over her new life's sell-by date.

Morton Jackman. Jacko.

He was her star pupil in her weekly drawing classes, though there was little she could teach him beyond the basics. He was a natural. Somehow he was always around, giving a hand in closing up at the community center, offering to drive her to the supermarket when her car broke down, fixing her leaky faucets and cleaning out the grout. Putting in fancy new locks in her doors.

She had no idea why he stuck around her so much when she clearly made him uneasy. Spooked him, even.

Though she should be the one spooked. And she had been, the first time they'd met. Suzanne had sent Jacko to pick her up for their first business meeting. He worked for Suzanne's husband, who ran some kind of fancy security company, though Jacko looked precisely like the kind of guy a security company was designed to protect against.

He was pierced, tattooed, his head was shaved and his muscles had muscles. He looked like trouble. Your worst nightmare, come to life. And yet...

Morton "Jacko" Jackman had the soul of a poet, though he'd probably punch in the face anyone who said so.

Lauren had never seen anyone respond the way he

did to fine art and classical music. As if they had been designed precisely for him. He understood and reacted to art instinctively, in a way no education, however advanced, could teach.

And though not an untoward word had been spoken, though they barely ever touched beyond a handshake, Jacko had somehow become part of her life, too.

Well, she was going to stick with Jacko because sticking around Suzanne was dangerous. At any moment Suzanne could spill the beans over who had created the artwork on the walls and there would be a fuss, the spotlight of attention would turn to her and blood would be spilled. Hers.

Jacko could be counted on not to say anything, simply because she'd asked him not to. Jacko wasn't the kind of guy to accidentally spill anything.

She swerved and walked straight to him, happy to see a friendly face.

Well…friendly. That might be going a bit far. He wasn't *unfriendly* around her. He was just stiff and formal. But she liked him in spite of himself and he made her feel safe.

No one would touch her—could touch her—while Jacko Jackman was around. He didn't do it deliberately but there was a definite *don't mess with me* vibe around Jacko that was like a protective force field. Lauren recognized that she liked having him around partly because she relaxed in his presence. No need to be tense or worry about the outside world. He did that for her.

As she walked toward him, she could see white all around his dark eyes. She smiled at him, placed a hand on his big arm.

"Hi, Jacko."

He swallowed. "Ma'am."

Lauren rolled her eyes. Being with Jacko was always interesting. He was fun to tease, like pulling the tail of a dangerous tiger you knew wouldn't bite. "*Lauren*, Jacko. Not ma'am. I've told you a thousand times. Unless you want me to call you sir. Do you want me to call you *sir?*"

"No, ma'am."

She stepped closer and his eyes opened even wider. "Jacko, how long have we known each other?"

"Four months, three days and seven hours. Ma'am."

Wow. That was actually…true. She had to think about it for a minute but he was right. "So don't you think you could bring yourself to call me *Lauren?* Considering the fact that we've known each other four months, three days and seven hours?"

"Yes, ma'am."

"Lauren."

"Lauren. Ma'am."

She sighed again and looked around the room. No one was paying her any attention at all, which was precisely what she wanted. Nobody was paying much attention to what was on the walls, either, which was cool. Everyone was completely taken up with the hot hors d'oeuvres making the rounds on platters and the excellent champagne an army of servers was pouring into glasses. Allegra's music made for a gorgeous backdrop to the sounds of happy people drinking and eating and gossiping.

She hadn't really had a chance to see her work up on the walls. The work was hers but Suzanne had framed and hung the drawings and watercolors, and Suzanne had a wonderful eye for color and balance. Now that everyone was eating, drinking or listening to Allegra would be a good time to look at what was on those walls.

She leaned close to Jacko and was surprised to find that he smelled really good. It wasn't something as overt as a cologne. It didn't have alcohol overnotes. So it must be soap. Citrusy and fresh. And his own smell. Mmm.

"Jacko, will you walk around with me while I look at the drawings? I haven't had a chance to see them framed and hung."

"Yes, ma'am," he said and stuck his elbow out at an odd angle. She stared at it—was he going for a gun under his jacket?—and after a long moment realized he was offering her his arm.

Such an old-fashioned gesture from such a rough man, she hadn't even recognized it at first.

She took it and she relaxed another infinitesimal amount. There was just something so incredibly reassuring about Jacko. Holding his arm felt good. Really good.

She looked up at him and smiled and he flinched. Okay. She was relaxed, but clearly he wasn't. Somehow she made him uneasy. But still, he wasn't running away screaming, so she tugged him toward the west wall. She knew it was the west wall because it was painted blue with gilt letters in cursive writing on the top—*West Wall*. The east wall was taupe, the north wall salmon and the south wall mint. Gilt letters proclaimed each wall. Suzanne had chosen the frames according to the colors of the walls.

They walked. Walking with Jacko in a crowded room was a very interesting experience. She'd bumped shoulders with about twenty people before. The room was full of people and everyone was intent on something else—food, drink or someone more interesting than she was. She'd been jostled and stepped on and shouldered aside.

Instead, now, it was like Moses parting the Red Sea.

Everyone somehow made way for Jacko, shifting out of his way as if that were the natural order of things. Those who didn't instantly move got a glare that—once they saw it—made them scramble. No one jostled her; no one stepped on her toes; no one crowded her.

"Have you seen the works already?" she asked.

Jacko had been scrutinizing the crowd as if they were enemy insurgents, carefully and coldly. He looked down at her. "Yes, ma'am. Lauren. I helped hang them."

"So which ones do you like?"

His dark eyes met hers. "All of them. Every single one."

She faked a smile. Wrong answer.

"But the Morgenstern series is amazing," he said. "And so is the Lachland residence. Never seen anything like it."

Okay. Right answer.

"I'd really like to see up close what she did with the frames."

"Sure thing." He looked down at her and if she didn't know better she'd say that was a *smile* lurking in his eyes. Jacko smiling? Nah.

But he walked her to the appropriate wall, people parting for them. Jacko snagged a couple of flutes of champagne off a passing silver tray and held one out to her. It was very deftly done, considering the size of his hands.

It had amazed her during drawing lessons, too. The number 2 pencil looked like a stalk of straw in his huge hands, yet that hand sketched the most delicate images imaginable. He was an expert on hand-drawn maps, and his own were exquisite.

They stopped in front of the Morgenstern series. Suzanne had gone all out in the presentation. Over the series was a long acrylic rectangle with *Morgenstern residence—24 hours* laser-etched across the top. The watercolors were framed with a gold passé-partout within an elaborate wrought iron frame holding the entire ensemble together. She'd had the idea of the Morgenstern series as she sat on a park bench across from the façade of the home. It was a Belle Epoque building and by some miracle of light and shadow, each part of the day—sunrise, noon, late afternoon and dusk—highlighted different parts of the façade.

So she'd done watercolors of the four parts of the day, each a slightly different hue, each shift of the sunlight highlighting different aspects of the ornate façade.

"Suzanne did a really good job framing them."

That earned her an odd look. "The works are yours. Not hers."

There was nothing to say to that.

She sipped the excellent champagne, holding the flute up so it caught the light. The crystal felt good in her hand, catching the light of the overhead chandeliers, so fine it was almost as if the bubbles were caught in air instead of glass.

She twirled the stem. Her family had had flutes just like this in Boston. Fifty of them. Three lifetimes ago.

For just a fleeting second sadness descended over her. She'd trained herself, *schooled* herself against it. Thinking of the past not only did her no good, it was actively dangerous. She had to be present, fully in the moment, every second, because danger could come leaping out of the darkness at any time.

The only way to survive was to be on her guard and to be grateful for every second, because every second could be her last. No past, no future, only the present.

And if it hurt her, just a little, not to be able to claim the watercolors and drawings she'd worked so hard on, if it hurt her, just a little, to remember her charmed childhood in Boston that could never come back, too bad.

That was life.

"Let's go look at the Agarwal house sketches over on the east wall." She tugged at Jacko's arm.

"Sure. They're beautiful. My compliments." They were crossing the big room and he looked down at her and she thought she saw...again, could that be a *smile* in the depths of his dark eyes? Jacko was the most serious man she'd ever been around. His emotional tones ran the gamut from sober to grim and back again. Even the hint of a smile was extraordinary.

"Well, it was thanks to you." She gave him a sunny smile, straight up at him, and his face froze. It looked like something hurt.

The sketches of the Agarwal house had come out well, she had to admit. It was thanks to Jacko that she'd been able to sketch the house at all. The Agarwal house was an extraordinary structure built by an Indian venture capitalist heavily invested in green energy. The house was built on a remote vast plot of land on the foothills of Mount Hood and had been designed to blend into the forest.

Lauren had sketched it in fall and deepest winter and had extrapolated what it would look like in spring and summer. She'd spent three full days filling ten notebooks with sketches.

When Jacko had heard through Suzanne—who'd received the contract to design the interior decor—that Lauren intended to spend a lot of time on the isolated estate he had insisted on accompanying her. The first time, Lauren had balked. She liked—no, needed—to take her time. She didn't want to draw hasty sketches with a bored guy tapping his size 14 boot waiting for her to finish up. But it hadn't been like that, not at all. Jacko seemed to have enormous reserves of patience. He found a bench where he sat quietly, simply waiting for her. Five minutes after she arrived in the morning, Lauren had forgotten Jacko's presence and only came up for air in the early afternoon after an orgy of sketching to find him waiting in the exact same spot in the exact same position she'd left him in.

Something told her he'd be able to do that for days and maybe even weeks, not just hours.

And, truth be told, the fact that he was there, watching over her, allowed her to lose her sense of time and do it right. Without him, there was a bit of her that would have remained tense and alert.

"You were very kind and very patient with me. I appreciate it." She looked up and met his eyes and again smiled sunnily at him. He blinked and his face became even more wooden.

"My pleasure, ma'am."

She rolled her eyes at him. "Lauren."

"Lauren," he repeated dutifully.

God it was fun teasing him. She tugged at the massive arm under her hand. "So come on, let's go over to the blue wall." They turned. "From what I can see of the frames, she did a magnificent—"

And then it happened.

And it cut her life in two.

THREE

A BRIGHT LIGHT went off in her eyes, blinding her. Another light went off, then another.

"Great!" a cheery voice enthused. "Great shot! You're a fabulous, unusual couple!" The man holding the camera was tall, rail thin, dressed in a very tight lizard skin jacket with a crimson red satin shirt underneath. That Mick Jagger vibe, only in a young guy.

Lauren's knees buckled, the lights in the room dimmed and all sound was cut off, gone. She couldn't breathe; she was choking. It was exactly as if a huge invisible hand caught her around the chest and squeezed. Hard. She wheezed but no air came.

She couldn't stand. Her legs wouldn't hold her.

But she wasn't falling either. Something strong, around her waist, was holding her up.

A sound, close to her ear. *—ren?* She couldn't make sense of it. The world was frozen, she was frozen, right down to her core.

And then the world came back—brightly, painfully— in a nauseating rush.

The kid taking shots looked at her as if she were a specimen in a zoo and walked off.

No!

Her lungs unlocked; she drew in a deep gasping breath. Jacko was holding her up but she needed to be able to stand on her own two feet. Now. Grabbing Jacko's tuxedo lapels she leaned into him, keeping her voice low.

"The photos," she gasped. "Oh God. Get rid of those photos of me, please! Destroy them! All of them!" Her voice was shaking badly; her lips felt numb. Was she getting the words out right? She gulped in a deep breath, to explain—to find some kind of explanation that didn't make her sound insane—but it wasn't necessary. Because Jacko walked up behind the young Mick Jagger, took him by an elbow and in a second they disappeared from view.

Lauren searched the crowd frantically, turning as she heard a cry. There they were, behind a pillar. Jacko's big hands were quickly and efficiently manipulating the camera, eyes on the view screen, completely oblivious to the squawking of Jagger Junior. Jacko handed the camera back, leaned in close, and whatever he said must have been forceful because the photographer paled and nodded his head jerkily.

Jacko watched Jagger Junior's face for a long moment then he nodded and made his way back to her. Jacko had such a…presence. Partly because he was such a big man—not tall so much as immensely broad—and partly because he had the kind of face you don't argue with, the crowd just parted for him again. Not scrambling to get out of his way but just making an opening for him to come back to her in the straightest, quickest line possible.

Lauren stood, shaking, watching him.

What had she done? Foolish, foolish woman. She'd let her ego and her heart get away with her. No matter that she *knew* it was a bad idea to exhibit her drawings and watercolors, that it could cost her everything. Suzanne had pleaded with her, and let's face it, her ego had been stroked.

And it had cost her everything.

Jacko was beside her and she tilted her head back to look into his dark eyes. He wasn't as tall as Suzanne's husband or the man they called Senior, Allegra's husband. But she was in flats and he was a head taller than she was.

She looked around, mentally saying goodbye. It was an eclectic gathering, a good Portland mix of professionals and creatives. Friendly and welcoming, just like the city. She could feel the good vibes, feel the friendliness almost beating against her skin like a warm tide.

The process that had begun with Suzanne—tying her to this place with silken ropes of pleasure and affection—began to unwind, spool out. It felt as if she were in some kind of experimental movie where alienation was shown by the camera zooming out.

In the space of minutes, there was a wall between her and the happy crowd so thick she could barely hear their voices.

Home. She had to get home fast.

Then get out of Portland fast.

But first—home.

She placed her hand on Jacko's arm. She rarely touched him. He froze whenever she touched him so she made sure she did it rarely. Now was one of those times. She needed his attention.

"Jacko…"

It was only when he bent low to her that she realized she'd practically whispered his name. She cleared her throat. Breathed out the pain. "Jacko." There, her voice was almost normal. "Did you—"

"Every single one, all the ones with people. The only photos left on the card are of the buffet tables."

She stiffened her knees. Thank God. She wanted to sag with relief but that could wait until she got home.

She leaned into him. "Thank you, Jacko." She hadn't had to beg him or convince him in any way. For that she'd be eternally grateful because she'd have ended up sounding insane. She'd probably have followed young Mick around, trying to steal his very expensive camera with about a yard of lens, hung by a leather strap around his neck.

"I, ah, I have—" Her mind shorted. What did she have? What was best? Sudden onset of blinding headache? Stomach flu? Uncle Elmer just passed away? "A headache. Migraine. I think I'll say goodbye to Suzanne and grab a taxi—"

"No," Jacko said. His deep voice, his dark eyes were calm.

Lauren blinked. "I beg your pardon?"

"You're not taking a taxi, not if you don't feel well. I'll drive you."

"But…" Lauren waved her hand at the scene in front of her. The show was in full swing. Everybody who was coming had arrived and nobody had left yet. It was the best moment of any successful exhibit, people talking, eating, drinking. Happy. "I can't take you away from the show. That wouldn't be fair."

"I'm driving you home." It was as if he hadn't heard her. He was impassive, as if stating some kind of universal law. The only sign that there was some emotion was the slight Texan accent that became stronger. *Draaaah-vin.*

Fighting him required more energy than she possessed. And a tiny part of her was glad. She was walking away from a life she loved. Her world had flipped in the space of a minute. It would have been almost more than she could bear to cut all the ties to her life here in the time it took a taxi to arrive.

At least on the drive home with Jacko she could pretend she still lived here, just a little longer.

"I need to say goodbye to Suzanne." Lauren looked up at him, trying her best to keep her face expressionless when the idea of it was ripping her insides. "Then we can go."

He nodded and this time took her elbow instead of offering his arm. Thank God. Her legs felt rubbery, her head light. Her heart was pounding so hard it was a miracle nobody heard. She felt as if the noise should be bouncing off the walls.

Suzanne was near the north wall, which contained Lauren's sketches of Suzanne's corporate interior designs, including the Lo Corporation's glass lobby. Lauren had loved sketching it—all grace and light.

Her heart gave another huge painful thump when she realized that she could never do this again. Never draw public buildings. Never, ever have a show, not even anonymously. That door had suddenly closed shut with a bang.

She swallowed. Saying goodbye to that and to Suzanne suddenly seemed like too high a price to pay. Like saying goodbye to life itself.

But it was what it was.

Suzanne was talking to the corporate spokesman for the Lo Corporation, a young, spiky-haired woman dressed in black, head to toe. The woman said something and Suzanne threw her head back and laughed. Even her husband, who was standing with his arm around her, smiled.

John Huntington, smiling. Wow. He was another one

of the grim-faced brigade, the founder of Alpha Security and, like Senior and Jacko himself, a former SEAL. He was tall and broad and good-looking, in a slightly dangerous way, his dark hair silver at the temples, making him look like a distinguished pirate.

Lauren had been astonished when she first saw the Alpha Security International website with its photograph of a dark-haired John, without a trace of white in his hair. John never spoke of his military service, but presumably as a SEAL he'd been in battle many times, which he'd apparently taken in his stride. He said that all the white hair came from being a husband and father.

Oh God. Suzanne's little girl, Isabel. The most beautiful baby on the face of the planet, absolutely adorable. She gave a huge toothless grin every time she saw Lauren.

Lauren would never see Isabel again. Never watch her grow up. Not get to watch John freak when she started walking. He'd be snow white by the time Isabel started dating. It would have been so much fun to be a part of all that.

But she'd be far away. In another world, another life. Mourning this one.

Suzanne held out a hand to her, smiling, as she walked up. She held out an arm. "Lauren. There's someone I want you to meet. I was just telling him what a talented artist you are. He wants to see your portfolio."

Suzanne was visibly quivering to tell whoever this guy was the truth. Not letting Lauren take the credit for the artwork was driving her crazy.

Sweet, sweet Suzanne. Funny, smart Suzanne. Loyal, affectionate Suzanne. She shimmered in the bright light of the exhibit space as Lauren blinked back tears. She looked at her friend, absolutely stunning in a pale peach satin gown, dark blond hair drawn back in some kind of complicated bun that on any other woman would have required three hours at the hairdresser's. Suzanne had an innate style, a natural elegance. She probably scooped up her hair after the shower and styled it herself in two minutes.

She was classy and smart and warm, a woman in a million, a friend in a million—and Lauren would never see her again.

This was breaking her heart.

Suzanne's eyes honed in on Lauren's face and her smile faltered. Oh God, Lauren had forgotten how incredibly perceptive she was.

"Is something wrong, Lauren?" Suzanne looked around, as if there could be muggers lying in wait among the petit fours, ready to spring out and do Lauren harm. Her husband, who was rarely far from her side, picked up on the vibe and moved even closer to his wife.

Lauren hesitated for a second. John—known for some reason as Midnight to the men he worked with—was frowning too as he studied her face. It was a characteristic of the Alpha Security men—John, Senior, Jacko—and their friend, Portland PD detective Bud Morrison. Most men didn't notice much outside themselves but these men did. And being noticed was dangerous.

Lauren found herself leaning heavily against Jacko, against that reassuring warm wall of muscle. She straightened, brought a hand to her head. "Suzanne, honey, I am so sorry, but I have this killer headache."

Suzanne frowned. "I can see that you're not feeling well. You're very pale. I'm so sorry." She looked up at her husband. "Do you think you can drive Lauren home?"

"Sure," he answered easily, as if leaving right in the middle of his wife's successful show were nothing. *Just driving my wife's crazy friend home, all across town. In terrible weather. No biggie.*

"Oh no!" Lauren was appalled. "I was going to take a taxi but as it happens, Jacko offered to drive me home."

Suzanne's frown didn't change. If Lauren didn't love her so much she'd hate her. Even frowns looked good on Suzanne. "I don't know." She looked from Lauren to her husband and to Jacko. "I don't like the idea of leaving you home alone if you're not feeling well."

The music from heaven had stopped and Allegra appeared at Suzanne's side, one graceful musician's hand reaching for Suzanne's shoulder. Senior trailed behind her. "Is something wrong? I saw Lauren looking pale. Are you okay?" she asked Lauren.

"Metal's a medic," Senior said in his rumbling bass. He pointed a big thumb at another one of Alpha Security's men in a bespoke tuxedo, the only kind that could accommodate his massive shoulders, scarfing down smoked salmon on toast points. "Can he help?"

As if operating on an invisible signal, Metal raised his head, toast point in hand, and looked at Senior, then at Lauren, ready to come over and help.

This was getting out of hand.

The whole group had simply adopted her, welcomed her into their fold, and Lauren had no doubt that if her headache were real instead of an attack of stark raving terror, and she asked for help, she'd be accompanied home in an ambulance. Suzanne and Allegra and Claire would start sending along gallons of chicken soup. Knowing them, they'd probably come in to fluff her pillows for her. Put a mint on the bedside table. Rub her feet.

Friends like these were priceless and she was losing them. Had already lost them—they just didn't know it yet. Lauren was a walking ghost, already gone.

Oh God.

She coughed to loosen up her throat enough to be able to speak. "It's nothing serious, don't worry." She coughed again. "I think I might be coming down with the flu, so it's best for me to get home." *Now.*

Suzanne looked troubled, but nodded. "Okay. But I hate to see you go." She cocked her head, a sudden mischievous gleam in her eye. "Because there was this guy I wanted you to meet. He's the new head of PR at the Isabel and—"

"Another time," Lauren choked. Meaning—never.

That was another thing, Suzanne and Allegra's endless attempts to pair her off with a suitable man, not realizing that she couldn't be paired off. Ever. It would be like a death sentence for the man, whoever he was.

Suzanne and Allegra and Claire were walking advertisements for wedded bliss. Though their guys looked rough and tough—and from what she could see they genuinely *were* rough and tough—they made their wives very happy.

It hurt, just a little, to be around them when their husbands were around. They were such—such *couples*. Devoted to each other, counting on each other, helping each other. She'd never actually lived that in her life, had never even seen it before. Her father had been devoted to his collection of first editions and her mother had been devoted to his money until it ran out, and then she'd been devoted to Alfonso's money. No one in Alfonso's family had been devoted to anyone but themselves, including Jorge, of course. Being around Suzanne and Allegra and their friend Claire she'd discovered something, something about that whole man-woman thing, that she'd never seen before and that made her yearn, just a little.

As long as Jorge was alive, she'd never have it. Couldn't have it.

Her knees were trembling. She had to get out of here. Fast.

She stepped toward Suzanne and hugged her. Suzanne hugged her back. "Take care of yourself now," Suzanne said.

Lauren was shorter and was wearing flats, so she could bury her face against Suzanne's shoulder, hiding the sudden rush of hot tears that pricked her eyes. For an instant she gave in to her emotions and clung to Suzanne. Soft, soft perfumed Suzanne. Loving friend, wife, mother. Who was a buzz saw when it came to business.

Lauren clung too long. She could feel Suzanne's bewilderment when the moment to pull away came and went. Lauren simply couldn't let go, not for the life of her.

Because, well, this was it. Her life was over.

If anything this past disastrous half hour had taught her, it was that she had to stay far away from everyone. The nicer they were, the farther she had to run.

What yawned before her was a friendless future of complete solitude. Keeping her head down, surviving. Relentlessly alone.

This might be the last time she hugged a friend. Maybe in her entire lifetime.

She squeezed more tightly. Suzanne understood that something was going on. Damn it, she was perceptive as hell.

This had to stop. Lauren forced herself to open her

arms, step back, before the temptation to just cling forever overwhelmed her.

"Hey." Allegra smiled, put a hand on Lauren's shoulder. "I get one of those hugs, too, right?"

Oh, yeah.

This time Lauren was disciplined. The hug lasted the exact right space of time. When she stepped back, Allegra kept her hands on Lauren's shoulders and frowned. "Is something wrong?"

Lauren swallowed, nodded. "Headache."

"No." Allegra shook her head. "Besides that."

Damn. She was so freaking perceptive, too. All that harp playing. Messed with her, allowed her to tune into more frequencies than most people.

"No, no." Lauren shook her head, gave a shaky smile that they would put down to a massive headache. "I just need to lie down in the dark for a while."

Suzanne looked at Jacko, beautiful face serious. "You'll walk Lauren to her door," she said, "and see her in." It wasn't a suggestion.

"Yes, ma'am," Jacko replied. Suzanne acknowledged that with a hard look and a nod.

Suzanne turned to smile at her. "It's going to be a busy weekend, but I'll call on Monday. Maybe we can have lunch together." She shot a look to her right. "Allegra's practicing for a concert but I think we can bribe her to take some time off."

"Alcohol and food? I think I can be bribed." Allegra laughed and Lauren did her best to laugh, too. All that came out was a sick croak.

She would give years off her life to make that luncheon.

Suzanne mimed a telephone with her hands. "So I'll call on Monday, then."

"Sure," Lauren wheezed. On Monday she'd be in Denver or Cheyenne or Cleveland. Or North Dakota or Utah. If her mysterious friend who provided her with documents was able to swing a passport, maybe she'd be in Toronto or London.

Lauren took a second, just a second, to mentally say goodbye to her friends in Portland. This was becoming her old life with every breath she took. She had an artist's eye and she wanted to keep this picture in her head, take it out when the loneliness overwhelmed her in her next life. Right here, right now, she had a little living tableau of friendship and community in front of her.

Suzanne and Allegra with their husbands, looking at her carefully in case she needed something they could give her. Willing to do that with every breath they took.

Oh, damn. This hurt so much! *I have to go,* she thought. *Right now. Before I break down.*

She smiled, turned around and walked away before she said something dangerous. Jacko was right by her side.

It was a crowded room but, again, walking with Jacko meant no jostling, no having to sidestep. He stuck out his elbow again at that odd angle and she slid her hand into that warm space between his huge biceps and his powerful forearm.

It made her feel a little better. She was walking out of a life she loved, but it was in style, with an escort.

She needed that support. Each step felt like her feet were made of lead, carrying her uphill where she desperately did not want to go—into a sere and barren new life, wherever that would be.

She got her coat from the coat check, though Jacko didn't seem to have checked any coat in. He had only the tuxedo jacket.

They stepped outside and Lauren would have been nearly knocked over by a sudden gust of wind if she hadn't still been clinging to Jacko. It was so cold her breath froze in her lungs.

They were outside on the white ultramodern marble porch that had turned slippery in the icy wind. Shivering, Lauren started picking her way to the steps, but stopped, snagged on Jacko's arm.

"No." Jacko hadn't moved and Lauren turned to him in surprise. "It's too cold out here." He shrugged off his massive tuxedo jacket and put it around her shoulders. It was like being enveloped in a warm blanket.

"What about you?" He was dressed only in a blindingly white shirt and black satin bow tie.

"Not a problem." Jacko turned her around, put a hand to her back and gently pushed her back into the warm lobby. "Wait here and I'll bring my vehicle around to the front. Don't move."

Her eyes widened. "Aren't you going to be cold without your jacket? It's warm here in the lobby. I can give you your jacket back."

"Nah." Amazingly, he smiled. It was brief, really brief. A flash of white teeth in his dark face and it was over, but it had definitely been a smile. The first smile she'd seen on his face in the four months she'd known him. "I don't mind the cold. Now don't go anywhere."

She shook her head. No, she wasn't going anywhere. Where would she go?

Jacko disappeared around a corner. The second he

was lost to sight, Lauren's anxiety level rose. She was so exposed here.

The vestibule was a glass-enclosed space with white marble floors, like a movie version of heaven. There was no one in the vestibule and the glass must have been thick because it was soundproofed. It was as quiet as a cathedral. She glanced over her shoulder at the sight of revelry in the huge exhibit space behind two-story glass doors. Everyone looked like they were having a really good time. Only Lauren and Jacko were leaving.

There was something heartbreaking about watching the huge throng inside, laughing, chatting, eating, drinking, like a movie with the sound turned off. Before, in her previous life, it was the kind of party she'd have loved. If you were there, it meant you had some kind of interest in interior decor or at least a passing acquaintance with art. It meant you enjoyed beautiful things and you belonged to Lauren's tribe. She'd loved exhibits like this, where everyone was dressed to the nines and really intent on enjoying themselves.

Take a good look, she told herself. Because it was the very last time she would ever voluntarily be in a crowd. Crowds were dangerous in these times of Facebook and Pinterest and Twitter. Crowds shared.

Inside, everyone was spotlit, colors more intense, clothes fancier, smiles brighter than in ordinary life.

Inside everyone was enjoying life, their greatest care whether shoes matched purses. No one was running for their lives inside.

She was cut off from them by more than thick plate glass walls.

As long as her life was under threat, events like this

were forbidden. As was rising in a career, any career. As was friendship or marriage or—God!—motherhood.

The thought of her life as it was now, continuously on the lookout, on the run, with a child in tow to protect—well that thought made her slightly nauseated

From now on it would be all about solitude and staying indoors and working through a computer under her assumed name for her book cover art. Working as Fabiola Chenet, who lived in France.

Nothing but work and solitude, for the rest of her life. Or for the rest of Jorge's life.

The external doors suddenly opened. She hadn't even seen Jacko arriving. For such a huge man, he was extraordinarily fast and light on his feet.

He was by her side in an instant. He pulled the lapels of his tuxedo jacket tighter around her neck. "It's really cold. I've got my vehicle right outside with the engine running and the heater on. Watch your step outside—it's slippery."

Lauren wanted to roll her eyes and answer "Yes, mom." Except it *was* really cold and the marble steps *were* really slippery.

There was no question of her slipping though, because Jacko had a big arm around her waist and he wasn't going to let her fall. Her feet barely touched the marble stairs. Before she knew it, she was sitting in Jacko's huge SUV, enjoying the heated cabin.

The backseats were all turned down and a big gleaming thing was back there, a mass of shiny steel and chrome, glinting in the darkness.

"What's in the back?"

"My bike."

Oh. The famous motorcycle everyone talked about. She turned her head and studied it. It was huge and looked more like a rocket than a bike. A car turning around in the driveway shone the headlights into the back and she could see it was lacquered a bright red. It looked dangerous, powerful. Sexy.

Jacko was looking at her, big hands dangling over the top of the steering wheel.

"Home?" he asked.

She nodded, throat tight.

Home. *Not for very much longer.*

He seemed to understand that she didn't want to talk. Couldn't talk, actually. If she opened her mouth, the words choked in her throat would come tumbling out. So she turned her head and watched the landscape go by as he drove her back to her house, blinking back tears.

Such a pretty city, Portland. Cool, in every sense of the term. Less overwhelming, less snooty than Boston. And a million times better than the hot, money-soaked Florida her mother had wallowed in.

The snow that had been threatening all day started drifting down. Damn. Even the snow, on her last night in Portland, was pretty, turning the parks and lawns into a fairy-tale world like Narnia.

Enjoy it, she told herself. She'd loved her time here, loved the vibe of the dynamic yet laid-back city. Portland offered tons of cultural opportunities while remaining friendly and walkable. She'd sketched in all corners of the city, not just the wealthy homes Suzanne decorated— skateboarding parks, the tiny gate to the tiny Chinatown, and she'd even followed the changing light in Pioneer Square, though for that she'd worn a big floppy hat that hid her face.

She'd felt instantly at home here and it hurt so much to know she could never return. Not only that, it would be best to go to another kind of city entirely, so Seattle was out. Certainly the entire Pacific Northwest was out, maybe even the whole West Coast.

She should go to one of those Sunbelt places where old people lived and iguanas roamed the earth. Or maybe somewhere up north in one of those empty states where winter lasted eight months.

Somewhere where she would finally heed what her rational mind had been telling her all along. Make no connections. Make no friends. Stay home as much as you can.

At least she had Felicity. Anonymous, faceless, virtual. But a friend.

She watched the neighborhoods go by, memorizing the buildings, knowing she could never come back. And knowing that her life would be an empty shell from now on.

It occurred to her that she would never have a love affair, ever again. The past two years had been of necessity chaste—though she'd never had a wild sex life anyway. Time to face the fact that sex and love were out of her life, possibly forever. Like most women, she'd had it in the back of her head that someday her Prince, or if not her Prince at least a really nice guy, would come.

But that was crazy thinking. She had to stay unattached. If nothing else, she'd put the man in mortal danger. Unless…she sneaked a glance at Jacko, handling driving in the snow with ease. He handled most physical things with ease. She'd heard Suzanne and Allegra talking about him. He'd been a sniper in the military, was a superb shot. Apparently he was also an expert in several martial arts.

He'd be a hard man to kill, even for Jorge's thugs.

Jacko... Hmm.

Well, why not? Her last night in Portland, spending perhaps the last night of her life in a man's arms. Jacko was attractive in an unhandsome kind of way. He was certainly sexy. And though he was stiff and formal around her and acted almost as if he were scared of her, which was ridiculous, something told her he wouldn't say no.

When he started hanging around her all the time, she thought maybe he would make a play, and the idea of sex with Jacko had flared up in her head, lodging there. But he hadn't made a play. He'd actually avoided touching her unless he absolutely had to, so clearly he wasn't interested in her that way.

Maybe she could interest him now, though.

Oh God, yes. A night of heat and passion when she felt so cold and alone. Who would it hurt? If Jorge's goons showed up for some reason having somehow tracked her down here, she'd be long gone. And Jacko knew how to handle himself.

Could she do it? Could she seduce him? Did she have the nerve?

And...how? Well, start by inviting him in for coffee. Or better yet, alcohol. She had a nice bottle of aged whiskey a grateful student had given her. Would it be hard to seduce him? She definitely didn't have the nerve to strip and curl her finger at him, but maybe that wouldn't be necessary. Perhaps they could talk a bit, sitting close together on the couch and...

Jacko pulled up in her driveway, much too soon. She

still hadn't fully planned her mode of attack, thought it through. If he said this, she'd say that…

He unlocked the doors with a whump, put his hand on the driver's side door.

She was taken by panic. Suzanne had asked him to walk her to the door, and he would. And then he'd turn and drive back. The thought of watching through her living room window as his vehicle drove away, the thought of never seeing him again, was almost more than she could bear.

She wanted sex with him, so she had to man up, fast.

"Wait." Her voice came out a hoarse whisper. Her throat was almost vibrating with emotion. "Would you—"

"Yes." His voice was so deep she almost felt it in her diaphragm more than hearing it.

Lauren gave a half laugh. "What?"

"Whatever you were going to ask, the answer is yes."

"Yes?" She blinked in surprise. He'd taken her aback. "No matter what? Suppose I asked you to paint my house? Or—or to give me a million dollars?"

Jacko turned his head to look at her full in the face. His dark eyes were steady on hers. "I'd paint your house, no question. I don't have a million dollars but if I did, I'd give them to you if you asked."

Her heart gave a huge thump. She smiled shakily. "Then it's a good thing I was just going to ask if you wanted a coffee or a nightcap. My headache's better."

"I guess you know the answer, then."

He got out in the snow in only his shirt, rounded the front of the vehicle and opened her door. He held out a huge hand and she took it gratefully. The ground was a long way down.

He looked down at her, still holding her hand in a warm, strong grip. His face was sober, even grim.

"Yes," he said.

LAUREN TREMBLED AS they walked up to her front door. Okay. Jacko had basically already said yes, to anything she proposed. So how hard could this be?

Very hard, it turned out. Because that rush of conviction in the SUV driving over here had dissipated, leaving her feeling sad and foolish.

She'd heard the stories about him from Suzanne and Allegra, though they'd tapered off lately. But still, they'd been plenty colorful.

How he was a player and he liked them young and super sexy. Biker chicks, mostly. That wasn't her. She wasn't very young anymore and she was anything but sexy. A B-cup at best, in her more optimistic moments.

She wasn't even that good in bed, or so she'd been told. What did she know? It all seemed so very mysterious, right now, walking up to her porch, with a light snow falling around them. That whole Sex Thing seemed alien, something Martians did.

Another woman would know precisely what to do and would be a firecracker in bed. *Firecracker.* That was the term one of her stepfather's goons had used to describe a wannabe model-du-jour he'd bedded. What did firecrackers *do?* Sex was such a basic activity, what room was there for improvement?

And yet there had to be room for improvement because Lauren knew, without a shadow of doubt, that no one would ever, ever call her a firecracker in bed. Not even a sparkler.

Oh God. This was a really really bad idea. They were

at her door and the whole Sex Thing loomed behind it. And really, in her experience sex wasn't *that* great. Maybe it would leave a bad taste in her mouth, cloud up her happy memories of Portland.

Had Jacko realized that for a brief moment of lunacy she'd contemplated dragging him to bed? Because though he always looked impassive and impervious, he was actually pretty observant. How humiliating if he realized it, shuddered at the thought, politely accepted a shot of her whiskey and made a fast escape.

And, and even if he did throw her—what was it called?—a mercy fuck, what would that gain her? She'd never see him again. She was going to embark upon a long trip tomorrow with no idea of the destination. She'd need a good night's sleep, not a night faking orgasms.

Thoughts buzzing in her head like angry hornets, she scrabbled uselessly in her tiny evening purse for the key. She was close to a full-blown anxiety attack and her hands were numb. Ah, there the key was, on her silver paintbrush fob. But her hand was trembling; she couldn't fit the damned key into the lock, one of those fancy ones Jacko had bought for her and had installed himself.

Something big and warm and hard enveloped her hand, stilling it. His hand, gently removing the key from the crazy lady's hands and opening the door himself.

Lauren looked up into that hard, expressionless face, wishing she had a clue what he was thinking. How to make a quick getaway, probably. So he could go home, change out of his formal clothes, hop onto his massive bike that all the men at Alpha Security International envied and go to a biker bar. Where he'd pick up a biker chick.

Who'd be young and sexy and fantastic in bed.

"Breathe," Jacko said, that deep voice heard in organs other than her ears.

She wheezed in a breath. At the same time, Jacko opened her door, ushered her in, then closed it behind them.

She didn't have time for any more anxious thoughts because a second after the door closed, her back was against it, Jacko's considerable weight pressing against her, and he was kissing her.

And kissing her.

FOUR

GOD, HER TASTE. Champagne and woman.

Lauren.

He'd spent way too many nights these past months staring at the ceiling, thinking of her mouth, sporting a massive hard-on that just wouldn't go down. Just wouldn't. Nothing he could do about it, either. His dick didn't want his hand, it didn't want another woman, it didn't want anything but her, under him, and that wasn't going to happen.

Except now, maybe it was.

He was going to take Lauren to bed. Something he'd wanted for months, fiercely, was going to happen.

But...fuck. He had to be careful because he was overexcited. Maybe it hadn't been a good idea to go without all these months for the first time in his life. The only times he was abstinent was on missions and his dick, like everyone's dick, stayed down when bad guys shot at him. Blood in your groin instead of your head during a firefight was a surefire way to the grave.

But other than that, he liked sex, a lot, and never went without. Until he met Lauren where he got that double whammy of wanting her and not wanting anyone else. And...she scared him.

For all the fucking he'd done in his life, this new thing didn't have any rules for him to follow. He wanted her so intensely he didn't know if he could control himself so he found himself stiff and formal around her. He didn't dare make a move because then when she rejected him he couldn't be around her anymore and he'd rather cut his own balls off. And she would reject him, no doubt. The kind of woman who wanted him wasn't subtle about it. Most women in bars just walked up to him and asked. Maybe they'd accept a beer or two but the reason they were with him was never in doubt. The rules were clear. He'd buy the beers and the dinner, spring for the pool table, no question. And he was going home with them, no question.

There wasn't any dancing around the topic. No long discussions. Not much talking at all, actually.

One chick he met in a bar in San Diego walked up to him, looked at his crotch, smiled and walked out. He followed her, they went up to her apartment, had sex, and he left early the next morning, deployed on a mission to Colombia. They never spoke and he had no clue what her name was.

So in his experience, women were pretty easy to understand and what they wanted was pretty clear. A stiff dick and stamina. Great. He could provide that.

Lauren? Shit, who knew what she wanted?

Not him.

After that first meeting where he scared her, she got it that he wasn't going to hurt her. He worked for the husband of her best friend. But she sure as hell didn't look at his dick and curl her finger at him.

And then, it was the damndest thing. She started… talking to him. Asking his opinions on things, things he knew nothing about. He answered in as few words as possible but she pondered them carefully, those gorgeous blue-gray eyes that turned silver in sunlight watching him carefully.

Nobody really listened to Jacko except teammates and then the topic was usually shooting. Sometimes tactics and strategy, for a change of pace. Bikes, too, because Jacko was a known expert.

But Lauren talked to him about *everything* after she got over her fear of him. And she listened to what he had to say. He found he really liked that. He also found that he'd rather spend one minute talking to Lauren about anything at all than spend hours fucking someone else.

So getting to talk to her was already better than anything else that had ever happened to him and shit, now he was kissing her.

She tasted so delicious. He breathed her in, nose next to a satiny cheek. He licked slowly in her mouth and stiffened when she stroked her tongue over his. Jesus! He had to tighten his groin muscles because he nearly came. Like some randy teenager about to pop his cherry.

This was not good if a kiss made his dick twitch, hard. He couldn't touch her anywhere except her mouth. Not yet anyway, not until he got himself under control. But fuck, how was he supposed to do that?

He pulled away slightly and looked down at her. His hands were planted on either side of her head. He had big, strong hands. And he was really excited. Couldn't touch her right now, didn't dare.

She looked up at him, her face mere inches from his. He'd never been so close to her before. She was so amazingly beautiful. Even up close her skin was perfect, smooth and pale, now slightly pink. Luscious mouth swollen from his kiss. Her eyes were an incredible silver blue with that dark blue rim and they flashed light as she shifted them left to right and back, reading his face. He always had the impression that she could see right into his head, which scared him. But didn't scare him enough to walk away.

"I was hoping you'd do that," she whispered.

"Do what?"

"Kiss me." She gave a small smile, watching his eyes. "I planned for it while we were crossing town but couldn't figure out how to do it. How to ask you."

It took a second for the words to penetrate. "You were *planning* how to get me to kiss you?"

She nodded, never taking her eyes from his.

"Breathing did the trick." She could look all she wanted—all she'd see was the truth. "And you didn't have to ask after all."

She could feel that. He was leaning against her. Not with all his weight, but he was close enough for her to feel his hard-on. It was massive and it freaking hurt. Every night since he met her that he hadn't had sex was now very present; he was feeling all those nookyless nights like one huge mountain. It felt like he'd never had sex before. He was going to have to play this carefully because, right now? He wanted to throw her to the ground, run his hands up her legs, with the silky material of her skirt riding his hands, rip her panties open and slide right into her.

Her eyes widened because he must be pumping testosterone into the air by the ton. He was breathing heavily, every single muscle tense.

He had to do something, fast. He didn't want to scare her. Of all the women in the world, this was the one he wanted to treat like a queen. He wanted to worship her, pet her gently all over, coax her into his bed. And at the same time he wanted to fuck her senseless.

So, yeah, control was key.

Jacko was all about control. You don't pass BUD/S without huge amounts of self-control. But right now it was slipping through his fingers, draining his head, inflating his dick.

Slow, he told himself. This has to be slow. Because though the images running through his head were definitely X-rated, Lauren hadn't actually signaled that they were going to have *sex*. They'd kissed. That was it. So before he strategized how he was going to have sex with her without going wild maybe he should try to find out if he was going to have sex at all.

It would kill him if she said no. He was as worked up as he'd ever been in his life. But if she said no, he'd accept that and…go out and shoot himself.

"Do you—" His voice was hoarse. "Do you want to sit down? Talk?"

Her eyes were still searching his, flashing silver in the dim light. "Actually, um…" She turned a bright red. "I was wondering whether you want to make love."

Hell yeah! Jacko stifled the shout in his throat because, well. Screaming probably wouldn't do it for her. So he cleared his throat and scanned his empty mind for something to say that wasn't *hell yeah*. "Yes," he said. "I'd, uh, like that."

Like he liked breathing.

"Okay." She relaxed, smiled a little. She'd been worried he'd say no? It flashed on him that being so aroused around her all the time had made him stiff. In all senses. And maybe she'd interpreted that as indifference.

He wasn't indifferent. Man, no way. It was as if she walked around with a big red arrow pointing at her from the sky. Spotlit by a light so bright it hurt his eyes and he couldn't look at her directly.

She was still watching him, a little frown now between her eyebrows. Moving carefully, Jacko reached out and smoothed it out with his thumb. He didn't want her frowning because he was being a jerk. No sir.

"Kiss me," he said and she frowned again.

"What?"

"Kiss me." He needed to hand her a little power.

She smiled again, faintly. Man, he wanted to see huge smiles on her face, wanted to see her sated and happy, having had a million orgasms.

She didn't smile enough and he could never figure out why. They were going to have sex and he didn't want sadness in the bed, no sir. He wanted joy and heat.

She cupped his face, still watching his eyes closely as if checking to make sure he didn't escape. He didn't move, barely breathed. Her hand felt soft and warm against his cheek.

"Kiss me," he said again. Putting everything in her hands.

He held himself still because he wanted to grab her, grab her hard. Right now, he was holding on to the wall and his self-control by his fingernails. She lifted herself on her toes to get closer to his mouth, pulling herself up by her hands on his shoulders. Her show, all the way. All Jacko did was stand there, fingers curved, holding on to the wall and to his control, trying not to groan when her hips rubbed his dick as she lifted herself up.

She was a little clumsy, slightly missing the mark, kissing the corner of his mouth. He didn't care. She could kiss any part of him because his entire body was now a huge erogenous zone. He'd read somewhere that the skin was the largest organ of the body, and he believed it because he could feel every inch of it, on fire. His dick was the second largest organ, it felt like.

Then she got it right, tilting her head, her mouth perfectly aligned with his, open, warm, wet. When she licked his lips he once again nearly came.

Shit, this wasn't working. He was going to have to get naked fast because he did not want to come all over his tux trousers.

Naked. With Lauren. The image in his head came fast, completely uncontrollable. The two of them naked, him on top, moving in and out of her, her pale slender legs hugging his hips...

Whoa, again he pulled himself back just in time; one second more and he'd have disgraced himself. Though he wouldn't have shot his wad, no no. Even if he'd come, he'd still be hard, It was entirely possible that he'd have wood for the rest of his natural life if what he was feeling right now was any indication.

Not being aroused felt like an impossibility if Lauren was anywhere in the vicinity.

She was making love to his mouth. That was the only term possible. On tiptoe, she moved her mouth over his, licking into his mouth, retreating to kiss a corner, coming back openmouthed for another deep kiss. He held himself still, *willing* himself to stillness when what he really wanted was to crush her against him so as much of her was touching as much of him as possible.

Nice thought but the images in his head weren't nice. They were on the edge of rough and he didn't want that with Lauren. He didn't want rough or hard. He wanted to be gentle because that's the kind of woman she was but...it was like there was a hot wind in his head blanking out everything and he wasn't one hundred percent certain he could keep control.

Which was crazy because Jacko was all about control.

So he stood still, hands on her living room wall, moving only his lungs and his mouth.

Lauren pulled away, dropped down. Looked at him uneasily.

Shit. She thought he was uninterested. He wasn't uninterested. His dick was radiating interest that could probably be picked up on the moon. But how could she know that? She'd just kissed a guy who barely responded.

Jacko had a very specific skill set that came in really useful if you wanted to whack enemies of the state. Not so useful when it came to relationships.

If he wanted this, he was going to have to go after it, and he had no clue how to do it.

He pried one hand off the wall, with difficulty. As if he were Spider-Man and his Spidey-fingers were fixed to the wall. Slowly, he brought his hand to her face, ran the back of his finger down her cheekbones. Jesus, her skin was so soft. How could anything human be this soft?

Lauren was still looking at him uncertainly, a little frown between her eyebrows. He smiled, wondering if it was an okay smile. He showed teeth; was that enough? He was trying to regulate his features while regulating his breathing *and* his dick and it was like patting his head and rubbing his stomach at the same time. Because all his attention was on her, on the pale oval of her face, the feel of her against him, small breasts against his chest, moving as she breathed.

She sighed, breasts rubbing against him again and he swelled. Lauren's eyes opened wide, flashing silver.

"Yeah," he said. There was no filter in his head. He

usually measured every word he spoke but now his mouth opened and what was in his head just popped out. "You breathing has that effect on me. Everything you do is such a turn-on I'm scared..." He drew in a deep breath himself and felt every inch of her along his front. "I'm scared I'm going to come."

"You want me," she whispered.

He blinked, swallowed. A thousand words tangled in his throat and only one came out, and it came out in a croak. "Yeah." He pressed his lower body against hers. "I, um, I thought you could tell."

She'd lost that slightly anxious look and gave a small smile. "I mean, you want *me*. As opposed to a generic woman."

A generic woman. Weird way to put it. Right now, Jacko couldn't remember what any woman he'd ever met looked like. He got as far as one head, two arms, two legs and then blanked out. There was only Lauren and he knew every single specific for her. The way her eyes flashed silver in a certain kind of light. The way her skin glowed as if she were lit from within. That delicate little knob at the corner of her narrow wrists. How her hands were so slender and how the tendons on the back of her hand danced when she drew. How she could blind him with her smile yet her eyes always remained slightly sad.

He remembered every single word she'd ever said to him.

Every cell of his body pulsed with desire. With *lust*. This wasn't sex after a dry spell. This was as if he'd never had sex before.

Was this going to work?

It had to or either his heart or his dick was going to burst with suppressed desire.

He cleared his throat. "You're—you're not a generic woman. You're Lauren Dare and I have wanted you since the second I met you."

Her eyes flickered. Was this news to her? Then her mouth turned up slightly. "That's, um, interesting. I hadn't actually understood that."

Jacko nearly sighed as he realized that huge divide between men and women. His bosses, Midnight and Senior, talked about this often. Metal, too. Metal looked as much like a thug as Jacko and could never find a woman who wasn't either scared of him or wanted to fuck him precisely because he looked so rough. It bothered Metal, but it had never bothered Jacko. He lived in a world of men and exited it long enough to fuck, then went right back in.

Inviting a woman into his world hadn't really occurred to him. Only now that he wanted Lauren, he realized that though he wanted this like he wanted his next breath he was opening up a real hornet's nest, because men and women didn't speak the same language.

Lauren thought he was indifferent to her and every man at ASI knew his dick was dragging the floor following her around.

By the same token, women's words all seemed to mean something different. It was going to be a problem, which he was definitely going to tackle after he'd had Lauren about a million times and got this major wood out of his system. Maybe two million times.

He took the hand he'd unclamped from the wall and placed it under her elbow. He touched only cloth, which was probably a good thing. Because right now? He wanted to throw her to the ground and jump on top of her.

Don't fuck this up, he told himself.

He moved away, every cell in his body stiff, directing

her by his hand on her elbow. He drew her away from the wall. "Jacko?" she said, making the word a question.

"I thought we could—we could take this to the bedroom." He looked at her carefully. She wanted to fu— to make love. They should be in a bed for that because though for him up against the wall, down on the floor, bent over the sofa, naked in a field of snow—all those worked for him, Lauren was a lady and he wanted her to be comfortable, and that meant a bed.

Didn't it?

Hell if he knew. Nothing about any of this was familiar to him.

"Bedroom," he repeated, whole sentences now beyond him. The house was small and he had an excellent sense of space. Though he'd only been in the living room and the big room where she worked, he knew where the last room was, though he'd never been inside. But having her lead him there would again put some control in her hands.

Her head tilted. "That way."

Yep. That way. He nudged her across the room, down the corridor, stopping at the threshold of her bedroom. There was a little light filtering through the snow from the streetlight outside her bedroom window. Bed, chest of drawers, rocking chair. But it wasn't those that told him he was in the right room—it was the smell. The whole frigging room smelled like her skin. Fuck.

He couldn't do this and not breathe; that wouldn't work. But every time he took in a breath it was as if he breathed in Lauren.

He walked her to the bed, stopping just short of it, feeling as if he were strapped with bricks of C4, just about to detonate. Lauren was looking up at him and in the dim light she seemed unearthly, some shimmering creature sent to earth to torment him. Beautiful, magical, unattainable.

She reached up on tiptoe again and kissed him, moving her mouth over his, tasting him. Not unattainable, no. But still beautiful and magical.

Jacko cupped her head with his hands, soft warm hair tumbling over them, and deepened the kiss, sliding his mouth over hers, tasting her, breathing through her. She curved her hands over his wrists, anchoring him, as if he might run away.

No, he wasn't going anywhere.

He lifted his head, looking down at her, her skin glowing in the semidarkness like a pearl. His body was split into two. Above the waist he could just stand here forever, looking at her face. Below the waist his dick was screaming—*get going you asshole! What are you waiting for?*

A sign. That's what he was waiting for. A sign that her excitement was one billionth of his.

He kissed her again, slow and deep, raising his head just a little, feeling her breath wash over him. Her eyes were closed, mouth a little swollen.

"Jacko," she whispered.

Okay. That was a sign. Wasn't it?

He let go of her head, lightly ran his palms over her shoulders, down her sides to her narrow waist, touched the zipper at her back. Looked at her.

She smiled.

Yeah.

Slowly, Jacko unzipped the dress, spread it. It fell unnoticed to the floor and he stared. Oh man. She had on a lace bra, pretty and delicate. There wasn't enough light to see exactly what color it was—something pale. Pink or yellow, maybe. There was plenty of light to see that it had a front opening. Jacko reached out and touched the fastening, watching her eyes. He could do this by touch, no need to watch his hands. Watching her eyes was enough. It came apart easily under his hands. He could field strip his rifle blindfolded. A bra snap was nothing, if it weren't for the fact that his hand was shaking lightly.

She couldn't know what that meant—for a sniper's hands to shake.

The two cups rested on her breasts. They were surprisingly full for such a small woman, filling his hands nicely. He opened the bra and it slid to the floor, too, and his hands were on her, soft and warm and perfect. He flicked his thumbs over her nipples, felt them harden, heard her breath speed up.

Panties. Fast.

His hands were shaking a little more now, had lost dexterity. He fumbled a bit, fitting his fingers into the elastic at her hips, careful not to rip. Very careful, because they felt like silk and looked expensive. They fell to her feet and he kneeled, lifting each foot until the panties were off. A moment and her soft slippers were off, too. That left only black thigh-highs, and he stopped for a second, kneeling before her, just looking, because it was the most erotic thing he'd ever seen in his life. Lauren, naked except for those dark stockings with the lace at the top hugging her thighs. Pale and soft and perfect. A wet dream.

Slowly, slowly, he rolled the stockings down, face so close to her mound he could smell her desire. When he got her stockings off, he kissed her flat belly and stood, wincing at the boner.

When he stood back up again it felt like a club hanging off the front of his body. She was beyond beautiful.

It was as if life had reached inside his head and pulled out a picture of the kind of woman guaranteed to drive him wild then came up with a match. Soft, slender yet curvy…just perfect.

And…blonde. She was a natural blonde, a strip of pale pubic hair covering her mound.

She didn't try to hide herself, didn't position her hands to cover herself. She just watched his eyes and must have seen something in them that made her smile.

"Me, now," Jacko said, voice rough.

She blinked.

"Undress me."

"Oh!" Lauren cocked her head to one side, stepped closer to him. He could feel her body heat all along the front of his body. She thought he wanted her to undress him as a form of foreplay, but that wasn't it. He wasn't sure he could get naked in a way that wouldn't scare her. Ripping his shirt and trousers off would probably scare her.

So he stood, trying not to pant, as she reached up to unbutton the super-white dress shirt he'd had tailor-made together with the tux because he couldn't find sizes that fit him. He was glad he'd sprung for the outrageously expensive Egyptian cotton because he could tell the feel of it pleased her. When she'd unbuttoned him to the bottom and unbuttoned his cuffs she placed her palms against his chest and rubbed her fingers over the material.

"Off," he ordered and she gave a secret little smile, as if she understood she'd reduced him to one-syllable words.

In a second, his shirt was fluttering to the floor, the heavy cotton making a slight sound as it hit the ground. Her fingers moved to his pants and he bit back a moan.

His dick, swollen beyond any reasonable measure, made it hard to unfasten the tux pants. Every time her fingers brushed him beneath the cloth, his dick moved, trying to get closer to her.

Finally she got him unfastened and unzipped. He actually had briefs on, something rare for him. But he was glad he did because it made him seem more civilized than having her unzip him and having his dick spring out in her face.

She looked down at him. Tactics. He was really good at tactics. And strategy. Goal: getting naked. How? That was where tactics came in. He reached down and unzipped the sides of his boots, again glad he'd sprung for brand-new ones. He and Metal both disliked shoes, being too used to combat boots. These didn't lace up but that was fine. He toed them off and stood in his stocking feet.

Christ. Why did people have to wear so many fucking clothes? He should have had a loincloth that he dropped and he could pick her up, drop her on the bed and drop on top of her. The whole process taking about two seconds. But no.

And she was so freaking slow. Or at least that's what it felt like. She pulled his pants down and he obediently lifted his feet, and she actually turned and placed the trousers on a chair, neatly folded. He couldn't have managed that, not in the state he was in. She pulled off his socks, slowly, laying those neatly on top of his boots.

Lauren stood, eyeing him. He stood at a modified parade rest, except he didn't have his hands folded over his crotch as soldiers usually did. He had on a white tee and black briefs and he thought he could actually see the options flit through her mind. Tee first or briefs? Tee. She lifted the hem, tugged, and he obediently bent forward so she could pull it off then stood straight again.

Her eyes went right to his shoulder. She'd seen his wrist tats of course. Unless it was freezing, Jacko usually dressed in a tee and vest. She'd never seen the tribal tats that covered one shoulder, down over his pec, one swirl surrounding a nipple. A Samoan American buddy of his had drawn them for him, each inch symbolic of something in his life, though right now he was too blasted by lust to remember anything.

"That's beautiful," she whispered, running her hand over his shoulder, over the tribal tats. They were dense and dark. "Did it hurt?"

"Some," he admitted. *Like a bitch..* "You're missing an item of clothing."

Her gaze lowered and her eyebrows lifted. She caught her thumbs in the sides of his briefs and tugged them down. They caught on his dick and he closed his eyes when she pulled out the material so it could slip over him. The briefs fell and he kicked them aside.

Lauren's eyes were fixed on his dick and he didn't blame her. It barely looked like a human organ. It was bigger than he could ever remember it being, huge and red and inflamed. He could feel her gaze on him as if it were her hands, and his dick moved.

"Just from me looking at you?" she murmured.

"Touch me," he ordered and her hand lifted to him. Her skin was very pale against him as she stroked him from base to tip. He jerked and hissed, completely uncontrollable reactions.

Lauren jerked her hand away as if she'd touched a red-hot stove.

Oh God. How excited was she? He was normally big

and now he was huge. He didn't want to hurt her. He looked her over carefully. How the fuck could you tell with women? She looked slightly flushed but it was too dark to be sure. Her nipples were small and hard, darker than the pale pink skin surrounding them, but was that enough?

Only one way to find out.

He placed his dark hand over her belly, smooth and sleek, ran it down, cupped her. Slid a finger in her and... *yes!* She was slick and soft. But small. He frowned and reached deep inside the wet softness, stroking, and felt her contract around his finger. Saw the muscles in her belly pull.

Lauren let her breath out in a long sigh.

"You're tight," he said, voice ragged.

Her eyebrows raised and she studied his face. "It's... been a while."

At her words, his dick swelled impossibly bigger and her eyes grew large. "You like that. That I haven't had sex in a while."

"Hmm." It felt like a huge band of heat constricted his chest. He could barely breathe, let alone speak.

"Isn't that politically incorrect?"

He shrugged. Yeah, he liked it a lot that she hadn't had sex in a while. And he was going to make damned sure she didn't have sex with anyone else but him for the foreseeable future. But right now there was something else on his mind.

"Don't want to hurt you," he mumbled.

Lauren watched his eyes and stepped toward him. Her breasts brushed against his chest and her belly rubbed against his dick. He blew out a breath.

"You won't hurt me, Jacko."

He could feel her breathing against him, breasts and belly lifting against him slightly with every breath she took.

"Jacko? Are you going to make me beg?"

On a scale of the top ten things he wanted to do, having sex with Lauren was the top nine, riding his bike coming in last. What the fuck was he doing? She thought he didn't want her. How crazy was that?

But…if he moved he'd explode. And he didn't know what he wanted to do first. Sliding into her immediately was out of the question. She said he wouldn't hurt her but he would. At least she'd be uncomfortable until he got her more excited. He didn't want her to feel uncomfortable, not for one second. He wanted her wet and hot, completely open and ready.

So…how? How to have foreplay without his head and dick exploding first?

"Lie down." Lauren's eyes widened again. His tone was rough, guttural. He cleared his throat to modulate his voice but she was already lying on the bed, quietly watching him.

Jesus. *Just look at her.* She was relaxed, one hand lying on her belly, breathing easy, waiting. Incredibly beautiful, every line of her just perfect.

It was like having a bed full of C4 and she was the detonator.

Jacko placed a hand and a knee on the bed and prepared to blow up.

THE MATTRESS DIPPED to take Jacko's heavy weight. He moved slowly and cautiously as if he expected her to run away any second now. But she wasn't going to run away. This next part was probably going to get really interesting.

If she thought Jacko would roll on top of her like any other man would, she was mistaken. He lay at her side, propped up on one massive arm, looking at her. His entire body was like a heater—warmth emanated from him, penetrating skin, penetrating bone.

He bent his head and kissed her shoulder while his free hand skimmed down between her breasts, over her stomach, down to between her legs.

"Open your legs," he whispered against her skin and her legs slid apart, as if they were there to do his bidding. That big hand disappeared between them. All she could see was his brawny forearm with the barbed wire tats around his thick wrist but she could feel him touching her. Slowly, carefully. Running a callused finger gently around her opening.

He thought she needed foreplay, needed warming up? Surely he could feel how slick she was, feel moisture coming with each stroke of his finger. And foreplay wasn't necessary with a naked Jacko in her bed. He was living, breathing foreplay.

She turned her head to look at him, take him in. He was grim-faced as usual. Well, she was familiar with his face. He wasn't a handsome man but then his attraction didn't lie in his face. His attraction was that overwhelming maleness.

When they'd kissed in her living room she'd felt him, felt those hard muscles, but it had been through layers of clothing. Now she could see what she'd only felt before and it was just…amazing. His dark skin was tough, like leather. Each muscle was clearly delineated, thick ropy raised veins running under the skin. He had so little body fat that in some places she could see the striation of muscle tissue. With all that he had a bodybuilder's physique he didn't look blocky or awkward. He looked like a Platonic ideal of man, perfect.

He was lying on his side, his shoulders so broad that he blocked out her vision. All she could see, stretching from horizon to horizon, was dark-skinned muscle, her world reduced to a cage of man.

Everything fell away. Her problems remained, but as distant clouds on the horizon. There, menacing, but not a threat right now, zooming out to the distance while the foreground of her consciousness was heat and desire, not cold, empty loneliness.

Fine by her, let Jacko drown out the world. The world had taken huge bites out of her. Jacko wasn't going to hurt her in any way. If anything, he was being too gentle. His fingertip circling her was barely touching her flesh. Her hips were gently moving, trying to deepen his touch.

She opened her mouth, though she wasn't sure what she wanted to say, and he leaned over and kissed her breast, and all that came out of her mouth was a deep sigh. Everything was happening in slow motion, slow movements, lush and languid. Except for those moments when his thumb brushed her clitoris and sent electricity through her. But then he moved right past, the beast.

His mouth, too, teased her as he nibbled his way around her breast, soft lips with the slight bite of stubble giving her goose bumps.

Clearly Jacko wasn't going to do anything fast, and she couldn't imagine making him do something he didn't want to do, so she let herself enjoy the slow—very slow, *glacially* slow—seduction. It was so silent in the room, no noises from the street. It was a quiet street and the gentle snow ate up all sound. The only sounds were the incredibly erotic sounds Jacko was making with her body, as if she were some musical instrument—his lips on her breast, his hand on her sex.

She felt cocooned in some magical place where no worries were allowed. The only things allowed in the room were heat and desire, Jacko's hands and mouth bringing them up from someplace deep inside of her. A place that had been deserted for so long.

Jacko's mouth found her nipple just as his finger penetrated her and that lazy warm feeling of floating on water changed, sharpened, and she started contracting around his finger in an electric climax.

Usually it took her a long time to climax. She'd feel it coming from a long way away and would coax herself to it. Now it shot like a lightning bolt through her, her body taking over completely.

"Yeah," Jacko muttered, mounting her. He held her open with two fingers and slid deeply inside her, then stilled.

Amazingly, Lauren was still coming, clenching over and over again around him as he held still for her. He was kissing her deeply and every sense she had was infused with Jacko. With the feel of him, the smell of him, the taste of him. All dark and delicious and so exciting she could barely breathe.

"Need to get deeper," he whispered into her mouth and she arched her back and opened wider for him, and just as the spasms started dying down he held her head still for his kiss and started moving inside her, hard and fast.

LAUREN WANTED TO open her eyes but, whoa. Way too much of an effort. She felt really really good exactly where she was.

Where was that?

Wherever it was, it was a great place to be. She was lying on something hard and warm. And that smelled really good. And felt even better.

Jacko.

God.

With a huge effort, Lauren didn't tighten her arms around him, though she wanted to. Her head was cradled against his shoulder, one arm stretched across his massive chest, the other along a huge biceps. The temptation to snuggle, to get as close to him as humanly possible, was almost irresistible because right now? In his arms? Nothing could touch her.

For the first time in two years, she felt safe.

This was so dangerous. It was a completely false sense of safety, like those kids who couldn't feel pain and got burned all the time. Safety didn't exist, would never exist for her. Safety, just staying in Jacko's arms forever, was like some kind of seductive drug. One that was bad for her, one that—like all drugs—could cost her her life.

He was deeply asleep, the kind of body language that couldn't be faked. Well, he'd earned it. A full blush bloomed all over at the memory of all the things they'd done. By rights she should be in a semicoma, too, but the twin demons of fear and anxiety were waking up in her, stretching their arms, looking around with interest, noticing her new love, faces stretched in evil smiles because they knew it would all be snatched from her very soon.

Like, now.

Because a monster was after her and he would never stop. As long as he was alive, she would never be safe. No one around her would be safe.

Where a moment ago upon waking she'd felt like every

cell in her body had been away for a week at the spa, now she felt cold and shriveled. Alone, in the truest sense of the term. More alone than before, because now she knew what it meant to be truly joined to a man. It felt like her previous sexual experiences had been two people politely uniting genitals, not the earth-shattering sex she'd had all night.

She had no idea what the previous night had meant to Jacko. He'd been a more than willing participant, sure, but from the talk in Suzanne's husband's company, he was a highly sexed man. A player. So he'd had fun, that was clear, but it was probably business as usual for him.

Not for her, not by a long shot. She had never felt so close to anyone in her life, and it was more than the fact that he'd been inside her almost all night. She'd felt like she was a part of him, felt his heart beating in his chest the way she felt her own, had breathed to his rhythms, had moved with him as if she could read his mind. She certainly felt as if she could read his body.

His body had given her endless cues as to what pleased him. Which had been more or less everything Lauren had done.

She'd been blown away. It was probably a function of her extreme loneliness, but still. It had been overwhelming and she mourned the loss of it. In all likelihood nothing like this would ever happen to her again.

Actually, nothing like this ever *could* happen to her, because she'd have to walk away from it, and once was proving painful enough as it was.

She slipped gently out of bed, slowly, so she wouldn't wake him. There was no way she could steel herself to say goodbye right now; she was way too shaky, way too connected to him. Every move she made reminded her of him. Her whole body was a map of the night.

A little time, a little distance was what she needed. She also needed a shower. How could she smile and wave goodbye forever when she smelled of him?

Her eyes suddenly welled with tears and she shot into the bathroom, leaning against the sink, looking at herself in the mirror, willing the tears back. She had willpower and she could do this. She could. All it took was not thinking of Jacko. Hard, but possible. Barely.

But not right now.

Lauren bowed her head, staring into the white porcelain sink, and tried to walk herself through the next hour. She'd feed Jacko breakfast—that was only polite. And she'd smile and nod at the things he said, though she probably wouldn't hear anything over the drumming of her heart. She'd see him to the door, promising that they'd meet on Tuesday for the usual lesson at the community center. He'd been coming for as long as she'd known him, even though he didn't really need her coaching. He had an instinctive talent.

He'd do just fine without her.

A drop fell from her cheek and she stared at it coursing down the white porcelain side of the sink. Another fell, then another.

This was crazy. Angrily wiping her cheeks, she dropped her dressing gown to the tile floor and stepped under the shower. She made it as hot as she could stand because she was going to wash both her Portland life and Jacko off her skin. Portland left easily but Jacko was harder to eliminate. Though he'd been enormously delicate, he'd left signs. Five faint bruises on either hip, where his hands had gripped her hips. A light red spot, like a circular blush, where he'd sucked and bit the skin of her breast.

She'd nearly had an orgasm from that alone.

Oh God.

Even when she closed her eyes, he was still imprinted on her body. The washcloth between her thighs brushed against sensitive skin that was still swollen, still weeping moisture at the memory of him inside her. She swiped the washcloth over herself there and her knees nearly buckled. She was more aroused at the memory of Jacko than she'd ever been with any of her lovers at the moment of penetration.

How wrong could you be? She'd imagined a pleasant sexy night with Jacko, sort of her goodbye to sex for an unknown period. Maybe forever. She'd imagined the night as a sort of farewell treat for her, some good memories to take along with her as she walked into the darkness.

Who knew it would be so overwhelming? It hadn't been a treat; it had been something that turned her inside out, changed her profoundly. This wasn't going to be a fond memory she'd keep with her going forward into her new life. It was like a huge boulder blocking her way, rather than a stepping-stone. Jacko was this enormous presence standing astride her life. Too tall, too broad to go around. Simply there, something she'd have to deal with.

But how?

This was crazy. Choosing her new life, where to go, how to make her living once she got there, how to stay not low-profile but no-profile…all these things would take every ounce of energy and ingenuity she had in her.

She shouldn't—*couldn't*—spend all this energy dealing with Jacko in her head.

She had to get him out. Get him out of her head, out of her house, get going, without thinking of him at all. It seemed impossible but she had to do this. Simply had to.

The only way to do that was to put all her emotions into a kind of lockbox, seal it away until she was established somewhere else. Then she could pull all these feelings out and try to deal with them. But not now. Being hugely distracted now would be a disaster. Maybe cost her her life.

By the time she dried off, Lauren had herself under control. The control was thin, tenuous, but there. It should see her through today at least. Who knew where she'd be tonight, or tomorrow or the day after that? Wherever it was she landed, she'd deal with Jacko then.

Lauren dressed and stood for an extra moment in the bathroom, facing the closed bathroom door. She straightened her spine and stared at it for a minute. She could do this. She could.

Pasting a bright smile on her face, she opened the door and walked through.

"Hey." She made her smile broader when she saw Jacko sitting up in bed. It seemed as if his bare shoulders nearly covered the entire headboard. The headboard that had beat against the wall as he pumped inside her.

Pure heat flashed through her body and her knees felt liquid. Thank God she was already pink from the hot shower, so he wouldn't notice the sudden rush of blood to her face. She hoped. Jacko always surprised her with the things he noticed.

"Hey back." His voice seemed to penetrate her diaphragm.

She couldn't get a read on his expression. None at all. His face was impassive, with a slight upturning of his lips, which could be construed as a smile. Sort of.

Maybe her frantic lectures to herself were delusional. Maybe—maybe he was just waiting to get up and go. She didn't think he regretted the night of sex. But maybe it was just his usual one-night stand. Maybe he was forgetting the night with every passing second.

That would be good. It was the best possible situation for them both. She could leave knowing she had a good memory but hadn't turned her back on a new love. And if that thought hurt, just a little, too bad.

He was looking at her, patient and stolid.

"I, um—" Lauren licked dry lips. She nodded at the bathroom. "Go ahead and have a shower and I'll fix break—breakfast." Her voice wobbled. She forced her mouth into a smile. "I imagine you usually have a big breakfast. So I'd better—" She waved a hand awkwardly. "Yeah."

This was terrible. She turned and shot toward the kitchen. Before Jacko got out of bed naked and she could be reminded all over again of what she was leaving behind. Before she burst into tears.

By the time Jacko got out of the shower, breakfast was on the table. Basically Lauren just emptied most of the fridge. She wasn't going to take any food with her. So Jacko had a four-egg omelet, fried ham, two whole wheat baguettes, a big slice of cheese and hot oatmeal with brown sugar and raisins.

Her own stomach was closed up tighter than a fist. Even the smells of the food made her nauseated. She was barely keeping down the vanilla tea she'd made. She hadn't even set a plate for herself.

"Nice spread," a deep voice said. Lauren gave a start as Jacko sat down. She hadn't heard a sound. He was not there and then suddenly there. He opened up one of her pretty floral napkins and spread it on his massive thigh. It looked dainty there, and utterly incongruous. "So how come you're not eating?"

She met his dark eyes, so sober and steady and watchful. What was needed here was a smile but for a second she forgot exactly how you did that. It had been two years since she'd had much to smile about. Various parts of her face weren't cooperating. She curved her lips upward but knew the smile didn't touch her eyes.

Lie, she told herself. "I'm—I'm not really hungry. I have a bit of a headache."

He lost that impassive look and scowled fiercely. "Did I overdo it last night? Is that why you have a headache?"

Lauren's eyes opened wide. "Oh, of course not! No, I—" Her mind whirred. Words clanked around in her head. She wanted to reassure Jacko but she couldn't tell him the truth, and it was like a logjam, paralyzing her. Finally, she landed on an old standby, the nuclear bomb of excuses. "I, um, I got my period this morning." There. Most men recoiled and asked no further questions when you brought up the Great Female Mystery. Plus it would reassure him that not even *his* sperm could make the leap across latex.

But somehow it didn't mollify him. He simply took another long look at her, as if he could go in and check her ovaries to see for himself what was happening, then finally settled down to his breakfast. He ate neatly and fast and demolished everything set before him.

Lauren sat and watched, remembering to sip her tea now and again.

She'd never see him again. The thought rolled around and around in her head like some huge, toxic ball bearing, destroying everything in its path. She was incapable of wrapping her head around it. She'd just found him and she was going to have to leave him. Today. This morning.

He was dressed in his tuxedo pants and white dress shirt, no black satin bow tie. He looked tough despite the fancy clothes and as she watched him, Lauren couldn't figure out how his attractiveness had slipped her notice for so long.

How had she overlooked the sheer male appeal of him? The huge shoulders and arms, the strong neck, the strong, dark features of his face. They all added up to such a sexy package. How had she not noticed? Even the shaved head was sexy. And the tats, hmm. The tribal tats had been a huge surprise and had turned her on enormously.

Tough guys weren't her usual type but there wasn't a woman alive with a pulse who could be indifferent. Why had it taken her so long to see that sexiness?

Maybe because he had acted so standoffish when he was around her. It sometimes felt as if he leaned *away* from her when she was with him. Which was cool. Not every man on earth had to be attracted to her. But even so, even being stiff as a board around her, he had always been …*there*. And she'd been attracted; she just hadn't realized it.

She realized it now. And how.

His huge body seemed to occupy more space than it should, like some high-density planet, and like a high-density planet with a moon, her natural inclination was to lean into him. She had to hold herself stiffly to keep still, because she wanted to lean forward, lay her hand on that massive forearm. For warmth, for reassurance. For sex.

Because, well…she'd be up for sex with Jacko again. Oh yeah.

Who knew sex could be like that? Overwhelming, life-altering. She felt like she'd discovered her body for the very first time. Something that hadn't existed before Jacko's touch.

Oh man. Leaving was going to *hurt*.

What she was feeling must have been putting out vibrations or something because his gaze grew even keener. He was about to say something. Jacko didn't talk much but what he did say was smart. He was picking up on her distress.

No no no.

She pasted a huge smile on her face, rose, started putting the breakfast dishes away. This was pure habit. She was going to leave the dishes and most of the pretty things she had accumulated behind. No baggage going forward. It was going to be a minimalist existence from now on. Renting a furnished unit and keeping personal belongings to a minimum. So wanting to put the dishes in the sink and wash them was pure muscle memory.

Jacko rose with her, bread and milk pitcher in hand. Oh God, he was *domesticated*?

"No, no." She made shooing motions with her hands. He had to leave right now before she burst into tears. "I can do that more quickly on my own. I have some work to do so, um, maybe you'd better get going." She looked him over. "You're not going into work in your tux, are you?"

"No, ma'am," his deep voice intoned. So we were back to ma'am? He narrowed his eyes. "What time do you think you'll be done?"

She blanked. "Done? With what?"

"With work. With what you have to do."

What she had to do was throw her clothes, computer and artwork in her car, take off and drive as far as her strength would allow. "Um, probably all afternoon."

"Okay. Do you want to go out for dinner?"

"Um, sure." Her voice wobbled on the word. She coughed. "Yeah. Sorry, I might be catching something. But sure. Let's go out for dinner."

He was searching her face, looking for something. She made her face a happy place, using every ounce of pre-varication in her. Happy, happy. Woman who'd just had sex with an interesting new guy. Who wanted to see her again. Happy, happy.

He grunted and picked up his tux jacket.

He was leaving! She wanted him to leave, absolutely. There was a lot to do and many miles to travel today but…*he was leaving*.

She'd never see him again. She wanted this but she wasn't ready for it. Would probably never be ready for it.

Her smile was blinding. He was leaving and her heart was breaking. Her hand wanted to reach out, touch him, hold on to him, and she had to make a fist to keep from touching him.

She offered her cheek for a kiss but Jacko cupped the back of her head with one big hand and drew her to him. It happened fast but there was nothing in her that would have—could have—resisted his kiss. She stepped forward, into his embrace, and was lost. His mouth was as soft as she remembered. He hadn't shaved and the heavy beard—now stubble—scratched her skin and she loved it. The first touch of his lips to hers was electric. Far too exciting. She pulled away before she could lose herself in that kiss.

Before she asked him to stay.

Before she changed her mind.

She showed her teeth. That was a smile, wasn't it? And swatted his arm, as if playfully flirting. "Go on now. Get out of here."

Before I beg you to stay.

Showing him $20,000 of orthodontics worked. He searched her face for another long moment then lifted one side of his mouth. "Can't wait to get rid of me, huh?"

The opposite.

She made a gun of her thumb and forefinger and shot him. "Work. To do. Now scat."

She accompanied him to the door, with a friendly hand on his shoulder. Actually, she just wanted to touch him one last time. While touching him, the monsters were kept at bay. No fear, no terror. Just hard warm muscle.

She ushered him over the threshold, still touching him. It was so hard to let go. She wanted to touch him forever, but she couldn't. Her hand dropped. He turned back, dark face serious, dark eyes searching hers.

She turned herself into a bright, shiny mirror, nothing visible underneath. *Nothing to see here, folks. Move right along.*

"What time?" Jacko said.

"What?"

"What time should I pick you up?"

Her mind whirred uselessly. Pick her up?

"For dinner," he said. "Tonight."

"Oh!" A spear of grief, sharp and uncontrollable, shot straight through her heart. Tonight she'd be as far away as she could drive. Out of his life forever. Tonight would never happen. "Sure. Six, say?"

He nodded, stepped forward.

She stepped back.

She didn't want a goodbye kiss, because it would really be goodbye and she didn't want to burst into tears in the middle of it. Jacko was unnaturally perceptive. Already he was looking at her in unlover-like terms, head tilted, eyes sharp. Like he was studying her.

"Okay!" she said, her voice suddenly loud. She clapped her hands, hoping she wasn't behaving like a loon. "See you this evening."

One last, slit-eyed look and Jacko nodded. He turned and walked to his huge SUV, which he'd parked right outside her garage door, blocking her. She couldn't leave until he drove away.

God, he was enticing even from the back. Insanely broad shoulders, thick strong neck rising incongruously from the satin collar of his tux, huge hands surrounded by an inch of white dress shirt cuffs peeping from under the fine black wool of the jacket sleeves. Hiding the barbed wire tats around his wrists, but she knew they were there.

He looked like he was walking slowly but in an instant—far too soon, in fact—he was at his vehicle's door. Once he was behind the wheel he paused for a second with the door open, looking across her small front yard at her.

She turned her lips up and made a little wave like a kid going bye-bye. Jacko nodded, got in, slammed the door shut and she lost all view of him behind the smoked glass.

Lauren swallowed, feeling suddenly sick. This was it. She'd never see his face again.

Jacko backed quickly out of her short driveway and drove off fast. She stood stupidly on the porch until she couldn't even pretend to see his vehicle, the unshed tears finally pouring down her face.

Inside she stood for a long moment, unable to summon the energy she needed to do this. It felt like her feet had been nailed to the pale hardwood floor. She couldn't move, could only sway there, tears dripping down her face. Her living room, which she'd lavished such love and care on, became a blur. Her heart, which had started beating hard as she said goodbye to Jacko, slowed, became a cold hard stone in her chest.

She swiped at her cheeks, trying to relegate Jacko to the back of her mind. There was no time to think of him, to mourn his absence. There was a life to end and another to begin.

She stared at the ceiling, willing the tears to stop. Finally, finally, they did.

Jacko was gone. Soon she'd drive away from this pretty little house and never come back. When he stopped by at six to pick her up for dinner she'd be at least four hundred miles away.

This was so hard. Yet this was going to be the rest of her life. Not making ties so it wouldn't be so painful leaving.

Even leaving her things behind hurt.

The curtains she'd made from Italian cotton bedspreads, the rescued coffee table she'd restored herself, the battered silver bowl from a garage sale she'd polished to a high sheen and filled with homemade potpourri. Small inexpensive things that had turned the house into a home. All wasted efforts, it turned out, because she was going to turn her back on them. She'd leave with the bare essentials for a new life—clothes, laptop and artwork—and that was it.

But first there was someone she had to tell. Someone she'd never met but who had saved her, and was her friend.

Opening her laptop, she found Tor and keyed in the
steps necessary to access the darknet. At times it felt
like descending down, down, down into another world.
An even darker and more dangerous world than this one.
Except for one small corner of it.

Felicity.

It wasn't her real name. Steeped in pop culture, Felicity loved *Arrow* and named herself for Felicity Smoak.
It seemed apt. Felicity Smoak always saved the day with
her smarts, and so did Lauren's Felicity.

She had no idea who Felicity was in real life, where
she lived, even what she did for a living. But she felt as
close to her as she would to a sister. Though she never
spoke about the details of her life, Lauren had the dis-
tinct impression that Felicity was as alone in the world
as she was. And that Felicity knew trouble, firsthand.

The secret impregnable chat room had an orange-and-
teal header because Felicity was a film buff. On the right-
hand side of the header was their symbol. Two feminine
hands, fist bumping. Bright orange fingernail polish on
one hand, bright blue polish on the other. Lauren had
designed it.

She saw that Felicity was online, as usual. She never
seemed to sleep.

Lauren signed in.

Runner: Runner here. Pulling the plug on this life.

The reply came almost instantaneously. Felicity didn't
ask any questions. Lauren had chosen the handle *Runner*
for a reason. She was on the run. Felicity knew that if
she needed to pull the plug, she needed to pull the plug.
Felicity also knew that she would need to change identi-

ties. Lauren Dare was a Felicity construct. Felicity had done it before; she'd do it again.

Felicity: Tell me what you need. Let me know when you get to where you're going then contact me. I'll get you whatever you need.

Runner: Not sure where I'm going. Doesn't matter as long as it's far away. And I need a new life.   .

Felicity: You need the TARDIS. Failing that, how about an eye in the sky? Who's on your tail?

Lauren sometimes wondered whether Felicity worked for the NSA. Several times she'd been able to provide overhead surveillance. Though she was good enough that maybe she'd hacked the NSA.

Runner: No one's after me right now. But it's time to go. I made a mistake last night. Let my guard down.

Felicity: A preventive bail. Smart choice. Nowhere is safe for long.

Runner: No, nowhere is safe for long.

She closed her eyes. Somehow Felicity knew, understood. Lauren could feel the sadness coming off the monitor.

Felicity: Docs. You'll need new ID. I can get you anything you need, girl. Just say the word. You want to be a PhD

in quantum physics? Done. You want to be a surgeon?
I'll have you in the operating theater in no time.

Lauren smiled. She was Lauren Dare thanks to Felicity, who could make her a doctor or a physicist or Italian.
She was brilliant.

Runner: Thanks. Will ask for new docs when I get to
where I'm going. Probably be best if I don't operate
on anyone.

Felicity: If you're going to go, do it fast. Speed is life.

Runner: Don't I know it.

Felicity: Sorry you're ejecting. Sounded like you had a
really good deal going there. Hard to give it up.

Runner. A very good deal. V sorry to go. Breaks my heart.

She wiped wet eyes. The screen was blank for a moment.

Felicity: OMG. A guy! You found a guy and now you
have to dump him and run! Bummer!

Pity Felicity was so very smart. Lauren had to put a
spin on it to save her heart.

Runner: Probably wouldn't have worked out anyway.
Hard to be with a guy when you're on the run.

Felicity: So how was the sex? On a scale of one to ten?

Lauren typed before thinking.

Runner: 100

Felicity: Sigh. You can't take him with you?

Taking Jacko with her. Heat shot through her at the thought. Heat and hope. Feeling safe all the time. Hot sex at night. Oh yeah. She'd give anything to take Jacko with her. But of course that was impossible. In another life, in another universe, maybe. But not in this one.

And, frankly, she couldn't imagine Jacko wanting to abandon his excellent job and his life here to follow her into exile.

Runner: Double sigh. No.

Felicity: Take a lock of his hair with you. For memory's sake. And maybe I can clone him from the DNA. Make sure to get follicles.

Lauren laughed and wiped away a tear. Felicity probably *could* clone him. All this time she'd imagined Felicity as some super analyst somewhere but maybe she was a lab rat in a white coat who could pipette a new Jacko into life. Of course Lauren would have to wait for Jacko to be born and grow up and she'd be sixty when he was thirty. That would totally work for Doctor Who but not for her.

Runner: Can't. Shaved head.

Felicity. Yum. Tats?

Runner: Tribal. Shoulder. Barbed wire around wrists. V sexy.

Felicity: Take some pubes with you. That guy definitely needs cloning.

Runner: I wish.

Felicity: Get going. Like I said, if you have to go, do it fast. When you land, get in touch. I'll be here.

Runner: On my way. And thanks.

Felicity: np

Their chat page blinked out. Lauren powered down her MacBook Air, resting a hand on the cover, fingers caressing the smooth Apple logo. It felt, for just a moment, as if she were still connected to her virtual friend. It was crazy but she could feel Felicity's support coming over the ether. Pixels and digits and friendship. She knew nothing about Felicity except for the important things. Felicity was smart, she had secrets, too, and she was on Lauren's side, always.

At least Lauren could plug back into the chat room when she finally landed. Jacko and her friends here were already in the wind, lost. This virtual friend on a secret network was the only constant in her life now.

God, it was already nine and she hadn't packed yet.

Good thing her wardrobe was deliberately small. Good pieces, but not many of them. Everything she owned fit into a midsized suitcase. She wheeled it out to the garage and went back in for her artwork. Her artwork could possibly be used to track her down if any of Jorge's people searched her house so everything she had went into the car. All her computer-generated graphic work was stored in the cloud under a fictitious name.

By ten she was ready to walk through the house for the last time, hand lingering over various items, as if touching them would store them better in her memory. The house was so pretty. She'd fallen in love with it immediately. Basically, a living room/kitchen, bedroom and a huge room with a skylight where she worked. More than enough. Snug and cheerful. The place where she'd hoped to make a life for herself, and damn it, she *had*. She'd made a wonderful life for herself.

Lauren angrily wiped a tear away. She never cried, never allowed herself to, and this morning she was leaking water like a faucet.

At the door to her bedroom she stopped. This was the last time she'd see where she'd made love with Jacko. It had been the best thing to happen to her since her mother and stepfather had died and this whole mess started.

She looked at the bed across the room, reliving some of the highlights of last night. Maybe the memory of last night would fade, as memories did over the years. Right now, though, the memory was vivid, hi-def, 3D.

Never again. Never again a mind-blowing love affair. Never again would she have friends in the flesh. Never again warmth and closeness with others.

Goodbye house.

Goodbye life.

Goodbye Jacko.

It had started snowing again, light flakes that drifted down like afterthoughts, the world outside light gray, nebulous. Pretty. Dangerous. She wasn't a good driver. Driving in the snow was terrifying, one more horror.

South. She'd head south. Maybe somewhere with a beach. San Diego would be perfect but it was still West Coast. Maybe it was best not to repeat herself. Florida was out, of course. Texas, Louisiana? Time enough on the road to decide.

Lights out, heat off.

She shivered in the garage, cold seeping into her bones. The car was packed, ready to go. She was lingering, not wanting to take off. Wanting a few minutes more here, in this magical city where she'd met some magical people.

She was going to hurt them by disappearing. For a second, crazily, she thought of going back in to leave a goodbye note.

No. That was dangerous thinking. No more stalling. It was time.

She reached into her purse for the keys and didn't find them. She scrabbled a bit around the bottom, frowning. She kept a neat purse. Car keys in one internal pocket, house keys in another. The house keys weren't there because she'd left them on the kitchen table. And…the car keys weren't there, either.

She searched again, more thoroughly. Clearly, she'd missed the car keys because she was hurting, worried. So she looked again. But they weren't there.

Sighing, Lauren opened her purse wider, angling it so it would catch the meager light of the overhead bulb.

No keys.

How could she leave if she didn't have car keys?

Search one more time.

This time she carefully placed the contents of her

purse on the car fender. Wallet, fake driver's license, fake ID, makeup case, her ereader with a thousand books on it. No keys.

This was a disaster. The snow was falling more heavily now. If the keys weren't in her purse—which they *should be*—then she had no idea where to look. It could take her hours to scour the house, hours she didn't have.

Now that she wasn't in the Jacko Force Field of Safety, danger was drumming in her head. She'd made a huge mistake last night and she was going to pay. She could feel it; she could almost smell it. Her neck prickled with the sense of impending danger. Jorge's goons could be coming for her *right now.*

She had to leave *right now.*

She huffed out an angry, scared breath, turning to walk back into the house, when a huge hand appeared in front of her, car keys dangling from thick fingers.

"Looking for these?" Jacko's deep voice asked.

FIVE

Palm Beach, Florida

THE NEXT DAY Frederick found it on the front passenger seat of his car. He was on his way to the airport where he'd fly under another identity to George Town. His Caymans' banker had contacted him for an "interesting proposal," which would have to be discussed in private and in person. He suspected the banker had somehow discovered Frederick's gifts and was proposing a money laundering scheme. This was perfect. The profit potential would be huge and above all, Frederick wouldn't get his hands dirty. He knew how to cover his traces. And it probably meant several trips to the Caymans a year, which was a pleasant thought. What was wealth in the United States was unimaginable riches in the Caymans. He could live like a king, outside the jurisdiction of the United States.

Finding something in his car was interesting in and of itself. Frederick's security everywhere was superb, and that included his car, a Lexus LS whose already-strong security system had been tweaked. The car door opened to his electronic key but it also required his thumbprint.

So if someone left something for him in the front seat of his car, that someone was serious.

A sat phone. Bigger, bulkier than most smartphones. He recognized it immediately. The latest Thuraya. Guaranteed non-hackable because it operated off a Saudi-owned satellite and the Saudis were not in the habit of sharing intel with the NSA, or anyone else for that matter. The Thuraya was an expensive, difficult-to-obtain piece of tech.

A small slip of paper with laser-printed words was on top of it. *Password: money.*

Okay. Good password.

He fired it up, put in the password and saw that it was preprogrammed with one long number. He didn't recognize the prefix and was sure that it didn't correspond to any specific geographic location. It was a connection to a forwarding service. The number itself would be of no help in understanding where the person on the other end was located.

Someone had gone through time and trouble to talk to him.

Frederick made his considerable living helping those in trouble. He pressed the call button and waited.

"Hello." The voice at the other end was mechanically altered. There were no hints as to identity. He couldn't even tell the sex.

"Hello," Frederick answered. "I'm listening."

"I understand you work for Jorge Guttierez."

"In a manner of speaking," he hedged.

This was tricky. Was this one of Jorge's many enemies? Was he going to get an offer to work against Jorge? Frederick had no loyalty to Jorge at all, but generally speaking it wasn't a good idea to get a reputation as someone who'd betray a client. If this was Jorge's enemy, though, he wouldn't play by any sane rules and wouldn't take no for an answer.

Damn. Why did Alfonso go get himself killed?

"This is not about Jorge. It is not even about Alfonso. It is about his wife, Chantal." Mechanical Voice dropped the little bombshell.

Frederick wasn't an easy man to surprise but this did. *Chantal?* To his knowledge Chantal had been a beautiful clotheshorse whose only real talent was spending money, and nothing more. What would some Mafioso want with Chantal?

"What about Chantal?"

"She had a jewelry collection. A famous one. Some pieces are designer classics." The mechanical voice all of a sudden sounded pained. "My wife wants the collection. Badly."

"I'm sorry," Frederick answered. He was sincere. He was *very* sorry. If there was money to be made knowing where Chantal's jewelry collection was, he wasn't going to get it. "I have no idea where that collection is."

"Chantal's daughter does," the voice said.

Frederick blinked. "Anne?"

"Yes. Anne. Chantal said that her collection was in a safe place and only she and her daughter knew where."

Ah. Frederick straightened in his seat. This was getting interesting.

"I am actually looking for Anne." He put that forward cautiously.

"Yes, I know. For that moron Jorge. Jorge wants her dead. I don't want her dead, certainly not before she has revealed where the jewelry collection is. I don't know how much Jorge is paying you, but I'll make it more than worth your while to find her, so long as you remember that a live Anne trumps a dead Anne."

Who will become a dead Anne as soon as wifey gets her bling. The subtext was unspoken but there.

"I can't start right now. I can only start in three days. Seventy-two hours, take it or leave it."

He couldn't do anything on the road; it would never be secure enough. He traveled clean and he always worked from home.

At home he could take precautions. His keyboard was TEMPEST-proof. His computer had a firewall that, if it were a real wall, could be seen from the moon.

The walls of his home had a special cladding that bounced any type of electronic surveillance, and the windows had a molecule-thick graphene film coating that protected against laser listening devices.

Essentially his house was what intelligence agencies call a SCIF—a Sensitive Compartmented Intelligence Facility. What happened in his home stayed in his home.

Everything on his computer was saved to a cloud managed in Estonia, guaranteed anonymity for ten thousand USD a year, cheap at the price.

His home was as secure as he could make it, and he preferred to work there.

Long silence. Then finally Mechanical Voice spoke. "Word has it you're the best."

Damn straight. "Yes," he said.

A mechanical sigh. "All right. But I want results soon."

"You'll have them. And now…about the fee."

"Two hundred and fifty thousand."

Not enough for what would eventually lead to a dead body. Frederick didn't care what happened to Anne Lowell but bloodshed was always more dangerous than shifting bitcoins around. The police were more tenacious about blood spilled than money lost. There was a remote possibility that this could somehow boomerang.

"Half a million," he replied.

Another pause, then— "Done."

"Half now and half when I make her available to you."

"Ah." The mechanical voice stopped. "I was thinking you could, um, extract the information yourself."

Frederick was many things, but he wasn't a thug. Nor a torturer. He shuddered at the thought. He was a civilized man. "No," he said firmly. "I hand Anne over to you and you do the honors."

A slight hesitation. "Done. Text your account details to this number."

Nail it down, Frederick thought. "Two hundred and fifty K, up front."

"Yes. The second half when I take possession of the girl."

It was clear that Mechanical Voice wasn't going to let Anne live after he got his hands on the jewels. Whether by Jorge's or MV's hand, Anne Lowell was already dead. The only difference was that one option would net him half a million dollars more. This guy sounded serious. Frederick didn't think Jorge had much money anymore. There was no question which boss Frederick was going to choose.

"So I call this number when I have the girl?" he asked.

"Yes." The connection was broken.

Frederick texted his Caymans account number and waited. Gratifyingly, the money showed up in minutes. In untraceable bitcoins.

It was always good dealing with a better class of criminal.

Portland

LAUREN SCREAMED AND turned as white as the snow outside. She stumbled.

Fuck! Jacko hadn't thought it through. He took a fast step forward and put his arms around her.

"Whoa." She was shaking so hard she vibrated against him. He held her tighter. "Hey. Sorry to scare you. Let's get you inside. It's cold here in the garage."

She didn't move. "Jacko?" she whispered, voice trembling. She pushed against him weakly. "How did you—you don't understand. I have to go."

Jacko looked down at her. He hated the look on her white face. The same look she'd had last night when the fucker'd taken her photograph. Drawn, terrified. His instinct then was right. She was scared to death of someone. Jacko had no idea who that fucker could be but he was a walking dead man. And he wouldn't lay a finger on Lauren, guaranfuckingteed.

She was panting with distress, breath a cloud around her beautiful head in the freezing garage. She was shaking so hard her teeth were chattering.

The hell with this.

"Come on, honey." It was really hard to keep his voice even because just the thought of someone after Lauren, someone wanting to hurt her…shit.

Jacko knew he had a deep, rough voice. Nothing he could do about that. But he tried to modulate it, keep his rage out of it, be reassuring. He wasn't good at the reassurance thing, he was better at being a badass, but this was Lauren and whatever she needed, he needed to give it to her. Right now she needed him to be calm and reassuring. "Let's go back inside. You can't stay here—you're freezing to death."

She pulled away, movements slow, uncoordinated. Jacko recognized shock. He'd seen enough of it in his life. He kept her trembling, ice-cold hands in his.

Even terrified and shocked, she was still so fucking beautiful. Those frosted blue eyes searched his. He didn't know what she was looking for but she wasn't finding it. She wheezed, pulled in air. Though she tugged at his hands, he wasn't letting go. His hold tightened, painless but firm.

"Jacko, you don't understand. I have to go. Have to. Right now."

Jacko brought her hands to his mouth, hoping he was transferring some warmth to her. "No, I don't understand. Tell me about it. Make me understand. Whatever it is, we can face it together."

Her hands jerked in his; she became even paler. "No!" Lauren shuddered deeply. "God no. He could hurt you, too."

Man, whoever this fucker was, he was dead meat.

"I'm hard to hurt, honey," he said gently. "Now come inside and tell me what this is all about."

She must have seen that he meant business, that she wasn't going anywhere, because when he pulled her toward the door leading back into the kitchen, she didn't resist. Good.

The first thing he did was sit her down on her sofa and drop his tux jacket over her knees. It would retain some of his body warmth, which she needed. He got up briefly to turn her heating back on. She jumped at the *whump!* of the boiler switching on.

When he sat down beside her again and held her hands, she pulled away.

"You need to let me go." A small slender hand covered her mouth. "You don't understand, Jacko. He'll find me again. He killed two people to get to me. I'm putting everyone in danger by staying. I can't do it. Please don't ask me to."

Two people had been killed? The hair on his forearms stood up. This was worse than he thought.

Lauren, dead.

The image bloomed in his head, in vivid colors. Jacko had seen a lot of dead people over the years, some by his hand. It was never easy, never pretty. His head couldn't wrap around the idea of a murdered Lauren.

Sure, she would die some day. A beautiful, white-haired Lauren seventy years from now, gorgeous and peaceful in her casket. Dead in her sleep.

Jacko knew, bone deep, what people who'd been killed looked like. Violent death was his thing, what he'd trained all his adult life for. He knew it inside out and it should never be anywhere near Lauren.

Violent death was grotesque. Lacerations, burned skin, blood everywhere. He couldn't think of that in relation to Lauren—it messed with his head. That pale, perfect skin, slashed. Beautiful head, the pink mist of a head shot surrounding it. Slender limbs, broken.

Someone killing her, then walking away. It was bad enough thinking of her being hunted before he knew her. Now that he knew her, now that she was his—no. It drove him crazy, just the thought of it.

Something big had come into his world with Lauren. Bits and pieces of it had slid into his life as he spent time with his bosses' women. Quick glimpses of a new world, a different world. Beauty and grace and stillness and peace. Things he had never had in his life. And then Lauren had arrived and a door had been thrown open. He hadn't actually thought of walking through that door. It was enough to see what was on the other side.

But last night he'd walked through that door and there was no going back.

He didn't believe in God and he didn't believe in heaven or hell. But if he did, he could say he'd glimpsed heaven with Lauren. Which was crazy, of course.

But still.

She was watching him out of huge eyes. "How did you know? I thought you'd gone. How did you know to come back?"

Because the entire morning was a goodbye. "Instinct," he said. "I lifted the car keys from your purse. When I left, I parked around the corner and doubled back, picked your garage lock, waited for you." It had been child's play. For a woman on the run, Lauren had no notion of tradecraft. No matter. She didn't need it. She had him now. "On my way in, I disabled the security cam across the street. There were no others. Right now there are no eyes on you."

Her eyes widened. She'd had no idea of the existence of the vidcam on the front porch of her neighbor's house.

"Okay. That—that's good."

"So you wanna tell me what's going on?"

Lauren's face turned serious. "I don't know, Jacko. I've never told anyone. It's—it's so hard. Once I tell you, you're involved."

She studied his face and he let her. He didn't think words would do the trick, and he wasn't good with words anyway. All he really had was himself and what he felt about her, which was that he was a mean motherfucker and that he would lay down his life for her. It had to be enough.

She took her time, which was okay by him. If he was running from someone he'd be careful who to trust, too.

Finally, Lauren gave a sigh, turned her hands in his

and held his hands tight. Her body told him before the words did that she had decided.

"My name isn't Lauren, Jacko," she started. Jacko wasn't too surprised. In the military there were lots of guys who were running from their background and they all had nicknames.

He nodded. "Jacko's not my name, either."

"I know," she said. "But you didn't change yours to hide from a madman."

He was listening to her voice but he was also listening to the pattern of her breathing, watching the blinking of her eyes. He casually held a finger to her racing pulse. Those things told him as much as the words did.

She was stressed, terrified.

He'd been trained in interrogation. He knew how to break bad guys, how to extract all the intel possible, and he wasn't gentle about it. He didn't want to break Lauren though, God no. But he *did* want to understand. So he wouldn't trick her out of intel or beat it out of her, but he could make her trust him enough to talk. He turned still, letting her take her time to decide. Stillness was a gift and he'd always had it.

For Lauren, he could wait forever.

She continued watching him and he turned himself into a still pool. No possible threat, just acceptance. Whatever she wanted to tell him, he was ready to hear it.

Quiet, inside and outside the small pretty house. Snow was falling steadily, damping sounds. He turned himself into a statue, breathing from his diaphragm, slow, steady, silent.

She watched him for a full minute, two.

Jacko wasn't used to opening himself up in any way to anyone, but he did it now. With most people he presented an opaque front. He had a rough background and he'd learned the hard way that you don't present any weakness to the world.

He'd been born to a druggie mom who dragged home a succession of "uncles" who rarely spent more than a weekday or two with them. One of the fucks had been his father, though he had no clue which one. Neither did his mom. He didn't even have a clue what race his dad was. One thing was for sure, though—the fucker wasn't white bread, no sir. Jacko looked like a mongrel with a hundred different ethnicities swimming in his blood. In the Navy he put himself down as *Mixed Race*.

He'd zipped fast and hard through adolescence where he'd been thrown out of high school for fighting so often he just stopped going, then straight into the Navy where he got his GCE. From there just kept moving faster and harder up into the SEALs.

SEALs weren't touchy-feely kind of guys. He didn't like talking about his childhood and he couldn't talk about his missions with the SEALs or for ASI, which didn't leave much space for small talk. Fine with him. He wasn't into emoting or group hugs. Right now, though, he tried to dismantle a lifetime of thick concrete walls, the ones that had saved him as a child and that allowed him to function in the hellholes he was sent to as an adult.

He wanted Lauren to trust him, instinctively. He wanted to be the guy she turned to, instinctively. So he sat, wanting her to understand she could trust him.

It wasn't that hard. His teammates knew everything about him they needed to know, which was that he was loyal and knew how to shoot. Lauren could know more. No walls with Lauren.

Finally, she nodded. "Okay. I grew up in Boston. My

parents divorced when I was ten and my father died soon after. My mother married a very rich man from Florida, originally from Colombia. Very, very rich. Alfonso Guttierez. He didn't make his money the nice way, though she didn't care. He had enough money to create a patina of elegance around him, but he was a crime lord. Drugs, guns, you name it. Officially, his money came from a string of casinos and hotels and restaurants he owned.

"My mother liked the money, and didn't care how he got it. I was sent to boarding school throughout my teens and then went directly to college in upstate New York and got a job at a museum in Chicago. I rarely went home to Florida. There was something creepy about my step-father and all that wealth. I didn't want any part of it. I would have died rather than touch a penny of my step-father's money. He had a big family back in Colombia and took a nephew in to what I guess you could call the family business. Scumbagitude. Alfonso was able to hide what he was under an elegant façade but Jorge was…" she shuddered. "Jorge was bad news. Violent and a little crazy. And unlike Alfonso he gambled and took drugs himself. Two years ago, my mother and Alfonso were in a car crash that killed them both. Alfonso had made my mother his universal heir. She outlived him by an hour and the entire empire came to me."

Lauren's head fell slowly forward to his shoulder. Jacko cupped the back of her neck and waited. He placed his thumb along the carotid and felt the fast pulse there. Her warm breath washed his neck.

She pulled back, looked him in the eyes. "I inherited millions. I don't even know how much. I didn't want it, but the law wanted to give it to me anyway. Six hours after my mother's will was read, Jorge tried to kill me.

He killed a girlfriend who was staying with me instead. And he killed another friend his goons mistook for me. I barely escaped that time, too. I survived this long in Portland because a—a friend got me new ID. But he is after me and he will never stop." For a second, Jacko was so filled with rage he couldn't think, which was bad. Elite soldiers don't have feelings. They don't *want* to kill. They could when they had to, no question, but that's not what SEALs were about.

But right now? Right now he wanted to rip this Jorge's heart out of his chest, see his blood flow, look down on his dead carcass and spit on it. He shook with the desire to kill.

Jacko had to wait a moment until his voice was calm. Inside he was raging but Lauren needed to see him in control. He pulled away, lifted her head so she could look him in the eyes to see the truth of what he said.

"That's over, honey. It's all over. No one is ever going to hurt you again, even come near you, not as long as I am alive." He waited for the words to sink in. "Do you believe me?"

"I—I think I do." She nodded jerkily. "I really really don't want that money, Jacko. I don't even know how to give it to him, which I would if I could. I think I could renounce it legally but I'd have to come out in the open and he'd get to me. That money is tainted—it makes me sick just to think of it. But he wants me dead now, no matter what."

Lauren put her hand against his face. He hadn't shaved so she'd be feeling bristly stubble. Her hand was cold against his cheek. She tried to smile. "I know you think you can keep me safe but you've got a job, Jacko. A life. You can't stick by my side 24/7."

Oh yes I can, he thought.

"I'll show you." Jacko put his hand under her elbow and rose. She rose with him, surprised.

"Show me what?"

"You'll see. Let's go. We're wasting time."

JACKO WAS FAST.

It had taken her two hours to pack her car but it took him only fifteen minutes to transfer all her car's contents to his SUV, even though there wasn't that much room with the huge bike in back. He brought his vehicle around, backed it into her garage and worked quickly and quietly.

When she asked if she could help, he said she could pack more of her stuff if she wanted, so she did. Including things it had broken her heart to leave behind. It felt good to be able to have more of her books, the two sets of linen Frette sheets, the posters of Picasso's bullfighters she'd had framed in light maplewood.

He came to get her in her bedroom, kissed her nose and lifted the bags from her hands.

Lauren looked up at him, at that dark intent face. As usual, she couldn't read his expression. He presented a completely blank slate to the world and for the first time, she wondered whether it was a tactic as opposed to his nature. Because the man who'd been in bed with her was not a blank slate. He was a man of fire and passion.

She put a hand on his forearm, savoring the power and the warmth, and said the hard thing that needed to be said. "Jacko, last chance. Some very powerful people are after me. Jorge has an army of goons. The last thing I want is for you to be hurt."

"Honey." He put his hard hand over hers and oh wow,

it felt like he was transferring strength to her by touch. "I'm not going to get hurt and neither are you. Guaranteed."

Guaranteed. Nobody could guarantee anything in this world. She knew that. Her mother and stepfather had been protected by vast amounts of money and a phalanx of thugs and in the end, they'd succumbed to a drugged-up teenager. Life at times was like a scorpion, stinging everything within reach. So no, Jacko couldn't guarantee her safety or even his own.

But she felt better. It was like a small lifeboat suddenly appearing in a storm where she was barely keeping her head above water. Crazy as it sounded, she felt reassured. And she didn't feel so alone.

It had been so very hard before Portland, completely on her own with her secrets and in hiding. Sure she had Felicity and Felicity was great, but Lauren liked being surrounded by friends. It had been the hardest part of being a runaway—being alone. It was why she had slipped up here in Portland, lulled by the friendship of Suzanne and Allegra and Claire. Enveloped in their warm embrace.

Jacko was watching her carefully, dark eyes intent. They stood there and she felt a surge of…rebellion. Jorge Guttierez, the scum of the earth, had made her life a living hell these past two years. He'd killed two people simply because they'd been close to her. He was a drug dealer and a psychopath.

It was time for this to end.

"Okay?" Jacko asked, deep voice quiet and firm.

"Okay." Lauren didn't know if it was really okay or not, but the word felt good in her mouth. It had been a long long time since she could say that anything was okay.

Jacko looked around her house. "I'll come back and pick up the rest of your stuff." He lifted his hand when she opened her mouth. "Believe me when I say no one will see me doing it."

She looked at that hard, tough face and believed him. She nodded.

It was snowing hard by the time she settled into the passenger seat of his SUV. She looked behind uneasily. Anyone who had eyes to see would note that this was a move. Luckily, he had darkly smoked glass almost everywhere, except in the front windshield. The windowpane was very clear.

"I know you killed the security cameras across the street," she said. "But when we do pass by security cameras, won't they see me? I know it's stupid to think of this now when I should have thought of it before, but now that I'm thinking in terms of cameras…"

Jacko turned to her, one big hand resting on the top of the steering wheel. "I have mapped out an itinerary of about three blocks without security cameras." He picked up his cell. "But I have something even better than a safe route."

Lauren looked on, puzzled, as he got out of the SUV and took snapshots of the entire front of his vehicle. Not selfies—he didn't appear anywhere. Just photos of the front of his SUV. The vehicle didn't dip when he got back in. Maybe it was reinforced.

Jacko showed her the screen of his cell. "Look carefully, honey, and tell me what you see."

For a moment, she didn't take in his words because her heart lurched when he called her *honey*. Such a simple word. Guys used it all the time. One friend in college told her he called all his women either *honey* or *babe* in case he forgot their names.

Something told her that wasn't Jacko's style and that he wasn't a big one for endearments.

She focused on the cell monitor to keep herself under control. She took the cell in hand, turned it so it was horizontal, but it still didn't make sense. What was she looking at? Vague stippled patterns.

"Can you see yourself?" Jacko asked.

Lauren frowned, studied the monitor carefully. "No," she said slowly. "I can't. Why can't I?"

"Because the front window is coated with a special film. It's invisible to the naked eye, which is why I see perfectly through it and why it doesn't raise any questions to outsiders or cops. But the film prevents vidcams or cameras from seeing inside. So no one is going to see you. No one. And images are slightly distorted to human sight, too. Not enough to raise a flag but enough to make it impossible to read who the passenger and driver are."

Lauren looked from the cell monitor, which showed an uneven camouflage effect to the window itself, which was perfectly transparent to her on the inside. On the film though, you couldn't even tell there were people inside.

"That's pretty nifty," she said. "Smart guy."

Jacko shook his head. "Careful guy."

Paranoid guy, too, but she wasn't complaining.

He pressed the remote and rolled out slowly, waiting on the curb until the garage door was closed again. Lauren looked back with a small pang. She'd been happy there.

Jacko shot her a narrow-eyed look. "I'm really sorry, but you're not going back again. Not until we're sure the danger is over."

He was protecting her. She tried smiling at him. It probably wasn't convincing but she did try. "I know, Jacko. I know. That house is the least of the things I've lost."

His jaw muscles flexed. "We'll get everything back for you. That's a promise."

Lauren nodded, throat tight.

Nice thought. But she didn't believe it.

SIX

IT WAS STILL snowing heavily by the time Jacko got onto one of the main roads, blending smoothly into the traffic. No one noticed his SUV and that was exactly as it should be. He'd even smeared some muddy snow on his tags. No one was going to get to Lauren through him.

Though he was concentrated on the road ahead—the snow was so heavy it challenged even his driving skills— he could see her perfectly well in his peripheral vision. She was sitting quietly, gloved hands in her lap, staring straight ahead. All he could see was her profile, steady and composed, but very pale.

It pained her to leave her little house and he understood completely. One night there and even he felt at home in it. She'd worked on it and she loved it, and a scumbag drug dealer was chasing her away. He tightened his hands on the wheel, wishing they were around the fucker's throat.

Well, he had a plan. He was good at strategizing and he was good at operational implementation, and as soon as humanly possible Lauren would be free and someone would be dead or in jail. The way he felt, preferably dead.

Lauren suddenly sat up straight and looked around. "Shouldn't we have taken Kearney? Don't you live in Roseway?"

"Yeah. We'll get there but first we have to stop by the office. I have some stuff to settle there. Then we'll get you set up at my place." He slanted a look at her. "My place isn't nice like yours."

She looked at him, luscious mouth upturned in a small smile. "I'll bet you have one of those mega plasma HD billion-inch TV screens."

"Bingo. 3D, too."

"And a huge sound system."

Badass sound system, yeah. "Bingo again. And an enormous bed." The words were out of his mouth before he could stop himself. *Damn!* He could kick himself in the ass. It made it sound like the price of his protection was sex.

Though…yeah. It wasn't the price, of course. He'd offer his protection for nothing because just the thought of someone hurting her made him a little crazy. So, not the price, no sir. He was protecting her because he couldn't do otherwise.

But man, if more of that sex he had last night was available, he wouldn't say no.

His dick stirred at the thought, the thought of sliding back into her warm silkiness. Right…*now.* God, he had to grip the wheel hard and concentrate on driving because blood was rushing to his dick, which never listened to reason. Because now was not the time.

Maybe later? He had to shift in his seat because his dick was getting stiffer by the second.

Lauren turned a bright shade of red.

What a fuckhead he was. "Forget I said that. Way outta line. Sorry."

She reached out and put her small hand on his. Even through her glove it seemed to burn. "Don't apologize, Jacko." She frowned, peering at a street sign as he signaled a turn. The sign was barely visible in the swirling snow. "Isn't this—" She looked at him. "Isn't this the street where Suzanne's office is?"

"Yeah." Jacko reached for his cell, put in the earbud, punched in a number.

"Yo." Metal, pulling office duty. Metal wasn't built for offices, just like Jacko wasn't, but they loved their jobs and if it required ass in chair once in a while, they could handle it.

"Coming in with package. Switch off vidcams."

"Got it."

Jacko relaxed slightly. Metal was a soldier and didn't ask dumb questions. He knew Jacko wouldn't make a request like that without a very good reason. And that very good reason was sitting next to him, pale, frightened, but composed.

And frigging gorgeous.

He nearly sighed as he rounded the corner and pushed the button to open the back gates. He was on a mission now and when he was operational, he was all business. Like most SpecOps soldiers, he could narrow his focus like a laser beam. The op. It was always about the op. Everything else was secondary.

Except now, for the very first time in his life, his attention was divided. Keeping Lauren safe was the op, but Lauren herself was distracting him. The idea of someone hurting her messed with something deep inside him, made him less…efficient. Scared him. Which was scary because Jacko didn't do fear. No sir. And yet here he was, sweating lightly, making sure the vidcams of his company were off because—though Midnight's cybersecurity was ace—you never knew.

Metal was waiting in the yard, impassive as ever,

though Jacko knew he was curious. No one asked for the security at Alpha International to be turned off, ever.

Jacko drove in and killed the engine, listening to the ticking as the motor cooled. He was absolutely one hundred percent convinced that what he was about to do was right. But it hurt, just the same.

Do the hard thing. A Navy SEAL motto that had never let him down.

"Jacko?" Lauren turned her face to him, pale and troubled. Her skin glowed in the dim light. "Why are we here? I need—I need to stay away from Suzanne. I don't want anything about my situation to touch her."

"We're not here for Suzanne," he answered, getting out and going to the passenger side. He opened the door and held his hand out to her. She stepped down, pointing her right foot like a ballerina until she touched the ground. She looked like a fairy princess in the snow, white flakes falling on her dark hair. She stood for a moment, hand in his, looking up at him and he saw…complete trust.

She was putting her life in his hands.

He swallowed. That trust was sacred. Nothing was going to happen to her; he'd stake his life on that, and he was. But before he could dedicate himself to her completely, the next step was necessary. Hard, but then nothing in his life had ever been easy. And he'd never had a prize like Lauren to fight for before.

Metal materialized by his side.

"Midnight in?" Jacko asked.

Metal nodded. "Waiting for you."

Yeah. He imagined that. The request to kill security would have been routed up to boss level.

"Senior's coming in a minute," Metal added.

Senior. One of the most effective senior chiefs in the history of Navy SEALs. And, like Midnight, a terrific boss.

For just a second, Jacko allowed himself a pang at the thought of leaving. Tiny, just for a second. But then he looked at Lauren, patiently waiting for him, trusting him, and the pang was gone. This was what he had to do.

Embrace the suck. A good rule in the military and in life. He was just going to put his arms around the suck and hug tight. Not the first time it had happened.

He put a hand to her back and they made their way in the swirling snow to the back entrance of Alpha Security International. It was the business entrance, where people doing actual work came and went. The fancy front office was for show and for clients.

Alpha Security International shared a building with Suzanne's interior design company, which explained how it was that ASI could be as sober and serious a business there was, while lodged in the most elegant surroundings he'd ever been in.

Alpha Security's employees were mostly former SEALs with the odd leatherneck tolerated. They were rough and tough men, used to hardship and Spartan surroundings, but they all enjoyed the space Suzanne had created for them.

Goodbye to that, too.

Jacko ushered Lauren over the threshold. As they walked down the corridor, she looked up at him. "It'll be okay," he assured her.

She gave a small smile and nodded.

They walked into the lobby of Alpha Security and the secretary, Alison, waved them through. "He's waiting for you, Jacko," she said.

Yeah.

Lauren was looking around and he realized she'd seen Suzanne's offices but not ASI's. She touched his arm. "We're here for a reason?"

He nodded.

Her voice was low, quiet. "I don't want Suzanne—or, God!—Isabel involved in any way in my troubles. Or Allegra. Or Claire. Promise me that."

"I promise she and Isabel will be safe. Allegra and Claire, too." He could make that promise. Midnight would see the world burn before he let anything hurt his wife or daughter. Ditto for Senior. Bud had already taken a bullet for Claire.

Midnight was waiting behind his desk when they walked in. His eyes widened slightly when he saw Lauren. For Midnight, that was a sign of huge surprise. He rose to his feet.

"Lauren?" Midnight looked from Lauren to Jacko. "Are you looking for Suzanne? Because she's out with a client."

"She's not looking for Suzanne," Jacko said after he settled Lauren in one of Midnight's comfortable client chairs. He himself stood, because what he had to say was going to be quick. And painful. The faster it got done the faster he could move on to the next stage. "She's here because I have something to say."

Midnight sat back down, leaned back a little in his chair. "Shoot."

"I quit."

Lauren took in a shocked breath, but Midnight simply narrowed his eyes.

"Request denied," Midnight said and that surprised *him.* He'd worked himself up to this and now…it wasn't going to happen? "At ease, sit down and explain yourself."

Jacko dropped into the chair.

LAUREN JUMPED UP at Jacko's words. Oh my God! Jacko was *resigning?* Over *her?*

The one thing she knew about him was that he loved his job. She couldn't allow this.

"Mr. Huntington—"

"John," Suzanne's husband said. He'd said it to her many times but he was so formidable she found it hard to call him by his first name. She nodded, forced herself to remember to use his first name. "Please sit back down."

She dropped to the chair. "John. This is insane. I can't let Jacko lose his job over my problems."

"No one's losing his job, Lauren. Least of all Jacko. He's too valuable to the company. So why don't you tell me what this is about? Is it related to the fact that you left the party last night when someone took a photograph of you?"

John's eyes were dark, but not as dark as Jacko's. There was a gunmetal sheen there that reflected light. But they were as observant as Jacko's.

She shot a glance at Jacko sitting next to her. He was stiff, impassive, the only sign of emotion his jaw muscles jumping. He looked at her and his message was clear. *Your call.*

Okay. She took in a deep breath. "Someone very bad is after me, John. He will stop at nothing. I've been on the run for two years, and sooner or later I'm going to make a mistake and he'll get me. Last night—" She swallowed hard. "Last night might have been one of those mistakes. This morning I tried to get out of town and go...somewhere. But Jacko stopped me."

"You're not going anywhere," Jacko said, deep voice hard. "The running stops now."

She was twisting her hands in her lap, but then pulled

her fingers apart. She met Jacko's eyes then John's. "I can't lie and say the idea of being protected by Jacko isn't appealing. But it's not practical." She turned to Jacko completely, looked him full in the face. "You can't stay by my side 24/7. Because that is what it would take. You've got a job, a life. You simply can't do it."

"I *can* stay by your side 24/7," Jacko growled. "No question." He looked at his boss. "Which is why I quit."

John was fiddling with a pencil, which looked out of place on his super high-tech designer desk with the six thin film monitors and the projected keyboard. "No, Jacko," he said. "You can't stay by her side day and night."

Jacko half rose out of his chair. "Goddamn it! Sir. Yes, I can and yes, I will."

"No. *You* can't." The pencil was suddenly pointed at him. "But *we* can. Now, sit."

Jacko's face turned blank as he lowered himself back to the chair. "Sir?"

John nodded at her. "Is she yours?"

At any other time Lauren would have protested the language, bristled at the tone. *Is she yours?* No, she wasn't anyone's. But this was something between John and Jacko.

"Yeah. She is," Jacko said immediately. He made a fist, bounced it off his knee.

"Then she's ours," John said simply. "And we look after our own. We'll keep her safe. ASI has manpower. When you're working we'll detach someone. We can work out a plan, shift schedules. This is what we do."

All of a sudden Jacko's face changed, lightened, and Lauren realized what relief he felt. He didn't look so impassive—a strong man making a big sacrifice, quitting the job he loved for her. His face was so grim and fixed all the time she hadn't noticed but now she did. He didn't look like he was bench pressing three hundred pounds. He looked relieved.

"Okay, Lauren." John turned to her, that handsome CEO look gone, the warrior underneath visible. She'd always seen him with his wife, and he curbed his essential nature when he was around her. Right now, he looked like Jacko, he looked like Douglas. He looked like all his men. Tough and mean and indestructible. And coldly efficient.

At any other stage of her life, seeing that look on a man's face would have scared her. Alfonso had looked just like that when he dropped that affable rich-guy affect he'd had. Dark and dangerous, belonging to a world of blood and iron. Only John was dangerous in defense of people, not against people. Like Jacko and Douglas and the rest of the team at ASI. Not criminals, good guys. But just as scary as the bad guys.

The instinctive part of her recognized a dangerous animal and she recoiled, then checked herself. These two men were going out of their way to make her safe.

Jacko she could sort of understand. For some reason he had placed himself at her service, like a knight of old. It had to be more than the sex they'd shared. Men didn't turn their lives inside out for a one-night stand. Underneath his impassive exterior, she felt he cared for her.

But John? What did John care?

"Why do you care?" she blurted, then bit her lips. But she needed to understand. Putting herself in Jacko's hands when he cared for her, that made sense. But John was about to be involved, too. *Why?*

He didn't take offense. He just sat back in his chair,

looking between her and Jacko. Jacko was staring straight ahead, but he reached over and held her hand tightly.

"We're all military men in this company," John said. He had a deep, mesmerizing voice. Well spoken but with a slight hint of the South. Not as much as Jacko, but definitely there. "We had each other's backs in the military and we have them now. A threat to Jacko and who he cares for is like a threat to my own family. I'd expect him to defend Suzanne and Isabel with his life, and he would. It's mutual. We're all in this together. And—" He shrugged broad shoulders. "Suzanne loves you. That goes a long way with me."

Something deep inside, something that had been frozen for a long time, suddenly thawed in a hot rush of emotion. She'd been alone for so very long. Jorge's pursuit had cut her off from everyone, leaving her in a cold bubble of fear and dread. Day after day of loneliness, keeping her head down, trying not to be noticed. Not answering the smile of the girl who poured her coffee, not responding to the nice guy who pumped the gas and who wished her a good day. Because any kind of human contact painted a huge bull's-eye on her and anyone who'd been nice to her.

Like Cheryl. Like Carla.

She clutched Jacko's hand, warm and hard, with a trembling hand. "Oh God. I—I'm having trouble coming to terms with this." Not being frightened all the time. Not being so relentlessly alone.

She held her other trembling hand to her mouth to keep in the sobs. But the hydraulic principle of emotion made tears well in her eyes.

John's eyes widened, almost in fear. She could see the whites all around his gunmetal eyes. Jacko simply held her hand tightly. Both men turned at the sound of the door opening.

"Senior," John said, relief in his voice. "Come in. We have a situation. Lauren's in trouble."

Douglas Kowalski moved quietly and quickly across the room, grabbed a chair and sat down beside John. He looked carefully at Jacko holding her hand and then at her. Unlike John, Douglas didn't have an avuncular CEO look as a default setting. His setting was tough warrior, always. It ratcheted up even more when he saw her.

"Sitrep," he said.

John nodded at Jacko, who sat even more stiffly in his chair, as if coming to attention sitting down. Jacko turned to Douglas. "Lauren has someone after her," he said. "A bad guy. Killed two people trying to get to her."

"Whoa." John held up a big hand, palm out. "This is new. We need to talk to the cops. Senior—"

But Douglas was already tapping on his cell. "Bud," he said. "Got a minute?" The answer must have been yes because a second later the image of Detective Tyler Morrison, known universally as Bud, Claire's husband, showed up on a monitor. Douglas angled it so everyone could see. Bud was in his office, Spartan and efficient.

"'Sup?" he asked genially. "John, you gonna bribe me with some more Trailblazers tickets?" He leaned forward a little. "Hey, Jacko. Hi, Lauren."

"Yeah," John answered, "but first we've got a problem. Jacko here's been telling me Lauren has a bad guy after her. Killed two people to try to get to her."

Like with John, the geniality left Bud's face immediately, his features sharpened, and he looked every inch a cop. Lauren remembered that he was ex-military, too. Not a SEAL, but a Marine. She'd heard the guys joke about the wusses in other parts of the military but never the Marines.

"Lauren," he said, curling his fingers up. "Talk."

"Yes…" Lauren swallowed the instinctive "sir."

She looked at the four men, three in the room, one on a screen, listening to her intently. Jacko looked impassive, as always, though she knew he was paying close attention. She held on to Jacko's hand tightly.

"My name isn't Lauren Dare. I've only had that name for the past year." No going into close detail on that. Felicity deserved her anonymity. "Basically, I inherited what I believe to be a criminal empire two years ago. My mother married a man called Alfonso Guttierez, who runs—ran—all sorts of nasty things from a hotel-and-casino empire. Guns, drugs, prostitutes, you name it. Alfonso and my mother died in a car crash. My mother died an hour after my stepfather. She was his universal heir and I was my mother's, so the whole thing came to me. My stepfather, who was childless, had imported a nephew of his from Colombia but he turned out to be a fuck-up." Lauren looked around. "Can I say that? It's what my stepfather—who might have been a crime boss but never used profanity around women except when talking about his nephew—called him."

"What's the name of the fuck-up? And where was this?" Bud asked. He was tapping on the keyboard of a monitor to the side.

"Jorge Guttierez, Palm Beach, Florida," Lauren answered and suddenly had an image of the next-to-last time she'd seen him, at the funeral, clearly drugged up and smelling of sweat and alcohol. The last time she'd seen him, he was trying to kill her. "At least Alfonso could control himself but Jorge…Jorge is in thrall to the products he sells."

"Yeah. Got him. Nasty fucker." Bud turned another screen to them. "Rap sheet as long as my di—er, arm." A flush of color appeared on his cheeks.

The three men in the room leaned forward to read off Bud's monitor. Lauren didn't bother. She knew what they were seeing.

If Bud's dick was as long as Jorge's rap sheet, Claire must be one happy woman. Actually she did look always happy. Despite his roughness, Bud seemed to be a really good husband.

A long list of arrests showed up, with Jorge's booking photos. He looked more and more disheveled as the photos scrolled down. His hair grew longer, beard going from chic stubble to unshaven mess.

"The arrests never stuck, though." Bud sounded angry. "What the—"

"Alfonso had set up a very good team of lawyers. 'The most expensive in Florida,' I heard him say once to my mother. Jorge was never officially charged with anything—he always got off."

"The serious stuff started two years ago," Bud said, eyes scanning what was on his monitor.

"Right after his uncle's death. He was scared of Alfonso, kept himself in check. But after Alfonso died there was no one to rein him in. I think he went a little nuts when he realized he hadn't inherited anything. That I'd inherited everything."

"A lot nuts." Jacko sat back after having carefully studied Jorge's dealings with the law. His lips were pressed tight. "Used to easy money, little work, thinking to in-

herit an empire. Certain kinda guy—yeah, it'd push him
over the edge."

"So, Lauren—do I call you Lauren?" Bud asked.

"Yes. I like the name. It was my grandmother's."

All four men scowled. At *her*. She scowled back.
"What?"

"Not good, honey," Douglas answered. "If you're
going underground, you should choose names that have
nothing to do with you."

Yes, that was exactly what Felicity had said. She'd
taken two seconds to find out that Lauren was her pa-
ternal grandmother's name.

Lauren sighed. "Yes. You are absolutely right. But—
I'd had everything taken from me. My past, my present,
my future. My job—I was a museum administrator, and a
good one. Everything was taken. And my first fake name,
I never remembered it. People would call my name and I
wouldn't answer. I loved my grandmother. I guess it was
a way to hold on to something of my past."

Silence.

Maybe they understood.

"So who are the dead bodies?" Bud asked.

Lauren shivered. Two women dead—because of her.
Jacko brought her hand to his mouth, kissed the back.
His touch steadied her, gave her warmth.

"The first is a friend of mine from Palm Beach,
Cheryl Goddard." Sweet, funny, too-rich-for-her-own-
good Cheryl, whose parents had given her money instead
of love. Cheryl, who'd never had loving grandparents
like Lauren had. "I was working in Chicago when my
mother's lawyer called up with the news of my mother's
death. And that I had inherited the house and casinos
and a slew of hotels."

Lauren pinched the bridge of her nose, looked at the three tough men before her, glanced at the monitor to one side. They were all leaning forward, faces tight with attention, including Bud.

"At the time, I didn't realize exactly what it was I inherited. I knew Alfonso was bad news but I didn't realize exactly how bad. My mother's marriage to him had created a rift between us. We rarely saw each other and I'd never seen the house, which my mother had just finished decorating." She tried a smile on for John. "Suzanne would be appalled. So much money, for so little style. So I traveled down to Palm Beach for the funeral and hadn't thought to book a hotel. After the funeral, this lawyer pressed a set of keys and some remote controls in my hand and said that I should stay in the mansion, start taking stock because I was the new owner. He'd send someone for me the next day. I was in a daze. I don't remember much. It was hot. All the colors seemed so outrageously bright. My head hurt."

Her heart, too, as she realized she'd never be able to reconcile with her mother. It was too late.

"Jorge was there. I barely noticed him. He was tall, good-looking in a sleazy kind of way. Dressed in black Armani. When he gave me the keys to the mansion, the lawyer whispered that I should watch out for Jorge."

"Jorge had nothing to do with it," Bud said. "If the estate had been deeded to you, he couldn't do anything at all. And even if you died, if you hadn't made out a will deeding everything to him, he got zilch."

"I know that and you know that but Jorge isn't too smart and not entirely sane." Lauren tried a shaky smile. For a second, she was back in the suffocating heat of Palm Beach, the smell of a billion flowers overwhelming, almost nauseating, the memorial facility filled to the brim with overdressed darkly tanned people she'd never met. Complete strangers, men and women drenched in perfume and cologne, embracing her. Murmuring platitudes while eyeing each other. Bling that nearly blinded her. Trying to come to terms with the fact that her mother— her vain and cold mother—was *gone*. Her entire family, gone. Father, grandparents dead. And now her mother. And she couldn't even begin to grasp what she was feeling. On top of it all, it turned out that she was rich, unbelievably rich, the money coming from the bowels of hell.

"My friend Cheryl attended the funeral with me and refused to let me sleep alone in the mansion. The place was huge, garish. We found two guest bedrooms that were larger than my apartment in Chicago, I took one, she took the other. I—I couldn't sleep. Around two in the morning I gave up trying and slipped outside to take a walk in the gardens. I saw two men dressed in black walking toward a third man. Jorge. Something told me to stay quiet."

She could never forget. The two men dressed for stealth. Jorge still in his black Armani. A full moon that showed his expression of vile malevolence. He was swaying as if in a full wind, stoned out of his mind.

Lauren tightened her hand around Jacko's hand. "They—they were reporting to Jorge that they'd 'found the bitch and taken care of her.' Those words exactly. He asked if they'd made it look like an accident and they said yes. He took two packets from inside his jacket. Payment. They took off. I went back in and found—"

Her teeth began to chatter. Jacko put an arm around her shoulders, pulling her against his chest. She felt his words more than heard them.

"That's enough for now," he said. "She needs some rest. We can go over this some other time."

"No, no!" Lauren pushed against his chest. She could never make him let go if he didn't want to, but he let her go immediately. She straightened, wiped her eyes. It was the first time she'd told the story to anyone. Even Felicity knew only part of it. She had to get it out now, get the grief and the guilt off her chest. She leaned her forehead briefly against Jacko's broad shoulder then lifted her head. "I have to do this," she whispered, meeting his eyes.

He nodded.

Lauren looked at John, at Douglas, glanced over to the monitor at Bud, then finally at Jacko. He was, as usual, impassive. No. On closer look, he wasn't impassive. He was totally focused on her, and she could almost feel his attention on her skin.

And she remembered—these men were warriors. They had faced death and dismemberment every day for their country. Most of the incredibly brave things they had done had been classified so no one even knew. She couldn't be a coward in front of them—she simply couldn't.

"I found Cheryl at the foot of the stairs. Her neck was broken. They'd thrown her down the stairs, but I couldn't prove anything. I ran upstairs, packed a quick bag and got out of there. My mother had a dozen cars. I took one of hers because when Jorge realized he had the wrong woman he'd come after me again. I thought it might take him a day or two to figure out I took one of my mother's cars."

"Cheryl Goddard?" Bud asked over the computer.

"Yes."

"Spell the name." She did. He held up a big hand for

silence, then started typing furiously. They were all quiet while he checked screens. He nodded abruptly. "Okay. They found it an accidental death." He looked up. "No one reported you missing."

Lauren swallowed. No. There wouldn't be anyone to report her missing. There wouldn't be anyone who really cared. The people who cared enough for her to take action were all in this room. And in a virtual chat room.

She shook her head. "Jorge certainly wouldn't report me missing once he realized he'd had the wrong woman killed. And I think Jorge must have bought someone off. I am absolutely certain he has plenty of cash even if he can't access his uncle's accounts. Or maybe not so much now but he would have had access to plenty of money then."

"I'll check into it carefully," Bud said, and she knew he would.

"You said two," Jacko said quietly. He was watching her intently, listening so carefully she was sure he could repeat what she was saying verbatim. "Two dead."

"Yes. And the second dead person is my fault, too." Lauren felt bitter bile in her throat as she spoke. Two people dead, because of her. "I—I was in shock. And I wasn't thinking clearly. I called my college roommate who lived in Indiana. Carla Whitman. Asked if I could come and stay with her for a few days. It never *occurred* to me—" Her voice broke; her throat closed. Jacko looked as impassive as ever but his hand tightened around hers again.

Lauren straightened. She had to own this. It was her fault entirely and she had to own it. She met the eyes of the three men in the room, checked the monitor. Bud was watching soberly. "It never occurred to me that I was endangering her. I was driving my mother's car. I was traveling anonymously. It just—I felt like I was safe. And I wasn't."

Jacko stirred. "Nothing in your background led you to believe you could be tracked."

True, but— "Still, I should have thought it through. But I didn't. I was shocked, stressed and I just wanted to get away. I thought if I could hole up somewhere, I could figure things out. Regroup. Call the police. Get out a restraining order or something. Then tell them what I'd heard."

"And instead?" Bud asked.

"Instead, I got Carla killed, too. We met at a café in town close to where she worked. She was worried—she heard the panic in my voice over the phone. I explained the situation to her and she was angry. Said that a friend of her father's knew someone who could help. I started calming down. I'd driven all night and I was exhausted. She said to come home with her and she'd call in a security company she knew through work to protect me." Lauren stopped, looked around the elegant premises, at the owners of the security business, John and Douglas. "Maybe like this one. It was just what I needed, safety. The time to think. We paid the bill and I needed to go to the bathroom. I left everything on the table, including—"

"Including your cell," Jacko said.

Lauren hung her head in shame.

"Yes," she whispered. That one careless, thoughtless act had snuffed out Carla's life. "Yes, except my cell. They killed her instead of me. I came back out of the bathroom to see two men walk into the café, right up to her. One took out a gun, put it against her forehead and pulled the trigger. Then they walked right back out again, fast. Everyone in the café was so shocked no one tried to stop them. Carla looked a little like me."

"Like this?" On the monitor, Bud turned another monitor around. And there it was—Carla's portrait photo that had been on her social media pages. Pretty, blond, lively.

Now dead.

Lauren nodded, chest burning with remorse.

"She's blond," John noted.

"So is Lauren," Jacko chimed in.

Lauren blushed, a hot rush of blood to her face and chest. Clearly Jacko had a way to know that. An intimate way. But none of the men showed signs of anything but concentration.

"I, ah. I have changed my hair color several times."

Polite silence.

"I should have gone to the police. But I had zero proof. It would have been my word against Jorge's, and he can hire the best lawyers there are. I didn't think of hiring a lawyer myself or, even better, bodyguards. All I could think about was getting away, as far away as possible."

"He would have gotten to you anyway," Jacko stated, voice flat. "No question. Throw enough money or men at the problem of getting to you and you'd be dead. You were right to run. Except…" Jacko gave a long hard stare at John, then Douglas. "The running stops. Right here. Right now."

"Damn straight." John leaned back in his chair.

"Oh yeah," Douglas said.

"So now you—" John pointed a finger at Jacko. "You're taking the week off. You've got a lot of accumulated leave you haven't taken. We're going to put together a protection roster and protocol to ensure 24/7 protection for Lauren when you come back to work."

"Thanks." Jacko bowed his head slightly, then lifted it. "And Bud's going to look into this Jorge, find out what's happening. Get some eyes on the fu—creep."

"You bet." Bud's stern face looked out at them from his monitor. The image was so clear he could have been in the room with them. "I'm going to start investigating this guy. From what Lauren says, he's probably breaking a million laws, not to mention two homicides. I know an LEO in Palm Beach, can't be bought off. He can do some digging. We're going to bring down a world of hurt on this Jorge. I'll check in with you later." His image disappeared in a wink.

"Oh." Lauren's head whirled. A few hours ago, she'd been packing to go somewhere, anywhere. To leave her friends behind, to leave her whole life here behind. Her new life would have been sere, friendless. Planned to be that way. Her heart had ached at the thought of what was before her. And now this. A reprieve. And maybe, just maybe a normal life at the end of it?

An impossible dream, only a couple of hours ago.

Her gaze shifted from John to Douglas and back to John. "I don't know how to thank you. But you must promise me that Suzanne stays away from me. And Douglas, Allegra, too. And tell Bud that Claire has to stay away from me. They shouldn't even know I'm still in town. You need to tell them I went out of town. I don't want any of them near me."

"Why don't you want us near you?" an indignant female voice inquired from behind her.

Lauren twisted in her seat. There she was. Suzanne. Wearing one of her perfect pastel suits that looked like a million dollars on her. And you couldn't hate her for it because she was so nice. The thought of anything happening to her—

Lauren jumped up, put her hands in front of her, palms up, as if staving off danger. And she was. Anything happening to Suzanne would kill her.

"Suzanne!" she called sharply. "You shouldn't be near me!"

Suzanne walked forward quickly, as if she hadn't spoken at all, and simply enveloped Lauren in a warm, perfumed embrace. Lauren pulled in a deep breath. Suzanne smelled so good. Not only of an expensive perfume, but of friendship and love. If those were smells, they would be Suzanne's.

She bent her head to Suzanne's shoulder to hide the sudden spurt of tears. Two years of not crying, and between Jacko and Suzanne, she kept breaking down.

"No," she whispered shakily into Suzanne's powder-pink jacket. But she clung even more tightly.

Suzanne lifted her head and spoke to her husband. "What's going on, John?"

Before John could answer, Lauren pushed herself away from Suzanne. It was hard to do but she'd gotten used to pushing away good things. "You've got to stay away from me, Suzanne. Someone is after me and you could get caught in the crossfire. Jacko and John and Douglas are going to try to fix this, but until it's fixed, I shouldn't be anywhere near you. Or anywhere near Allegra and Claire."

She took a step back, far enough not to feel Suzanne's body heat, or smell her perfume. It hurt.

To her surprise, Suzanne stepped forward again and put her arm around Lauren's shoulder. "Nonsense," she said briskly. She looked at her husband. "John won't let anything happen to me, will you, John?"

John stood up, walked toward them. He put a big hand on Lauren's shoulder. Douglas had stood up, too.

John's face was hard. A warrior again, not a highly successful businessman. "Nothing is going to happen to Suzanne or Isabel. We keep our women safe. Don't worry about that."

"Oh yeah," Douglas chimed in. His scarred face was hard, too. "Nothing's going to happen to you or Suzanne or Isabel or Claire. And no one on this earth is going to touch Allegra. You can bank on that."

Lauren believed them. There was a concentration of male power in the room that was more than testosterone. These were men who had been tested again and again and had come out victorious.

There was an aura in the room, a feeling of strength and purpose. These were serious men. Even Suzanne was serious. When Suzanne was in business mode and not in friend mode, she was invincible. Firm and smart.

All of a sudden, Lauren had a vision of Jorge. Instead of him looming hugely in her head, this gigantic monster, a Godzilla capable of swatting away her future, her life and the people close to her, she saw him as he was. Weak and petulant and a little crazy. An addict, too. All of this heartache was because he thought he could simply step into Alfonso's shoes. Whatever else Alfonso had been, he had been a hard worker. Jorge was a spoiled child. He'd gotten close to her twice because of luck and her own stupidity. Not through his own intelligence.

The presence of Jacko, John and Douglas—and even Suzanne—made her realize she had better and smarter people on her side.

For the very first time the thought crossed her mind—*I'm going to win this*. She'd been so grief-stricken at the loss of Cheryl and Carla, so caught up in the idea that Jorge could find her wherever she went to ground, it had distorted her thinking.

She was going to win this. She was going to get her life back.

Another male hand landed heavily on her shoulder. Jacko's.

"As long as I am alive, you'll be safe," he growled.

SEVEN

SOME COLOR HAD come back in her face. Jacko glanced over at Lauren in the passenger seat. Her skin had been the color of ice when they arrived at ASI.

He'd gone in fully expecting to walk back out without a job. Instead, he'd come back out with a *team*. Midnight and Senior—man. Those guys were real team leaders. A member of the team needed help? They stepped right up. Jacko was intensely grateful for that. But intense gratitude was nothing compared to the white-hot relief he felt knowing that ASI had his back. Lauren would be kept safe, no question.

Jacko could have done it alone—he knew that. He'd have locked them in his secure quarters forever if that's what it took. But he didn't have to. He didn't have to be on alert 24/7 because he'd be sharing the job of protecting Lauren with his teammates.

Basic principle of bodyguarding and of soldiering— never do it on your own. You work in shifts. Otherwise the adrenaline of constant alertness will eat you alive.

So not only were they going to keep Lauren safe, they were going on the offensive. Oh yeah.

It wasn't in Jacko's nature to hunker down. If he knew Lauren was protected, he and ASI could go take down this son of a bitch.

He'd give Bud some time to dig up intel. It was always good to go the legal route. But bottom line? If there was no progress soon, he'd leave Lauren with Metal—no one better, no one smarter, no one meaner when he had to be—and go off to Palm Beach and smoke the fucker who was after her himself.

He knew how to do it and leave no clues.

So sometime soon Lauren's nightmare would be over. Oh yeah.

"Jacko," she said, turning to him, "I don't know how to thank you—"

Jacko held up a hand in horror. "God, don't thank me." His throat tightened. He had a lot of skills. Get in his way and you'd be sorry. But words weren't what he was good at. "Just...don't."

Unspoken words choked him. *I would happily die to protect you. No will ever touch you again.*

I think I love you.

That last thought made him sweat. He gripped the steering wheel harder, his palms suddenly damp.

Fuck.

His hands were sweating. That never happened to a sniper, and sweaty hands had sure as hell never happened to *him.* He'd always been the meanest, nastiest mother-fucker around since he was twelve. No one messed with him then; no one messed with him now.

He'd shot and killed really bad guys without breaking a sweat. Sometimes he hadn't used a bullet but his bare hands. And now just look at him.

He weighed twice what Lauren did. He could bench-press her. Hell, he could bench-press *two* of her. Yet she somehow reduced him to a wreck, particularly when he thought of someone hurting her.

He could have put it down to sex, but he'd felt this way

for four freaking months now and they'd only had sex once. It was off the charts, okay, but still…

In those four months in which he wasn't getting his rocks off *at all*, just seeing her made him sweat but also made his day. He felt…different when he was around her, as if there was this force field around her that skewed his molecules.

No, that wasn't it.

Hell, he didn't know *what* was it.

All he knew was he felt good around her and missed her when she wasn't there and by God, no one was going to hurt her.

He couldn't say any of that. The words stuck in his throat and they fucking hurt because they couldn't come out. The words were like knives, cutting him. He swallowed and looked at her and she seemed to understand.

That was the thing about Lauren. She…understood him. She never treated him like a piece of meat or a walking dick like other women did. Well, Suzanne, Allegra and Claire didn't. But every other woman did. She listened to him, though he didn't speak much around her. But when he did he had her full attention.

He felt good around her. Wanted to be around her as much as possible.

Was that love?

Fuck if he knew.

Uncomfortable with the thoughts in his head, he was grateful when they reached the underground garage of his building.

He switched off the engine and turned to her.

She recognized instantly that he had something serious to say. When she turned to him, her entire focus was on him. It felt like a beam of light was on his face.

"Okay. This is how it's going down. When you want to go out, we come straight down here where no one can see you get in the vehicle. I will temporarily disable the security cams when we come down to the garage and I'll let the security guys in the lobby know. And I'll tell them that no deliveries come up except from them. Just in case you have to be out in the open, I know a guy who can manufacture hats with brims that beam down a special invisible light that messes with recorded images. No facial recognition software will be able to pick up your face. It won't be stylish but it will be effective."

He didn't even go into pancake makeup, which fooled skin-texture analytics and graph measurement software. But they were available and she'd make use of them.

"I should stay in as much as possible," she said softly.

"Yeah. But I don't want you to feel caged. If the weather clears, I can take you for walks in the country where there are no vidcams. I always keep my bike in back so maybe we could go for a ride. Would you like that?"

"I hear you're very good on your bike. Though I also hear you go about a million miles an hour. We'll have to go slower than that." She stretched out a hand to caress his cheek and leaned forward. The kiss was soft, warm, fleeting. She pulled back just a little and searched his eyes. "You're taking such good care of me, Jacko. Thanks."

His throat tightened and he swallowed heavily. "No problem. Let's go up and I'll show you around."

He left her in his apartment while he went back down to bring up the last load of her stuff. Crazily, though he knew for a fact that nothing was happening to her, he was anxious until he walked back through his door and found her putting things away.

Muscles he hadn't known were tense immediately relaxed the instant he saw her. Okay, maybe there was a way to save his sanity.

"Lauren," he said quietly. "Come here." He was able to put his hands immediately on what he needed and palmed it. He knew where everything was, at all times, because he was OCD when it came to gear. He sat down on his long brand-new sofa and patted the cushion next to him. "Sit down."

She came right away, sat down next to him. Folded her hands and waited for what he had to say. He loved that about her. She was always no nonsense. Never whiny or pouty. If she'd been busy with something she didn't want to interrupt, she'd have said so, firmly.

She treated him as a teammate, and as someone he could count on, always.

His heart thumped once, hard.

Jacko tried to look at his place through her eyes. "First of all, I hope you'll be okay here. I haven't, um, decorated." At all. He had a bed, a long sofa and a big screen TV. A table with his six-monitor computer set up. A table to eat on, with a couple of chairs. That was more or less it.

Luckily he was sailor-neat. Not that there could be a mess when there was nothing there.

Lauren smiled. "I'm not assigning decorating points, Jacko. I'm not the decor police. I'll be comfortable here—don't worry. And I can always order throw pillows online."

He smiled back. "Oh yeah. Do whatever you want. Consider the place yours. Throw pillows, curtains, frills.

Those flower petals in silver thingies that Suzanne has everywhere. I'm game."

She tilted her head. "We could start with food. Your refrigerator has ten bottles of microbrewery beer, a hunk of stale cheddar and a soft tomato."

He winced. She'd probably seen that his cupboards were completely bare, too. Well, he rarely ate at home, and when he did it was takeout. Didn't know how to cook. Now things had changed. He'd be taking most of his meals home, for the first time in his life. The thought didn't disturb him as much as he thought it would.

"There's a supermarket that does online ordering. When we're settled, we'll order. And I'm good at ordering takeout. I have the menus for Chinese, Thai and Tex-Mex. You won't starve."

"No." She smiled. "I won't."

He took in a deep breath. This next part was going to be tricky. He opened his hand to show her what was on it. "Here."

She picked it up, puzzled. He could understand that. It was a tiny piece of tech with a thin steel rim.

"What's this?"

"It's a tracker." Jacko held up his hand. "Now, I don't want you to feel weird or anything but I want you to keep it on you at all times. Just until we know what's going down." Or until that fuckhead Jorge was dead. "I'll be with you as much as possible and when I can't be with you Metal or another ASI guy will. But you know, there might be times when you'll be alone here. The place is secure, trust me. But if I'm not physically with you, I need to know where you are. At all times. So I gotta ask—you think you could do that? Keep this on you?"

There were so many things he wanted to add. *I don't*

even know if we're together, besides this crap that's happening right now. I'd fucking hate to be tracked myself. But please do this for me, so I don't go bugfuck crazy when I can't physically see you. It nearly killed me to go back down to the garage. But he didn't know how to say the words. All he could do was sit beside her with the tiny piece of silicon and brushed steel in his open palm and hope she didn't hit him across the face.

She didn't. She looked at it thoughtfully, studying it. Then she put it on her knee and reached behind her neck to unclasp a light gold chain. In a moment, she'd somehow threaded the chain through the tracker and put it back around her neck. She stroked it and smiled at him.

"There," she said softly. "It'll be on me at all times."

Oh man. He swallowed. A wave of something—heat, lust, *love?*—swept over him, like a solar wind in a sci-fi flick. Whoosh. Enormous heat. What felt like another realignment of his molecules.

He placed his hand over it, just below her collarbone. Her skin felt so satiny, so smooth. Not like normal skin, like something finer than that. He looked at his hand on her neck, fingers curling slightly. He had big hands, strong hands. Steady hands.

But right now his hand felt huge and awkward. Not part of his own body, more like a part of hers. He was unable to take that hand away, as if she were a powerful magnet and his hand was pure iron.

"Thank you for this," he said hoarsely. "I appreciate it."

She blinked. "Jacko, I don't think you're clear on what's happening. You just offered to quit your job—and I know you love it, don't deny it—for me. You're rearranging your entire life for me, to keep me safe, and you think I'd balk at making sure you know where I am at all times?" She edged closer to him. "And do you think I'd complain about you sharing your home with me?" She looked around at the huge emptiness of his living room and brought amused eyes back to his. "Though I really might be doing some decorating here. I promise no chintz."

He ran the back of his forefinger down her cheek. "You can make this place wall-to-wall chintz for all I care. Whatever the hell chintz is. As long as you're here, and safe, I'm okay."

"Thank you."

He shook his head sharply. "I told you, don't need thanks. Don't want it."

She leaned in even farther, smiled into his eyes. "Then what do you need? What do you want?"

"I'll show you what I want," he whispered. He lowered his hand. She had on one of those sweaters that buttoned up the front. They had a name but he couldn't remember it right now. He could barely remember his own name. He unbuttoned the sweater slowly, watching her, ready to stop if she wanted him to.

But she didn't stop him. She sat quietly while he opened the sweater and folded one side back. She had on one of those lady bras that looked sexy as hell. In some light purple color that probably had a weird name. Suzanne would know. She had names for every color under the sun. He unhooked the bra, brushed it aside and bent forward to kiss her breast.

Lauren gave a soft sigh and arched her back. One hand rose to his neck and she held him tightly to her, fingers caressing the back of his head. She tasted salty sweet, incredibly delicious. As he licked and sucked at her, he gently slid off the sweater and the bra, then lifted his head. Though he'd only sucked one nipple, both were erect and cherry red. The breast that was wet from his mouth was pinker.

Jacko reached out an unsteady hand and outlined the deeper pink. "Razor burn." He lifted his eyes to hers. "Sorry."

"Do the other breast," she answered softly.

Oh yeah. As he licked and kissed it, Jacko finished undressing her. She helped, lifting and moving and pulling, until she was naked on his couch, lightly flushed, smiling at him.

He couldn't smile back. His face just wouldn't. A smile felt small and inadequate to what he was feeling. She was sitting like a queen, pale and glowing, looking at him with softness in her gaze. No woman had ever looked at him like that. Women looked at him pre- and post-fucking. The pre-fuck look was speculative and the post-fuck look was, thank God, usually satisfied. But there was never any emotion there.

Lauren's feelings were written all over her face. Feelings for *him*.

He had no idea what was on his own face; he could barely feel himself, he was so concentrated on her. He had tons of feelings rolling around inside, so many and so strong he couldn't express them. He had no words to tell her what she meant to him. What he felt seeing her on his couch smiling at him as if he were the center of her world. He couldn't explain it to her in any way.

There was one thing he could say, though, and it came from the deepest part of him.

"I'll keep you safe." He wanted to say more but the words just wouldn't come.

"I know you will, Jacko." Lauren smiled at him, cupped his jaw with a hand. He shifted and kissed the palm of her hand, a little calmer now. She'd understood all those unspoken words. He didn't have to say them because she understood.

She understood him. He'd allowed her glimpses inside himself, something he had never allowed anyone before and instead of running away screaming, here she was, sitting naked on his couch, looking at him with softness in her eyes.

His own little miracle. Oh yeah, he was going to keep her safe.

Because she was his.

Heat rose inside him, heat and lust, desire so strong he'd die if he didn't have her, right now. In a second, he was naked, too. Some instinct, some muscle memory that didn't require thought, like switching out a mag in a firefight, something he'd done so many times he barely noticed, had him ripping open a condom and sliding it on, then he lifted her over him as if she were weightless. She was in that instant. He didn't feel the weight, just her softness as she settled over him. His hands pulled her thighs apart, then he positioned her with a hand on her back and he felt her, oh God yes. Felt her wet heat against his cock, opening to him. She was bracing her hands on his shoulders, looking down at him. Not smiling, eyes slitted. She blew out a breath, circling her hips with him just inside her.

Jacko's heart was hammering, muscles twitching. This was a moment for self-control. He knew that; he wasn't stupid. He was just blasted by lust, not quite in control of himself. Lauren was lifting away from him, then settling back down on him, a little deeper each time.

It was taking her goddamned forever. Sweat trickled down his back from the effort of staying still. When she rose back up on her knees, with him barely inside her, her head bowed over his, her dark hair forming a little curtain around them.

Jacko tightened his hands around her back, looked up into her silver-gray eyes glowing with an unearthly light.

"I have to—" he gritted.

She nodded and he pulled her down onto him while slamming his hips up until he was deep inside her, and the god of soldiers smiled on him because she was coming, pulling on him with sharp little strokes of her sheath. He started jetting inside her in spurts so strong he thought he'd pass out.

They were holding each other tightly, neither of them moving except where they were joined, panting, eyes closed, lost in their own world.

Jacko came back into himself slowly. When he realized he was clutching Lauren so hard he could be hurting her, he loosened his hold, letting out a long low breath. Man, it had been so freaking intense. For all the years he'd been having sex—more than half his life—nothing like that had ever happened to him. He'd lost all notions of self, of where he was, completely taken up by the woman in his arms.

He let out another long breath, relaxing a bit on the couch, feeling tight muscles loosen. Lauren slumped onto him, head nestled on his shoulder, and he rested his cheek on the top of her head. The sharp smell of sex rose, but it was a great smell, with an overlay of her perfume, something that smelled like spring.

He was still partially erect and he'd be up for a second round but he could feel Lauren relaxing and the feeling was so precious he didn't want to spoil it. She'd been through hell and if she could find peace with him, well… that was worth more than another round of sex.

And besides, they had all the time in the world.

The rest of their lives, in fact.

At any other moment, that thought would have shocked Jacko, but right now it just popped every single pleasure center in his head.

"That was quite a welcome, soldier," Lauren said and he could feel her lips moving in a smile against his shoulder.

"Hmm."

Lauren gave a little sigh and he could feel her slipping into sleep. Oh man. She was a warm weight against him, soft and light. He cupped her head and adjusted himself so she'd be as comfortable as possible.

Something warm and heavy and unfamiliar passed through him. It took him minutes to realize it was happiness.

EIGHT

Palm Beach

GEORGE TOWN HAD BEEN very interesting, Frederick mused. Two days of intense talks with the president of the Caymans Credit Bank, with a scheme that could net a lot of money over the next ten years. A lot of money. And it was even legal, marginally. He'd probably have to relocate at some point, but the idea was intriguing. There was even talk of becoming a citizen of the Cayman Islands. Which Alfonso had told him did not have an extradition treaty with the US.

Perfect. Just perfect.

While he was in George Town, Frederick had seen a mansion high on a bluff overlooking the sea, which the president had told him was called Cliff House. It had belonged to a minor British royal, and was for sale.

In his hotel room Frederick had looked it up on the site of a very exclusive Realtor's and it was indeed magnificent. And selling for a tenth of what a home like that would cost in Palm Beach.

Oh yeah. Frederick was going to retire in ten years' time a very rich man, living a life of leisure, untouchable by U.S. law.

In the meantime, though, he had a job to do. Mechanical Voice wanted results. He turned himself to the task of finding Anne Lowell, one lone woman in a country of over three hundred million people. Impossible, one would think. And yet...

What was a face after all? Most people imagined faces as endless iterations of a few facial features. Eyes, nose, mouth, chin. Expressions: happiness, sadness, rage, curiosity. Everything that makes us human can be summed up in the face.

But that wasn't what faces were at all. Faces were sets of data points. About eighty of them, in fact. Nose width, eye socket depth, length of the jawline, distance between the eyes. All data points. Algorithms making up faceprints like the data points of fingertips make up fingerprints.

You can run, but you can't hide.

Frederick had found Anne Lowell twice by small mistakes she'd made, but then Jorge's goons were morons and let her slip through their fingers. What did he care? He'd been quite happy to stay on retainer, no skin off his nose. But now he had half a million incentives to find the woman and deliver her.

Just not to Jorge.

Anne Lowell was adrift somewhere in a country of three hundred million faces. Three hundred million sets of data. A number-crunching problem.

Time to bring out the big guns.

Faces were data and all he needed was a big enough bot array to crunch the numbers, because somewhere Anne Lowell's face was on film. There were an estimated thirty million surveillance cameras in America, not counting the cams and drones operated by the NSA, the CIA and the Pentagon. Unless she was dead and in a hole in the ground, someone somewhere had filmed her, and recently.

She was a set of data in someone's computer and all he needed was enough crunching power to find her.

There was an app for that. An idea simmering in his head for a while, a secret weapon for when serious amounts of computer power might be needed. He'd put the idea away for a rainy day and now that rainy day was here. Frank Sinatra singing "Here's That Rainy Day" provided a nice soundtrack as he worked his way into QUANTUM.

QUANTUM was a shadow network with a vast hidden infrastructure of secret servers and routers used by government alphabet soup agencies, the NSA in the forefront. But the infrastructure was huge and had required years and thousands of man-hours to build. Frederick knew one of the coders, known as the Whiz, a talented young man with an unfortunate taste for drugs and debauchery. The Whiz had been responsible for building a small corner of QUANTUM, much like a mason who erects a minor wall in the construction of a palace. QUANTUM had undergone a vast expansion and required work from many talented coders just like the Whiz.

For the price of several months' worth of highs, courtesy of stolen goods from Jorge's deliveries, Frederick managed to buy himself a backdoor into QUANTUM. It was a small secret little hatch in a forgotten corner of the vast structure that, however, led into the palatial rooms, leaving behind no sign of intruders. QUANTUM had a built-in redundancy factor so that the theft of bandwidth, even vast quantities, never showed up in the system.

Getting in required delicacy and time. But Frederick had time and a very deft touch. By midnight, he was in and set to work. He had plenty of photographs of Anne from when she was a young girl and a college student. Her mother had been a cold bitch and actually preferred photographs to the person. Particularly since her daughter was photogenic enough that the beautiful silver frames looked good in arrangements.

So Frederick was able to scan over two hundred photographs into his facial recognition system, starting from age ten. He also had almost five hours of video from her graduation ceremony and several birthdays.

He brought up snapshots of her a few years ago, taken when she was in her last year of grad school. They'd been taken at a beach. She laughed into the camera, arm around the shoulder of the friend that idiot Jorge had killed by mistake. She had the face of one of America's upper class. Very pretty, excellent teeth, full figure. The expression reflecting invincibility—nothing could touch her and she was destined to sail through life without hitting any speed bumps. In one of the photographs she was holding a young man, her male equivalent. Blond, excellent teeth, the slight arrogance of the young and the healthy and the rich. He was her, only ten inches taller, without breasts and with a penis.

The system used a 3D model where bone was more important than soft tissue. Weight gain or weight loss made no difference at all.

The program then measured the underlying bone structure on a microwave scale and created a template. It was dawn by the time a 3D scan of Anne Lowell's face appeared on his monitor.

By midmorning he could make Anne Lowell's template smile, frown and laugh. So, a sprinkling of fairy dust, a little soupçon of algorithms and he could set his construct free. His finger hovered over the enter key. He was about to unleash the greatest concentration of virtual firepower in the world on to the search for one young woman, who had done no one any harm.

But, such was the way of the world.

He pressed Enter and waited.

His computer didn't hum, of course. But Frederick imagined humming going on somewhere underground, in refrigerated banks of servers somewhere in Virginia. Working for him, about to earn him a lot of money.

A blank monitor was boring. Frederick went out for an early lunch at Les Deux Renards, a charming French restaurant known for the chef's light hand. He allowed himself a glass of pinot noir because, well, he wasn't the one combing the internet, was he? QUANTUM was. A quick visit to his gym, a lovely massage and home by five, in time for a drink on the terrace. The red-and-yellow-streaked clouds above the horizon were slowly turning purple when a soft ping sounded behind him.

Ah. Found. Excellent.

Frederick took his glass of Pimm's with him as he sauntered over to his workstation. He had six monitors, top of the line, with incredibly sharp images. Spread over the monitors were thumbnail photographs, in chronological order. He took in the visual data at a glance, noticing that Anne had cycled through platinum white hair, auburn and, on the right-hand monitor, chestnut. She was a dark blond naturally. He shook his head. She'd spent a lot of money at the hairdresser's for nothing. His algorithms didn't even look at hair color. Not even part of the data set.

The thumbnails to the left showed where she'd been. He'd study them for patterns but he wanted to know where she was *right now*.

And there she was, on the far right monitor, in a Twitter feed dated three days ago.

He went to the Facebook page of one Monica Shaw,

sometime actress/artist, full-time caterer. She'd Instagrammed photos of an art show held in—Frederick leaned forward, squinting at the coordinates that the program instantly geolocated for him. He rocked back on his heels.

The art show was held in an art gallery in the center of Portland, Oregon.

Portland, hmm? Maybe not such a bad place to come to ground, all things considered. Small but large enough to hide in. Multicultural so nobody stood out. A percentage of the population newcomers, so one woman arriving sparked no interest.

Monica Shaw carried drinks and manned the buffet table while surreptitiously taking shots with her cell phone. She was interested in a famous harpist and singer, Allegra Kowalski. She was excited at the presence of event organizer Phillip Barton, a big shot in the art world. Manga artist Wu was there and she sneaked in a selfie with him.

So as of last night, Anne Lowell, who had evaded him for two years, had been at the vernissage of *Inside/Out*, a series of watercolors and gouaches of designs by one Suzanne Huntington.

The caterer had no interest at all in the actual works on the walls, or the star of the show, Suzanne Huntington. On another monitor, Frederick checked the website of Suzanne Huntington who, it turned out, was seriously talented. The Gallery section showed ninety offices and homes she'd decorated.

When he bought his mansion at the top of the bluff, he just might hire her and fly her out to the Caymans—she was that good.

And…there she was, at the gallery! Anne Lowell, or whatever she was calling herself nowadays. Brunette.

Not good enough, sweetheart, he thought. Anne had

never noticed the caterer taking shots from her cell phone. She was never in direct line of sight, but most of the shots were quite clear nonetheless.

She was still very pretty. Being a brunette suited her, with her silver-blue eyes and pale skin. She'd lost some weight, too. Maybe a little too much. Being on the run could do that to a girl.

The program isolated her face inside a red box. In all, there were ten shots of the evening where she appeared. In five of them she was holding the arm of a big bruiser. Not tall but immensely broad. Shaved head, dark complexion, grim expression. A rough-looking guy.

Really ugly mean-looking bastard. Hmm. The man looked—looked as if he'd be hard to deal with. It had never occurred to Frederick that she would hook up with someone. She was on the run, for Christ's sake. What was she doing having sex with someone? And someone who looked like *that*?

Anne Lowell, of the Boston Lowells, with a master's in business management of cultural institutions, choosing this person who looked like one of the more unsavory *Sons of Anarchy* in a tux—well.

They looked strange together, a *Beauty and the Beast* kind of couple. The man was wearing a tux but it didn't look right on him. Yet in two of the shots, Anne was looking up at his dark, ugly face and smiling.

The man was stiff, unsmiling. He didn't look like a guy who'd unexpectedly scored a beauty. Could he be a bodyguard? Could she afford one?

But no. Bodyguards stood back from their primaries, scouting the terrain. This guy looked as paranoid as a bodyguard—in each shot he was examining a different part of the room—but he was definitely escorting Anne.

In one shot, one huge dark hand covered hers in the crook of his elbow. Bodyguards didn't do that.

Interesting.

Hmm. So she had some muscle behind her. Well, brains trumped muscle, always.

Okay, time to get to work.

Frederick kept a number of identities on file. They were fully fleshed out, with websites and active FB pages. There were over three trillion websites in the world. His passed unnoticed.

He scrolled through his files like a connoisseur choosing the perfect bottle of wine from a well-stocked cellar. Ah, there was a good one. He tapped on the screen and a very distinguished head shot of himself came up. He remembered when he'd had the portrait photo taken. He'd made sure to get an excellent haircut, had had lunch at a 5-star restaurant and had been to the spa. He looked ruddy, self-satisfied, pampered and very rich.

Paul Andrews. Investment broker. Owner of Stonewell Financial. The website was a little vague as to exactly what he brokered and what he invested in, but he'd modeled it on the sites of other investment gurus, so it didn't stand out.

Paul Andrews was thinking of buying a major property in downtown Portland, Oregon, and he wanted it redecorated floor to ceiling. And he had heard such very good things about Suzanne Huntington…

Yes, that's how he'd play it.

He took out a throwaway cell that would show up on the other end as a number connected to Stonewell Financials. It was the little details that counted.

"Yes, hello," he said to the pleasant female voice that answered. "My name is Paul Andrews, of Stonewell Financial. I would like to make an appointment with Ms. Suzanne Huntington, tomorrow afternoon if possible. Yes, I'll hold."

He poured himself half a glass of Prosecco. No harm in that. He still had a cross-country flight ahead of him. The Prosecco would dissipate in his blood well before that. And, well, he had something to celebrate. He had that unmistakable feeling he got when his plans coalesced.

The secretary came back on.

"Excellent," he said, giving himself the plummy accent of the super rich, the voice of a man used to getting his own way. "Three o'clock. I'll be there."

He tapped another screen and an inset of his pilot popped up. "Sir?"

"Get the plane ready. We're leaving in two hours for Portland, Oregon."

Portland, Oregon

PRETTY CITY, FREDERICK thought the next day as he exited his luxurious downtown hotel. Cold, though. The snow was ankle height and it was below zero. However, Frederick was billionaire Paul Andrews and the rich didn't do cold. Billionaires had a Goldilocks existence, never too hot and never too cold. He was wearing a heavyweight cashmere Brooks Brothers overcoat, cashmere scarf and a genuine Borsalino. He stepped from the heated lobby of the Beresford Hotel where he had the Presidential Suite, directly into a town car he'd booked online. The car was heated, of course, the driver suitably subservient and in livery.

"Where to, sir?" the driver asked, meeting his eyes in the rearview mirror.

"The Beckstein Gallery. On Stratton Street."

Before presenting himself to Suzanne Huntington, he wanted to visit the art show where Anne Lowell had been photographed. He was a computer guy but he liked firsthand data whenever possible. He'd viewed all the photographs on the caterer's FB page and the official photographs on the gallery's website. It was interesting that besides the caterer's cell phone shots, Anne didn't show up once on any other photos, anywhere, including the official website photos that seemed to highlight everyone who'd been there, on principle.

Except Anne.

The car left him right in front of the gallery's ornate white marble entrance. The driver said he would park around the corner and to call when he was needed.

No bell rang when Frederick opened the gallery door. Bells were so passé. Instead there was a metallic sound of a drop of water echoing. Immediately a man appeared from an inner door. Elegant. Dapper, even.

Frederick held up a hand covered in a cashmere-lined black kid leather glove. "Just looking," he said.

The man gave a little ironic bow and disappeared again behind the door. It was clear that if Frederick wanted to buy something he would let it be known.

He clasped his hands behind his back and slowly walked the perimeter of the gallery, looking carefully at each picture. They were excellent; even he could see that. Each picture was of either the façade or the interior of a building Suzanne Huntington decorated.

The designs were exquisite and they were all superbly rendered.

He made the circuit twice. All of the paintings, drawings and watercolors had a small red Sold sticker. A placard stated that the proceeds of the sale went to a breast cancer research fund.

Frederick knew he was lingering too long, but there was just something about the pictures that tugged at him. They were all beautiful, yes, stylish, yes…but somehow *familiar.*

He would have even bought one. A watercolor of the façade of a sleek mansion in the foothills of Mount Hood was exquisite. The artist had perfectly captured the contrast between the streamlined outline of the house and the gnarled old forest lines of the branches surrounding it.

A flute appeared, half-full of champagne.

"Excellent, isn't it?" the gallery owner, presumably Mr. Beckstein, said.

Frederick took the glass and sipped. Not champagne but Prosecco and excellent. "Yes, indeed. I would have contemplated buying it if it weren't already sold." The small red sticker was discreetly placed in the lower right-hand corner.

"We sold out in the first half hour." The owner gave a small, satisfied smile. He shifted his drink to his left hand and held out his right. "Alfred Beckstein."

Frederick held his own hand out. "Paul Andrews, pleasure."

"Welcome to Portland," Beckstein said.

Frederick arced a brow. "It's that obvious I'm an out-of-towner?"

"With that tan it is. It's been raining and snowing for two months. You didn't get that tan here."

There was an unspoken question. If it went unanswered, Paul Andrews would stick in the gallery owner's mind. Frederick gave a light laugh. "Bingo. I've spent the last four months in my house in Cabo San Lucas.

Came up to Portland for some investment opportunities. Speaking of opportunities, I've been looking at some property here. I have a tour of the penthouse of the So-renson Building scheduled."

Backstein's eyebrows rose. It was by a factor of ten the most expensive residential building in the city. The penthouse was valued at fifteen million dollars. Condo costs were $10K a month. Frederick had checked.

"So, I was thinking of looking for a decorator and it looks like I just might have found one." He tapped the show's brochure with the photograph of Suzanne Huntington on the cover. "Judging by the interiors on the walls she is very talented."

Backstein smiled. "That she is. This gallery provides a lot of artwork for her interior designs. She's brilliant. It's a pleasure to work with her."

Frederick waved at the gallery walls. "And I will definitely commission artwork of the finished decorations."

A small frown appeared between Beckstein's eyebrows, then he smoothed it away. "Ah, yes. That would be an excellent idea." He drained his flute. "And now, if you'll excuse me, I have some work to do. Take your time enjoying the artwork. Pleasure meeting you."

Hmm. Interesting. Something there...

For form's sake, Frederick spent another ten minutes perusing the artwork on the walls, then called for his car and walked from the heated gallery to the heated backseat of his town car in three steps. His driver was of course holding the door open for him so he wouldn't have to do that himself. Frederick was exposed to the cold for about a second and a half. Rich guy tourism.

His next stop was the visit to the penthouse apartment of the Sorenson Building in the presence of a young and pretty real estate agent practically quivering with eagerness. Her conversation was peppered with "yes, Mr. Andrews" and "of course, Mr. Andrews." She agreed with everything he said because, though the property was stunning, it was still the tail end of the recession and there were probably not more than a couple of thousand people in the country able and willing to pay fifteen million dollars for an apartment.

If he had a spare fifteen million dollars, which he didn't, and if he wanted to live in Portland, which he didn't, he could do worse than this penthouse. It was over nine thousand square feet with five bedrooms and two fireplaces. He was certain it had views to die for when the sun came out. There was even a deck for the three warm sunny days a year during the summer.

The Realtor had obviously done her homework because she kept dropping references to Stonewell Financial. Pity it didn't exist. And pity he was going to have to disappoint the agent, who was truly attractive.

She was nearly panting with excitement. He doubted she got a commission—that would be for the owner of the realty—but she'd definitely get a bonus. She looked almost sexually aroused as she ran through the penthouse's amenities. Eyes bright, color high, mouth moist and open.

Hmm. *Really* attractive.

But no.

This was a business trip. In and out. In empty-handed and out with an unconscious but alive Anne Lowell.

Priorities, priorities.

He tuned out the estate agent's babblings and turned to the floor-to-ceiling bulletproof windows. It was pointless telling the eager young agent that bulletproof didn't exist unless it was a foot of concrete or several inches of steel. Windows could only be bullet resistant. There was plenty of high-end weaponry that could blow right through it. Not to mention an RPG. Or a hovering helo with a .50 cal machine gun.

The bulletproof windows was probably a rehearsed selling point, given the fact that top members of the Russian *Mafiya* were moving to Portland and were going to want high-end real estate. A *vor* would definitely want bullet-resistant windows.

But Paul Andrews wouldn't worry about that until the ninety-nine percent rose up and revolted. By which point Paul Andrews would definitely have already decamped on his private jet to Barbados.

Frederick really *liked* Paul Andrews.

It had been snowing on and off since he arrived. It had stopped, leaving a pristine snowscape, no colors, just shades of white to gray to black. Quite beautiful.

One of the pictures in the Beckstein Gallery had been a collection of four seasons of a country mansion, the winter version a stunning play of chiaroscuro.

He'd seen something like that somewhere. It had niggled at him in the gallery, too. Where had he—

He caught his breath.

God. Could it be?

"Oh!" Frederick tapped a nonexistent earbud and took out his cell. "Sorry," he said, turning his back on the agent, her pretty face startled. "Have to take this."

He moved into another room, took out his tablet from his briefcase and opened a couple of files, flicking through them. He was extremely thorough with his background research and inside of a minute he had what he was looking for.

Anne Lowell had a degree in museum curation but

she'd also taken art classes. And she'd taken part in an art show collective. Forty young artists, mainly conceptual. She was the only one of the forty who'd entered figurative art. Four watercolors, all landscapes. One a snowy plain. Pristine, shades of white through gray, no colors.

He carefully studied the four works of art, looking at shape, balance, color scale. *Yes*.

The person who'd done the landscapes and interior decors of the show at the Beckstein Gallery was the same person who'd exhibited four works in the collective art show. Same color palette, same architectural sense of proportion, same hand.

That was why Beckstein's forehead had scrunched. Suzanne Huntington hadn't done the artwork.

Anne Lowell had.

Jesus, he'd found her.

He sent the signal to his driver to bring the car around to the monumental front entrance of the Sorenson Building.

"Sorry," he told the pretty agent, "something very important has come up. I am however quite interested in the property. I'll get in touch tomorrow."

Tomorrow he wouldn't be coming back but he would definitely be half a million dollars richer.

Peanuts for Paul Andrews but good enough for him.

Once the car took off, he called Suzanne Huntington's office.

"Yes," he said when a pleasant female voice answered. "My name is Paul Andrews of Stonewell Financial. I called yesterday for an appointment with Ms. Huntington, a brief meeting for a commission for a place of business and a home. I would like to confirm the three p.m. appointment, thank you." He tapped End Call and leaned forward to address the driver. "Take me back to the hotel and then pick me up again at two p.m."

The driver nodded.

Frederick sat back in the comfortable leather seat, very pleased with events. Very pleased.

JACKO'S CELL RANG in his pants pocket. Christ, the pants were all the way across the room.

He was neat. He emptied his pockets and folded his pants and his cell was always within reach. Just like his gun. Lauren really messed with his head because he couldn't remember leaving pants in a heap on the floor across the room. He didn't remember much about getting naked, though he remembered every second after he'd gotten naked. Oh yeah.

You'd think that after a couple of days basically spent in bed having sex he would have gotten his groove back, but no.

He should be leaping out of bed and grabbing his cell. You never knew—it could be important. Was probably work, and work was the number one priority in his life. Had been number one priority.

But right now? Right now he was in bed with Lauren's head on his shoulder and his arm around her and he didn't want to move one single muscle. It was late morning but he had the day off, the week off, for the first time in forever. He had Lauren in his arms and he had no desire for anything other than a late breakfast.

She stirred, looked up at him, smiled. "You should get that."

Yeah, he should.

The cell stopped playing the refrain of Cee Lo's "Fuck

You" and went to voice mail. Then it started ringing again. Whoever it was was a persistent fucker.

"You really should get that," Lauren said, lifting her head off his shoulder.

Oh man. The moment was spoiled.

Jacko had been lying there with half a boner, thinking of when Lauren woke up. And now she was awake but someone wanted to talk to him, even though Jacko didn't want to talk to *anyone* except Lauren.

The cell stopped ringing for a moment then started again. And something like situational awareness pinged to life in Jacko's sex-saturated brain.

It could be news concerning Lauren. He could have missed vital news because his blood had gone from his head to his woodie. Christ.

He scrambled out of bed just as the cell went to voice mail. Then it started ringing again. Jacko grabbed it, looking at the display. Bud. Bud Morrison. Who'd promised to look into the fuckhead who was threatening Lauren.

"Yeah?" he barked into the cell. "What?"

"Took you long enough," Bud growled. "Go to your computer and link to KWXX. Local TV station in Palm Beach. Stay on the line."

"Jacko?" Lauren was sitting up in bed, propped on her elbow and oh Jesus, the temptation to crawl right back into bed with her, slide right into her and start moving…it was almost too big to resist. *Just look at her*, he thought. Shiny hair slanting across her face, falling onto her shoulders, slender hand holding the blanket up, covering her breasts. She could cover them all she wanted but he knew exactly what they felt like, what they tasted like. They felt like silk and tasted like salty strawberries.

Damn. The woodie was growing.

"Yo, Jacko!" Bud sounded impatient. "You seeing it?"

Jacko did the only thing he could do—put his jeans on and hope they kept the worst of the boner down. He looked away from Lauren as he pulled his jeans up, going commando as usual, wincing as the zip caught a few hairs.

He switched on his Mac, looked the link up on Google, and frowned at the feed. It was a helicopter shot, shaky footage of a big fancy mansion, swimming pool looking like a basin of Scope from on high. *SHOOTOUT IN PALM BEACH* read the chyron. Then the feed switched to a Latino bimbo journo sporting a ton of tanned cleavage.

No sound.

Jesus. He was slipping. His headset was connected. He yanked out the jack and heard the bimbo's breathless voice. "To recap, a SWAT team is now surrounding a mansion in Palm Beach—"

"Oh my God!" Lauren shot out of bed, naked. He looked over and couldn't help the smile.

"That's my mother's house!" she exclaimed.

"What?" For just a second, the news knocked a naked Lauren out of his head.

She reached into a drawer, pulled out a tee of his and slipped it on. It billowed around her, coming down almost to her knees. But at least it covered her up so he could concentrate on what she was saying.

She pointed a shaking finger at the monitor. "That—that's my mother's house. Jorge's house." She shook her head. "Technically, my house. Oh my God, a shootout! Turn the volume up, Jacko."

He did, putting the cell to his ear. Bud was still there. He put Bud on speakerphone.

"Sitrep," he said, putting Bud on video on another monitor now that Lauren was covered up.

Bud's face was grim. "What a fuckup. My guy has been conducting an undercover investigation into the 'accident.' He sent two of his men to ask some questions of Jorge Guttierez. He saw signs right away that there'd been a coverup. Evidence lost, interviews misfiled. The guy who covered it up is retired, has half a mil in his bank account, right there for anyone with a warrant to see. Moron. Turns out judges in Palm Beach are very sensitive to police corruption, so a warrant to search the premises of the Guttierez household was easy to obtain. And the bad cop is no longer enjoying golf but is now under indictment, and if found guilty, which the fucker is, I'd bet my pension on it, he'll spend the rest of his miserable life behind bars.

"So long story short, this morning PBPD sends two officers to question our guy Jorge, who apparently was coked to the gills. And the fucker opened fire, can you believe that? We have an officer down, he's now in surgery. There's a chance he can make it. The other officer called it in and there's a SWAT team there now."

Lauren was watching the computer monitor intently. "Jorge's crazy, Bud. Please tell the team to be careful. He's got an army in there."

Jacko hooked an arm around her shoulders, kissed her hair. Telling a SWAT team to be careful was perfectly useless. "These guys know what they're doing, honey. Don't worry about them. They're trained for this."

The feed switched back to the helicopter footage. An army of SWAT team members, looking like heavily armed ants, crouched in a perimeter surrounding the house. No sound could be picked up but Jacko could write the playbook for them. There was a fusillade that barely registered as distant pops over the noise of the helicopter, and Jacko knew it would be covering fire for flashbangs.

There you go. Two black-suited helmeted SWAT guys in front and two in back lobbed what looked like tin cans into the ground floor. A flash of light and streams of heat-distorted air and the SWAT guys rushed the place.

The feed switched to the bimbo anchor woman whose expression had sharpened—*live fire! Maybe dead bodies! Live, on air!* She was in anchor heaven, bleating. She had nothing to say but was saying a lot of it.

"Please, let the officers be safe," Lauren whispered. She looked up at him, face pale. "Jorge's such a whack job. And he takes drugs. No telling what he'll do."

Jacko didn't answer. The SWAT team undoubtedly knew what it was doing. They'd be really competent guys, really well-trained. But shit happened. For all he knew a drugged-out paranoid fuckhead could even have the place wired to blow.

It wasn't over until it was over.

So he didn't try to reassure her again. They simply watched the monitor, listening to the *pop pop pop* of small arms fire and the *ziipp* of automatic weaponry.

Suddenly, there was silence.

"It's over," Bud said over the speakerphone. He was clearly on a direct feed with PBPD. "Asshole thinks he's in some kind of movie like *Scarface* or something. Wait." On the video feed Bud pressed a finger to his ear, suddenly breaking out in a smile. "Fuckhead's *down*! Sorry about the language, Lauren. Jorge Guttierez is dead. Smoked. Caught thirteen bullets. Couldn't happen to a nicer guy. They found two underage girls tied to a bed and enough cocaine in the room to choke a horse. Eight of his henchmen are down, another two surrendered and are going away for a long, long time. You don't shoot at cops and walk. And my guy inside PBPD has a real jones for pedophiles. Likes to put them away forever, so his goons are never getting out. Ever. So, Lauren, looks like your troubles are over. I'll meet you guys at ASI in half an hour."

Jacko turned to Lauren, who looked shocked, a hand over her mouth. Her face was pale, blue eyes huge. She sobbed, choked it back. She was used to suppressing her emotions. Well, that was going to change.

He kissed her. "It's over, honey. It's all over. Your running days are over—you're free."

She breathed in and out looking stunned, as if she'd been hit. Jacko frowned, surreptitiously placing a forefinger over the outer corner of her wrist. Her pulse was racing fast and shallow, pupils dilated. She was in shock.

They wanted him and Lauren at ASI, but first he had to tend to her. He led her to the couch, pressed lightly with his hand on her shoulder. She dropped as if he'd shoved her down and he sat next to her.

He waited patiently as she cycled through her emotions. She shook, eyes unfocused. The thousand-yard stare. He knew that one.

Finally, she blew out a breath and shook her head sharply, as if getting rid of something. "I can—I can hardly believe this. Jorge is dead. I'm not on the run any more. I don't have to hide anymore. I can walk around freely, no need for special makeup or funny hats." For the first time a smile crossed her face. "Would it have been a stylish hat?"

Jacko sighed. What he'd seen in catalogs had been

like a Marine's beanie hat. She would have hated wearing it. "No. Sorry."

She giggled and the sound zinged through him. "I think the first thing I'm going to do is to buy myself a pair of high-heeled shoes."

"Yeah?" Jacko tried to suppress the image of a naked Lauren wearing only heels. Man.

"Oh yeah." She lifted a pretty, bare foot. "I haven't worn heels in two years. I need to be able to run at a moment's notice. Correction. I *needed* to be able to run at a moment's notice. Now I don't have to think that way any more."

"Nope. And you can walk in and out of here any time you want without me freaking if I don't know where you are."

She sobered instantly, turned to look him full in the face. "About that. About living here. I don't know…"

And though he knew his face wasn't showing anything, Jacko's stomach dropped to the floor. He wanted to kick himself in the ass. What the fuck was he thinking—that they had a future? That she'd just continue staying here with him, that they'd be a couple? He'd promised to keep her safe and he had. With a little sex thrown in.

That was what it had been for her but it had been a lot more for him.

This was the first time his heart had been involved and that had messed with his head, making him think things that just weren't true. Of course they weren't a couple, together forever. What would someone like her be doing with someone like him? And yet—how the fuck was he supposed to have seen the signs when everything had been so mixed up and stressful? So yeah, the sex had been off the charts, but that didn't mean—

She reached out to cup his face, searched his eyes. "Do you think you could stand living in my house instead of here? I need my skylight."

FREDERICK'S CELL BUZZED when he walked out of the shower. He'd stayed under the rush of water at the hottest possible setting for over half an hour. Short of going to a spa to get that flushed rich-man look, a scalding hot shower was the next best thing.

He stepped out of the shower, made full use of the fancy moisturizer the hotel provided and gave himself a close shave, happy that he'd recently had one of those $200 haircuts by a stylist who knew what she was doing.

Solemnly, like a knight donning armor, he dressed rich from the skin out. Nothing that wasn't silk, Egyptian cotton or cashmere touched his skin. The real estate agent had not been discerning. She'd been told he was rich and that was that. But Frederick was certain that Suzanne Huntington would be able to sniff out the real deal.

Well, Frederick was used to social engineering. And he *was* rich, after a fashion, just not billionaire league. So it was a question of degree not of kind. Plus, he could go gay. Muddy the waters a little.

Billionaire gay guy. Not so easy to read.

He was lacing up his thousand dollar Barker Blacks when his cell buzzed. An alert, not a call. He'd designed a nice little bot that scoured news feeds for about fifty key words, most pertaining to ongoing jobs.

The screen showed Jorge Guttierez. Which meant he was on the news somewhere. Frederick switched to the news feed with the most hits and his eyebrows rose.

The screen was too small. He turned on his computer and watched the monitor. He had to sit down to do it.

Jesus. This surprised even him.

Jorge finally proved what a moron he was. And a coke-head to boot. What a combo.

Listening to the news anchors, Frederick could easily piece together what had happened. For some reason the cops had come to the door while Jorge was hopped up. Of course lately, that was always. Jorge got mean when he was stoned. Crazy mean. And crazy stupid. It was a lethal combination.

From what Frederick could make out, Jorge had fired at two cops, wounded one. Seriously, apparently, because the officer was in surgery.

Well, no one fired at cops with impunity. From the feed from a news helicopter, Frederick could see the mansion surrounded by SWAT.

Alfonso would have been appalled.

This could only end one way because Jorge was too boneheaded stupid to give up when he saw himself surrounded. He'd watched *Scarface* way too many times. Right now, in his little pig brain, he saw himself a heroic figure, fighting off an army of cops. Going down fighting, like a man.

Pinhead. Really, too stupid to live. Darwinism at work.

Frederick sat on the edge of the bed, filing his nails, waiting it out. Watching events unfold on TV, as predictable as any cop TV series. SWAT, hunkered down. Two officers throwing something into the mansion from the front and two from the back, and a second later, a bright flash of light, a sound that could be heard over the helicopter rotors, smoke billowing out.

With anyone but Jorge, the next act would be the men holed up inside walking out with their hands up, being told to kneel, hands on their heads. Flexicuffs, the perp walk, officers putting a hand to their heads to get them inside the cop car.

But this was Jorge, who probably had fevered dreams of glory sprouting in his drug-addled brain. Sure enough—by the time Frederick was buffing his nails, body bags were being carried out of the house. Jorge and his goons, loyal to the last, poor dogs.

Well, there went his retainer. Pity.

But, on the whole, it was for the best.

Jorge was becoming so very tedious as a client. Money talked, of course, but even just seeing Jorge once a month had become a chore. Something very unpleasant and really—what was the point of being successful if you had to do unpleasant things?

Unpleasant was for the peasantry. A saying of Alfonso's, and quite right he was, too. Alfonso had had people to do the unpleasant things for him.

So, all in all, a very satisfactory ending. With Jorge out of the way, Anne Lowell would be lulled into a feeling of complacency, of safety.

How could she know he was about to deliver her to someone who would extract what he wanted from her and would then dump her body like a piece of trash?

She wouldn't. Couldn't. Anne Lowell's death was in the cards; it was just going to be by a different hand now.

Just like in that great story by whosis he'd read in college. "Appointment in Samarra."

What was that saying? *Karma is a bitch.*

NINE

THEY THREW A PARTY for her, right on the premises of
Jacko's company. Lauren and Jacko walked in through
the door and there they were, all of them. ASI employed
ten rough guys, two of whom were the bosses, and they
were all there. Plus Bud.

Plus Suzanne, Allegra and Claire. Smiling, laughing,
hugging.

The girls made more noise than the men, who stood
around looking slightly uncomfortable. It seemed celebra-
tions were rare things in the security company.

"Oh, I'm so glad you're safe!" Suzanne was the first
to embrace her, soft and perfumed and happy. Suzanne
held her at arm's length and she actually had tears in her
eyes. Lauren couldn't imagine Suzanne, who despite her
elegant looks was a tough cookie, crying. But there they
were—tears.

And Allegra, too, crying and hugging her. Then Claire.

And there was Bud, who'd orchestrated her freedom.

Lauren tore herself from Claire's hug and threw herself at Bud, holding him tightly. "Oh God, Bud, thank
you! Thank you so much! How can I ever repay you for
what you've done?"

She hugged Bud again. He was the one who'd set
things in motion. Like the ASI guys, he was a doer and
he was a good guy. Good guys were rare in this world.

In fact, all the good guys she had ever met were right here in this room.

Bud shuffled his feet and patted her back awkwardly. "No problem. Glad to do it. And the cops there are really glad that justice has been done."

"Thank you. I owe you a huge debt." She squeezed him again, glancing up. Way up. Bud was really tall, just like John and Douglas. It occurred to her that Jacko was exactly the right height for her. Bud looked uncomfortable, glancing around the room for help, but his wife was too busy chatting and laughing and wiping away tears and the other men just shifted their weight from foot to foot.

"Uh," he said. "Yeah." He patted her back again. "But I didn't really do anything. You should thank the Palm Beach PD and their SWAT guys."

"No, if you hadn't called them I would still be on the run," Lauren said firmly. "Still be at risk."

Suddenly Bud's face tightened, shed that lost look. "I *hate* bad cops, and my friend in Palm Beach does, too. That bad cop is going to pay. And another biggie—we've got one more scumbag off the streets. And we have you to thank for that, not the other way around. You were supposed to be protected and you weren't. Some heads are going to roll. Innocents shouldn't be on the run—bad guys should be."

Metal, Jacko's friend, huge and scary-looking but always oddly gentle, lifted a bottle of beer. "Yeah."

Suzanne put a glass of champagne in Lauren's hand. "Here's to bad guys on the run."

"And in a cage." Bud had opted for a beer, too, and drained his bottle.

Lauren walked over to Jacko, looked him in the eyes,

clicked glasses. "Thank you, Jacko," she said softly. He didn't smile, but leaned forward and kissed her forehead.

Suzanne, Claire and Allegra lit up like Christmas trees. They descended on her, a perfumed cloud of buzzing bees, and spirited her away to a corner of the room where they went into a huddle. A real one, like football players, arms around each other's shoulders. Lauren in the middle.

She was surrounded, trapped by these wonderful women who—yes—loved her but who were also intensely curious about her and Jacko and weren't going to let her go until their curiosity was satisfied.

"So," Claire said. She huffed out a breath. "Jacko."

"We thought he'd *never* make his move," Allegra said, bouncing on her feet with excitement. She rolled her eyes. "Guy's a sniper, probably killed more bad guys than smallpox and he was so *scared* of you. Amazing. Jacko a wuss, who would have thought? Took a death threat to force him to make a move. We were really frustrated."

"It was a lot of fun watching him suffer," Suzanne said briskly, "but we're really glad that stage is over. So—dish." She curled her hand up in a *gimmee* gesture.

"*Dish?*" Lauren brought a hand to her mouth, knowing that she was blushing down to her breasts. Oh my God! Images of her and Jacko on her bed and on his filled her mind. "I can't—I can't do that!"

"Well, we don't mean *details*," Suzanne began.

"Yes we do. Lots and lots of details." Claire's eyes gleamed. She looked around. "What?"

Allegra narrowed her eyes. "Okay, no details. Or not many. For the moment. Just—is he good in bed? I mean all those muscles…but he doesn't talk much." Allegra shook her head. "Of course Douglas doesn't talk much either and he's dynamite in bed."

"On a scale of one to ten," Claire demanded. "How good?"

"A hundred," Lauren blurted and covered her mouth again. Why did her girlfriends keep asking this question?

The three women sighed. "Do you think they teach that in SEAL school?" Allegra wondered.

"No." Claire shook her head decisively. She'd recently cut her long dark hair to shoulder length and it swirled around her head. "Bud was a Marine and a cop. And he's off the charts."

"How would you know?" Allegra looked at her with a sly smile. "He was your first and last."

"I just know." Claire smiled smugly. "Any better and I'd pass out."

"Girls, girls." Suzanne frowned and put on her CEO scowl. "You're not the point, Lauren is." She turned to Lauren. "Come on, talk!"

"I—you can't be—I can't!" This was so embarrassing. Even her *tongue* was embarrassed. "It happened so quickly!"

"Quickly?" Allegra exclaimed indignantly. "You call that quick? Glaciers melt faster."

"Allegra's right." Suzanne nodded. "I can't believe it took you guys so *long.* Four whole months!"

"Though we had fun watching you two," Claire said, and Allegra and Suzanne nodded. "Better than TV. Except for maybe *Game of Thrones.*"

"Douglas and I had sex the night we met." Allegra smiled at the memory. "The night they tried to rob the Parks Foundation jewelry show. Gunfire and hot sex. Amazing combination."

Claire nodded. "Same with Bud. We had sex right away. The night we met."

Suzanne smirked. "John and I had sex the night we met, too, and three days later I was pregnant."

Silence. That trumped everyone.

"So." Suzanne took pride of place and leaned forward. "Does he talk?"

Lauren blinked. "Does he *talk?*"

Suzanne nodded. "In bed."

Oh man. Lauren bit her lips.

"I'll bet he doesn't," Allegra said judiciously. "I mean he doesn't talk anywhere else—why should he talk in bed?"

"Has he told you he loves you yet?" Claire asked.

Lauren's jaw dropped. "I—ah—no, ah—"

All three women laughed. Suzanne patted her shoulder. "He will. It's just a matter of time. Guy's cooked."

"Ripe pear," Allegra nodded. "Dropping at your feet. Be kind to him. It's his first rodeo."

"Don't break his heart," Suzanne ordered. "John and Douglas count on him. He and Metal are their top operatives."

"Here." Claire reached over and put a full glass of champagne in Lauren's hand, taking the empty one. "Get smashed. Get drunk out of your mind, then go have wild monkey sex with Jacko. If anyone deserves to celebrate, it's you."

Allegra suddenly clutched her. Lauren spilled a little champagne onto the back of Allegra's dress but nobody cared. "We're so glad you're safe, honey," she whispered fiercely.

"And we're so glad you're with Jacko," Claire said,

eyes shiny. "He's one of the good guys. He deserves some happiness and so do you."

Now tears sprang to Lauren's eyes.

Suzanne wiped under her eye with one manicured finger and turned when someone tapped on her shoulder. "Yes?"

Alison, the receptionist for ASI and for Suzanne's interior decorating business smiled uncertainly. "Sorry to interrupt, Mrs. Huntington—your three p.m. is here. Mr. Paul Andrews."

"Yes, of course." Suzanne straightened her jacket. "Tell him I'll be right there."

"Yes, ma'am." Alison turned and walked away.

"Okay, okay. Whew." Suzanne wiped under her other eye. "I feel like I've been through the wringer. First we find out that killers are after you, then we find out the killers are dead and you're safe. My head is whirling. I don't know how I can talk estimates and materials after this, but I will."

She sure would. Suzanne's prowess in business was legendary. She advised her husband, who listened to her carefully. Allegra listened to her carefully when signing contracts for concerts and recordings. Everyone's business was thriving, in no small part thanks to Suzanne.

And now… Whoa. It just now occurred to Lauren. She could continue her business! Maybe in the open now! And she'd ask Suzanne's advice, just like everyone else.

She was going to have a life here. A real life. With a wonderful job and wonderful friends.

Jacko appeared by her side, her coat in his hand.

And a wonderful love, too, apparently.

A couple of days ago she'd been ready to abandon everything and leave, planning on living alone the rest of her days. And now she had an overabundance of great things in her life. From zero to hero. It was enough to give her the bends.

"Time to go, honey," he said, helping her on with her coat. He rested his big hands on her shoulders afterward. It felt good, warm, grounding. "We've got a lot of stuff to do. Midnight said I still have the rest of the week off."

They did have stuff to do. She did. No, *they* did. God, she was part of a couple now. She wasn't going to be facing things alone any more. Someone by her side. It felt odd and wonderful and scary, all at the same time.

A couple. Doing things together. Counting on each other.

Who'd do the dishes?

Jacko would, she decided. He'd do them naked wearing only a tiny frilly apron. Heat came over her so fast it was as if she'd walked in front of a furnace. There was going to be a lot of naked Jacko in her future.

She smiled up at him. He didn't wince and look away. He searched her face and gave a small smile back.

Wow.

Suzanne, Claire and Allegra kissed her, hugged her and dispersed. The guys from ASI had gone; only John and Douglas were left and they were checking something on a monitor, frowning.

The party was over.

Well, the party inside her wasn't over; she still felt the champagne bubbling in her veins. Or maybe that was—happiness. *Happiness*. She turned the word over in her mind. A couple of days ago she'd been listening to Jacko's plans to keep her safe essentially by keeping her locked indoors 24/7, which had been fine with her, since the alternative was a messy death. And before that she'd planned to disappear forever. Leaving all these wonderful people behind.

Happiness hadn't even been a consideration; survival was. And now—now she was looking at a life that was more than survival. A life with a job she loved, friends she loved, a man she…loved?

He was standing next to her, his arm cocked at that peculiar angle. She slipped her hand into the warm space between massive forearm and brawny biceps, feeling his strength and feeling his solidity. This man who'd been willing to give his job up for her, this man who'd been willing to stand between her and danger. Forever, if necessary.

Happiness. Love? Well…just maybe.

They walked out of the building just as Suzanne's three p.m. came in. He was unmistakably one of Suzanne's clients. Tall, slender, exceedingly well dressed. And giving Jacko a slow up and down.

Lauren smiled to herself. *Sorry, mister, but he's all mine. And he swings my way.*

Lauren leaned heavily into Jacko, squeezing his arm. He looked down at her and smiled again. Smiles looked odd on his face.

Maybe she'd get used to it, in time.

TEN

THERE SHE WAS!

Walking out of the building where Suzanne Huntington ran her business. Together with the business of her husband, which, alas, was security.

That was quite unfortunate. Frederick was hoping to conduct his business with Suzanne Huntington alone. He didn't want any input from a security guy. All security professionals in his experience were professionally paranoid.

Not good.

Particularly not good when Frederick was showing his face shortly before Anne Lowell disappeared.

So he shot laser beams at the two vidcams at the gate of the compound and at the two just inside the door and turned in time to see Anne Lowell walk down the driveway clinging to the arm of the man who looked like an ugly bruiser.

Looking good, our Annie. Well, she'd just learned that the man chasing her was now dead. She must be feeling that sweet sagging sensation of relief at a danger passed. She was intact, safe, and her nemesis was dead. The most fundamental, most primordial of sensations, that of a dead adversary. The human animal was primed to be awash in endorphins when danger was averted. Simple biology.

So her guard would be down, which was good.

Unfortunately, the guard of the man by her side was not down. He walked arm in arm with her, checking on her but checking on his environment as well. Calmly quartering his field of vision for any possible threats. The man's dark gaze swept to Frederick's face, lingered like a spotlight. It was very uncomfortable.

Frederick knew who the man was, besides clearly being Anne Lowell's lover. Morton Jackman. Frederick always did due diligence and had taken a look at the business website of Suzanne Huntington's husband. He'd even studied the faces and brief CVs of his employees and had recognized the man who'd been by Anne's side at the art show.

The headshot of Morton Jackman on Alpha Security International's website showed an unsmiling portrait with a number of piercings that were now gone. Former SEAL, which was *not* good news. More or less everyone in the company was a former SEAL including the two owner-partners.

SEALs were formidable adversaries. As they walked toward each other, Frederick gave himself an almost exaggerated feminine walk and simpered at Jackman. That usually worked with machos, amused them, distracted them. But this Jackman didn't let down his guard at all. Frederick got a full appraisal, head to toe, and he was very glad he wasn't armed because something told him Jackman would figure it out. Maybe by the way he walked.

And then they were gone and Frederick was walking into the building. He was wearing his Borsalino and kept his head tilted downward. There was no question of blinding the two vidcams at the entrance. Half the security company would come roaring out.

No, he needed to keep his eyes on the ground, face hidden by the larger-than-normal brim and continue.

The left-hand side door, he knew, was Suzanne Huntington's business. There was no security camera above
her door. He knew there would be one over the door of
ASI but all they would see was his back and an expanse
of very expensive charcoal-colored cashmere.

He was buzzed in, walked over the threshold and…
paused. In admiration. My, the woman knew how to create an ambiance. He was instantly taken with the room,
instantly put at ease by the colors and shapes, the soft
furniture, the faint smell of potpourri. Truly remarkable.

"Mr. Andrews." The woman coming toward him with
a smile and outstretched hand was stunning. Dark blond
hair caught up in a French twist, Grace Kelly face, slender figure. Wearing a Donna Karan suit if he wasn't mistaken. Warm and elegant. "Welcome. Do please take a
seat."

Instead of leading him to one of the two client chairs
in front of her desk she took him to a small damask-
covered sofa and sat down beside him.

The office was a very eloquent advertisement for her
services. It was highly decorated without being over-
wrought, modern without being stark. Every single object
struck just the right note, including its owner.

She smiled at him. "How can I help you, Mr. Andrews?"

"Well, I have a small investment firm…"

"Not so small," she said.

Very well done. It was a flattering comment while also
a warning. *I do my research.* Frederick looked again at
Suzanne Huntington and this time noticed the sharp intelligence in her gaze, not just the elegance and beauty.
This woman was not to be trifled with. He had to keep
his best game on.

He bowed his head in acknowledgment of her words.

Not commenting because a very wealthy man knew he was very wealthy and nothing else needed to be said.

"So." He leaned back, a man at ease with himself and the world. "I'm thinking of relocating, at least temporarily, to Portland. Portland makes a good hub. I need decent premises for my business and myself. I recently looked at a property that would be large enough both for offices and home premises. Each part would need a different look, of course."

"I'm familiar with a lot of properties in Portland, Mr. Andrews. Which one would this be?"

Frederick smiled. "Please, Mrs. Huntington. Call me Paul. I suspect we will be doing business together."

She cocked her head, smiled. "Of course, Paul. And you must call me Suzanne."

"Excellent, Suzanne." He watched her face carefully. "The property I was thinking of would be the penthouse at the Sorenson. Either a rental or I might just buy. Would make a good tax break."

By not a flicker of a long eyelash did Suzanne betray anything other than polite interest. She knew perfectly well that the decorator of the penthouse at the Sorenson would be landing a public relations coup. Big spreads on decorating websites, AD, you name it. Frederick knew her portfolio and it was already impressive. This would make her a nationwide name.

"That'd be an interesting job," she said with a polite smile, cool as silk.

He nodded. "I'd want the office to make a statement. Investment is as much about psychology as about data. And I'd want the home premises to be very comfortable. Other than that, I'm open to any designs you might care to offer."

She gave him a sharp glance. "I often do business with Ingram Realty so I'm familiar with the specs of the Sorenson penthouse. I could get some preliminary designs to you by next week. Give you several options, so we could narrow down what would be to your taste. I often find that clients recognize what they want when they see it. And it isn't always easy to articulate the kind of look you want. So I always give a range of looks."

Frederick beamed. "That would be *excellent*," he enthused. "By the way—before making an appointment with you, I happened to stop by the Beckstein Gallery. Which is how I got your name, by the way. I was simply blown away by the renderings of your designs. Whatever designs you do, I'd love to buy them. Even the ones we don't go for. It'd make for an interesting collection on one wall—variations on a theme. You have an extraordinarily fine hand. My congratulations."

If he was expecting her to take credit for the renderings, he was wrong. She smiled. "You're quite right, they are extraordinary, but I can't take the credit for them. They are all by a friend of mine, Lauren Dare. She is very talented."

Frederick managed to hide the leap of delight he felt. *Lauren Dare.* So that was the name she went by here.

Silly, silly girl, he thought. Lauren was her grandmother's name. How sentimental. Sentiment got you killed.

"Funny." He cocked his head. "I met the gallery owner, Mr. Beckstein. He gave me to understand that you were the artist."

She had the grace to blush, a very becoming rose. "That's because until very recently, Lauren had some… problems. Ah, fiscal ones. And it was easier to pretend that I was the artist. But now her problems seem to be, ah, over. And I'm sure she would enjoy the work." The blush was gone and she narrowed her eyes. "Her price just went up, though. Way up."

Frederick nodded. A price increase was no problem. He pulled out his cell. "Could I have her number?"

Suzanne opened her mouth then closed it. Frederick could see the calculations running through her head. Her friend was free and clear, the bad guy after her was dead, but still…

"Um. I think she is in the process of changing providers. I have your cell number and I will be sure to pass it on to her. She'll contact you herself."

No, my dear, Frederick thought. *I'll be contacting her first.*

He stood and she stood with him. He buttoned his jacket, put on his overcoat, heavy and warm and expensive. God, the rich had such a nice life. He kept his hat in his hand, ready to don it the instant he crossed the threshold.

"Well," he said. "I look forward to hearing from you both."

"Yes, indeed." Suzanne pulled open her door. "You'll definitely be hearing from me and from Lauren."

Yes he would. And Suzanne Huntington would be getting an email from the personal assistant of Paul Andrews in about a week. Paul Andrews was switching the focus of his investments to San Diego. It had been a pleasure, he would keep her in mind…yada yada.

Happened all the time in the business world.

On the way out Frederick kept his eyes on the ground, the brim of the Borsalino covering his face.

Outside the compound, he walked up the street and around the corner where his driver was waiting. He called his pilot and quietly made arrangements to have "the briefcase" delivered to his hotel.

The rich were different in many, many ways. The rules governing ordinary people didn't apply to them. He'd been cursorily examined upon arrival in the private part of the airfield, called general aviation, and the plane wasn't examined at all. Inside a compartment in the plane's hull was a briefcase with an untraceable weapon and several preloaded syringes of fentanyl.

Frederick wasn't operational, had no aspirations to being operational. He'd observed Alfonso's and Jorge's goons from a distance, and with great distaste. He himself was an intellectual and he solved problems with his mind.

Some problems, however, required action, and this was one of them.

The fentanyl was to put Anne Lowell under.

The gun was for the thug by her side.

"OH MY GOSH!" Lauren bounced in her seat. "I can buy that big wireless Mac desktop for my graphic work! No more laptops for me!" She rubbed her hands. "I can actually declare myself to the IRS, pay taxes." She slanted a glance at Jacko and scrunched her nose. "Believe it or not, that's a biggie. I hated evading taxes. And I'm going to buy myself at least three pairs of high heels! Louboutin! *Red!* And…maybe a puppy. But only if you promise to share in taking him out for walks."

She turned her head to look at him fully, smiling.

Jacko clenched the steering wheel and tried not to look at her. She was flushed with happiness, electrically alive, heartbreakingly beautiful. It took every ounce of self-control not to slam on the brakes and reach out to her.

But it was snowing and if he pulled over to the side of the road and killed the engine, she'd freeze. He wouldn't be cold, no sir. He was never going to feel the cold again, not as long as Lauren was with him. Near him. Even the thought of her filled him with blazing heat. They could put him in a snowy ice field naked and if she was nearby, there'd be a melted circle of water around him.

A puppy. Jesus. A dog. He'd never had a pet, never. As a kid there hadn't been enough to eat for him, let alone a pet. So he'd never had one, not even a goldfish. Pets required work and required his staying in the same place for more than a day or two. In his SEAL days it would have been impossible, of course. SEALs couldn't keep their wives, let alone their dogs. You could be wheels-up at any minute with no advance notice. And these last few years working for ASI? Well, he'd been one to volunteer for anything that took him out of town. Hotel rooms were more welcoming than his place.

Only now could he admit to himself that his apartment was spare and cold and depressing. He never really liked coming home, which was why he worked out of town as much as possible and when he fucked, he slept over at the woman's house, whoever the woman of the day was.

And now? Permanent girlfriend. Living in that pretty house with Lauren, sleeping with her every night. And a dog.

"Puppy, huh?" He pretended to scowl. "What kind?"

"Golden retriever," she replied. "The kind with the long eyelashes. The kind that—"

"Pees everywhere?"

She laughed. "That's the one."

Lauren was irresistible when she laughed. She looked like an imp, face alive with delight.

"We could do that."

She laughed again, sobered, put her hand on his forearm. He kept his face forward but in his peripheral vision he could see her looking at him..

"So…you'll be okay with living in my house? You wouldn't miss yours?"

Considering there wasn't much in his place to miss… "Nah. But I'll be moving in the TV."

"Okay." She considered. "I think it will fit on the living room wall. You wear a headset if you watch late at night."

He slanted her a glance. "Making ground rules already? That was fast."

"Yeah." She tightened her grip on his forearm. "But I think I'm really easy to live with, though I haven't lived with anyone since my college dorm roommate."

His heart leaped. She'd never lived with another man. He had no idea why that was important to him, but it was. "I've never lived with anyone, either." Though he couldn't count his sex partners, no one had lasted more than a couple of weeks. Most a couple of days. "I think I snore."

"Yeah, you do. I forgive you, though. Seeing as how you did everything you could to keep me safe. Thank you so much."

She waited, looked at him expectantly. Oh man, oh fuck. This was the moment, the perfect moment for him to tell her what he felt. He hadn't so far. He hadn't because…he couldn't. Everything was deep in his chest, so tangled and so hot it hurt. But nothing of that hot, wet tangle of feelings could make it up through his throat to tell her what she wanted—needed—to hear.

That keeping her safe was his top priority. That he'd defend her with his life. That she was now absolutely vital to his well-being. That he…he shied away from that thought. Telling her…*that*…would hurt. He'd never told *that* to a single human being in his life.

His whole life had been about being invulnerable, in every way. Nobody could hurt him, man or beast—he wouldn't allow it. He'd been like that since he was five, maybe even earlier. Nobody gave a shit about him so he learned to take care of himself right from the get-go and never depend on anyone. He grew big really fast so no one had bullied him, ever. He'd learned early to project that *don't fuck with me* vibe. It was ingrained.

So giving Lauren what she deserved—an indication of just how fucking important she was to him—well that was hard to do. But he had to tell her. How his chest would cave in if something happened to her or if she walked away from him.

He knew he didn't even really have to say The Words. She was smart. She'd read between the lines if he opened up to her.

But…he couldn't. He could fuck her nearly to death but he couldn't tell her what he felt. A lifetime of never expressing emotions stood like a huge, towering mountain of granite between them.

Lauren could sense something was going on inside him. Though his face was impassive—it took a freaking effort for him to show anything—inside he was vibrating with stress. She glanced at him, eyes wide. Waiting to see if he said anything.

No.

He couldn't. Fucking *couldn't*.

The only thing he could talk about was facts. The outside world—that he could do. "We're here," he said and swerved into her driveway. The first time she'd been to her house since they'd left a couple of days ago.

Lauren was talking again, a happy rush of words. He should be listening to what she was saying because she was always interesting—but right then all he could pay attention to was her flushed, happy, beautiful face. Hear the happiness in her voice. She chattered as he helped her down from his SUV and as they walked up her driveway.

Then she stopped, fell completely silent.

Jacko stood by her side as she reached out to touch her front door, as a primitive tribesman would a talisman. Touching it as if it contained special magical powers. And maybe it did because her face just shone. Something was touching her, deeply.

She glanced up at him and opened the door with the key in her purse. The door swung wide and she gestured with her hand for him to walk in.

She wanted him to go in first because—because this was going to become his home, too. It hit him with full force right then. She'd agreed to living together, to sharing a home. *This* home, which was now by some twist of fate going to be *his* home.

Shit. He'd never had a real home before. He'd moved from his mother's trailer, which was never clean and grew only more desolate and battered with each passing year, to barracks. The barracks were a huge improvement but basically he had a cot assigned him in an enormous space. Nothing was his, not even the cot. Just the Navy-issue trunk at the foot with a few belongings. Not many.

The Navy had been his home until he retired and rented his place in Portland. It wasn't his home. It was where he slept and watched TV and listened to music. If ASI had set up bachelor quarters somewhere, that's where he'd have lived.

And now…this. He hadn't had much of a chance to

look at her space. He'd been way too blown away by Lauren herself.

But looking around, feeling tense muscles relax, drawing in air that still smelled of flowers and her, it hit him like a sledgehammer that for the first time in his life he was *home*.

Lauren switched on the lights and turned the heat on. Somewhere a boiler kicked in. She trailed a hand along the back of the couch in the pretty living room, picked up something soft across the back of it, lifted it to her cheek.

"I thought I'd never see this place again." Her eyes were shiny when she turned to him. "I thought I had found a safe haven so I worked to make this place my home, and the other day when I left—" she gave a faint smile, "—when I tried to leave, it hurt. It felt like something was cutting me up from the inside. I couldn't bear the thought of leaving this place. Leaving Suzanne, Allegra, Claire. Leaving *you*."

Jacko let out a long breath. "I would never have let you go. I would have found you, wherever you went."

She smiled. She was crisscrossing the house, touching things, touching him when she passed by.

Though Jacko wanted more than anything to pick her up and throw her onto her fancy bed with the billion pillows and flowered sheets, he understood she needed to do this. Needed to connect by touch with the life she'd lost, but now was hers again.

"That's a nice thought, Jacko. But Felicity is good. Very good."

He cocked his head. "Felicity?"

She sighed. "I guess now I can talk about it. Felicity isn't her real name. It's sort of her internet handle, after the character in *Arrow*."

He raised his eyebrows.

"Felicity Smoak?" She laughed at his clueless expression. "Very pretty and very smart character on a TV show. My Felicity is just as smart as the character. She gave me a new identity and even my secret job."

Jacko did impassive very well. Or thought he did. But apparently Lauren saw right through him. She laughed again, which was good. Great even. If he could make her laugh, she could laugh at him for the next hundred years.

"You're dying to know—I can tell." Lauren pulled out her MacAir from her big purse, put it on the coffee table and switched it on. She sat down on the couch and patted the seat next to her.

He didn't need another invitation. He sank into the cushions, happy to be sitting next to her. Happy she was here. Happy he was here with her.

"Okay, pay attention. Felicity lives in the darknet. You know what that is."

"Yeah."

She pursed her lips. "Yes, you would. Of course you would. I don't know what she does for a living—I suspect she's involved in computer security. I've often thought that she might work for the NSA. For some reason, she understands innocent people on the run. She got me my new identity and she's really good at it. She spent a lot of time creating Lauren Dare, giving her an impeccable background and supplying perfect ID. She said she hoped I could be Lauren Dare forever."

"You can." Jacko reached out, wanting to cup her face. He settled for tucking a lock of dark hair behind her ear. Who knew if she wanted to go back to being blond? He didn't give a shit. She could go purple, or shave her head like him for all he cared. "You can be anything you want to be. Anyone you want to be."

"I can, can't I?" Lauren smiled. "Maybe I will just stay Lauren Dare. Anne Lowell wasn't too happy a person. Lauren Dare is. And there's yet another person inside me." She brought up Google and typed quickly. "Voilà!"

The screen showed a website in French, of all things, www.chenet.fr. She clicked on the small British flag on the upper right-hand corner and the site morphed into English. There was a carousel of pictures floating right to left. On the top of the site was a name in flowing script: Fabiola Chenet.

Jacko pointed. "Who's she?"

"My avatar. My alter ego. Here." She clicked on Bio and there was one of those Facebook-type photos that hid more than revealed. Half a face, the other half hidden by a long fall of platinum hair, dark sunglasses, face cropped just below the nose. Completely unrecognizable yet alluring. Jacko would never have been able to connect her with Lauren. "There you go. Meet Fabiola Chenet. She studied graphic art at the Paris Design School, did a year at the Royal College of Art, so her English is very good. If you check the schools, you'll find her CV. Got very good grades." She smiled faintly. "Though Felicity gave me some Bs, for authenticity."

Jacko leaned forward, acutely aware of the heat of her body next to his. "So…what am I looking at here?"

She smiled secretively and clicked on a thumbnail image. It suddenly filled the monitor and Jacko sat back. "Whoa."

A beautiful woman seen from the back, face in profile. Long black hair piled on top of her head. Arms out, in the process of twirling. She was dressed in a long black dress laced up loosely along the back, showing plenty of smooth satiny skin. As she twirled, the hem of her long black dress lifted and became sleek blackbirds. Like crows only with thinner beaks. The blackbirds lifted from her graceful hands, too. The overall effect was stunning, a woman who was magic.

"That's beautiful."

The smile broadened. "Thanks. It's the cover of a fantasy novel about a shape-shifter woman who can command animals. She has been exiled and must make her way back to the castle." She pointed a finger at a misty fortress on a granite hilltop in the background. "See?"

This was something entirely different from what Jacko had seen her do. This was artwork that told a story, that grabbed you and pulled you right into the picture. You could see the woman's power, the trek ahead of her, the wild animal kingdom that was hers to command.

"You did that." Jacko shook his head.

"I certainly did. Watch." She clicked and the carousel of images continued floating across the monitor, enlarging as they reached midpoint then reducing again to a thumbnail. Many of them were fantasy images, magical and enticing. Some were portraits, the faces always interesting, with an element on the cover that showed whether this was a tragedy or a comedy. The colors were perfect—sharp and clear and glowing.

She sat back, satisfied. "These are all book covers. So—that's how I've been earning my keep, thanks to Felicity who set me up, created me, created Fabiola. If anyone checked the website's IP address, it's in France. Fabiola is very successful and she pays all her taxes in France." Lauren wrinkled her nose. "Nobody should complain about taxes in this country. Not after being stuck in the French system."

"No, it wasn't thanks to Felicity. It was thanks to you and your talent," Jacko growled. "She just allowed you to use it."

Lauren sobered, turned to look at him, utterly serious. "I thought I'd lost it all. If I'd been forced to run I don't know whether I'd have had the courage to keep this business up, and it's just now taking off. I have more commissions than I can handle. And I love it. I love interacting with the author, reading the book to get the feel of it, giving the book a face. I was on the verge of losing everything and now—" She stretched out her hand to him and he took it. "Now I think I have everything I could possibly want."

Keeping his eyes on hers, Jacko brought her hand to his mouth. A romantic gesture, but it was not out of romance. He didn't have a romantic bone in his body. He just wanted to feel her skin on his lips.

Lauren sighed and without changing tone said, "What took you so long?"

Jacko blinked. "What?"

"You hung around me for four months. Every time I turned around, there you were. Apparently we drove Allegra, Suzanne and Claire crazy because you weren't making your move. Why not?"

Time for honesty. "You scared me," he confessed.

Lauren's eyes went wide. "I—I what?"

"Scared the shit out of me. You terrified me."

She looked him over and he knew exactly what she was seeing. He was 240 pounds of pure muscle, a trained killer. Though he didn't have the many piercings he'd had a few years ago, he was still heavily tattooed. Shaved head, the works.

Lauren, on the other hand, weighed less than half what he did and she was an artist. And a sweet woman on top of it. She probably had never hit another human being in her life. He'd grown up fighting bare-knuckled until he got into the Navy. Then they armed him.

Her eyes narrowed, face lit with mischief.

"I like the idea of terrifying you. I like it a lot."

Jacko fought a smile. "Yeah?"

"Oh yeah." She leaned forward, a few inches from his face. She pursed her lips and he thought she was going to kiss him but instead she said, "Boo!"

He jumped, gave an exaggerated shudder of terror. She laughed. God it was good to hear her laugh. Light, carefree. A laugh of delight.

Then she sobered and her hand tightened around his. "That was fun." She searched his eyes. "But I don't want to do that. I don't like to dominate." He gave a small nod. Her eyes remained steady on his. She was telling him something really important now. "And I don't like to be dominated."

"No." Fuck no. He didn't want to dominate her. BUDS training had been all about breaking strong men. Or trying to. Everything had been thrown at him—physical, verbal abuse, cruel punishments, DIs screaming in his face. They hadn't broken him, not even close. But he did understand bone deep what it was like to have someone try to break you.

He didn't want one molecule of anything like that near Lauren. In the same room as Lauren. She was magic. She made him feel better just being around her. He didn't want that magic gone. He wanted to protect that magic from the outside world; he didn't want to crush it. God no.

And maybe all things considered she was as unbreakable as he was. Maybe more. Because, shit, he couldn't have taken the pressure of being hunted for two fucking years. Looking over his shoulder day after day after day. He'd have taken the fight to the enemy, that was his nature and he'd been trained to do it, but Lauren couldn't do that. Two women had died. If he didn't shave his head, every hair on his head would have stood up when she told him that. She didn't have the tools to resist armed men so she'd done the only thing possible—run.

He couldn't say all that. He didn't have the words for that, but what was on his face must have been reassuring because she nodded sharply. "Okay."

"Okay." Something in his voice made her smile.

"So." She stood. He stood, too. "I'm hungry—how about you?"

It hadn't even occurred to him but now that she talked about food… "Starving."

"Good thing when I was running away from home I didn't take the time to empty the fridge out completely. I'll cook, you'll set the table."

Another thing he'd been taught in the Navy. Tactics.

"This is a test," he said. "You're seeing how domesticated I am."

"Bingo." She smiled but was still watching him carefully.

Well, this was easy. "I was in the military." He looked down at her, wanting to dispel the slight anxiety that he saw in her beautiful face. He reached out, smoothed the small furrow between her brows. "I take orders well."

ELEVEN

BEING OPERATIONAL WAS exceedingly tedious, Frederick thought. There was so much damned interaction with the physical world. He hated it. His world was virtual, rational and reliable binary code. It either was or it wasn't. And in his hands, it mostly was.

He could sit in his very comfortable, climate-controlled study with every possible convenience at hand, and shift the levers of the world.

Instead of sitting in his $800 Eames chair that did everything but make coffee for him, he was sitting in a freezing cold midrange rental waiting for his pilot to bring the briefcase.

The driver had taken Paul Andrews to the airport. Ten minutes later, Lawrence E. Macy rented a sedan, drove two miles along the perimeter of the airport and parked. That had been an hour ago. It was pointless calling the pilot. He knew he was supposed to be here an hour ago. He knew he was in trouble.

Snow was falling softly, visible only in the cones of light of the streetlights, invisible otherwise, until it fell on the windshield. Frederick glanced up sourly at the sullen gray sky, seemingly an inch above the roof of the car. He changed his mind about the charm of Portland. Miserable town. Provincial and *cold*. Frederick vowed never to go to a northern city in winter, ever again. How did people stand it?

He could switch on the engine, put on the heater, but he preferred to keep the full tank of gas. He didn't want to pull into any gas station with its video cameras. The plan was to drive to Anne Lowell's house, shoot her boy-friend if he was there, inject her with a syringe of fen-tanyl, bundle her in this car and drive straight to the plane. But anything could happen and he wanted to keep as much gas in the tank as possible.

But it was damned cold. And he was bored.

The thought of the half million dollars warmed him, though. Down to his bones.

It would have taken him two years of Alfonso to make half a million dollars and now look at him. A simple twenty-four-hour mission to Portland and 500K was going to be deposited in his account. Of course, Freder-ick was going to have to kill the bodyguard/boyfriend, and Anne Lowell would be smoked, but still.

And the Caymans deal. Man, if he played his cards right that was going to be a real moneymaker. Maybe he could establish the servers directly in the Caymans and—

He jumped when someone rapped sharply at his window. The pilot, holding out the briefcase. Freder-ick buzzed the window down irritably, face impassive, heart still racing.

"Here, sir. I apologize for the delay. The access road was blocked and has just been cleared." The pilot glanced up at the sky, snowflakes falling on his face, then bent down to Frederick again. "The control tower said that if it keeps snowing like this they're shutting the airport down by 10 p.m. So whatever business you have, it would be best to be back here in two-and-a-half hours at the most."

Frederick nodded. He intended to be very fast. Anne Lowell's house was about a thirty-minute drive away.

Forty, maybe, in this weather. She didn't have a land-line but he had checked power contracts in the name of Lauren Dare and bingo! One had come up. Then some more rooting and he came up with a cell phone number.

His business once at her house would be fast. Shoot the muscle, drug her and carry her outside to his car. Then drive to the airport, get her onboard, wait while the pilot drove the rental to the long-term parking lot—he was resigned to sacrificing his ID as Lawrence Macy—and took the shuttle back.

They should be wheels-up by 8:30 p.m.

"There will be another passenger onboard on the way back," he told the pilot through the open window. The pilot nodded. He was being paid three times the usual price for this trip. He wasn't going to question an uncon-scious passenger. Not if he wanted to be paid.

Frederick waited until the pilot left to open the brief-case. Not being an operator, he was more interested in the five insulin-sized syringes in their foam cutouts than the gun. Five syringes was overkill, but better to be safe than sorry. He'd bought the syringes from a dealer who also supplied Florida's professional elite. Fentanyl was a powerful drug that had to be calibrated carefully but it also guaranteed sleep, because fentanyl was a form of anesthesia. If you suffered from massive insomnia, as two of the dealer's clients did, you used fentanyl or one of its opiate precursors and you could be guaranteed sleep. Too much of it and you could be guaranteed death. But the kind of insomnia suffered by the clients was co-caine-induced so they were used to dancing on the abyss.

Frederick's dosages were carefully calibrated.

He hefted the gun with distaste. Beyond some lessons at a gun range he wasn't proficient with firearms. But that was okay. He wasn't going to try for a headshot. He'd aim at center mass. The boyfriend had a really broad chest. Frederick couldn't miss.

Frederick texted his client to expect to pick "the package" up at a private airfield near Palm Beach around 4 a.m. the next morning. All in all, he didn't expect to be responsible for Anne Lowell for more than eight hours. Everything had gone smoothly so far. This would all be over very soon.

Tomorrow morning, Frederick would be on his terrace, sipping an espresso in the sunshine, half a million dollars richer. And Anne Lowell would be singing like a bird, after which her dead body would probably be dumped into the big, wide ocean.

JACKO DID TAKE orders well. She told him what to do and he did it quietly, with no fuss, and extremely efficiently. She had splurged on a set of crystal wineglasses and crystal water glasses, which she'd left behind because crystal wouldn't go well with her new life on the run. Now she could use them again.

Though Jacko had huge hands, he handled the glasses delicately, precisely. The cutlery was lined up like…well, like soldiers. Perfectly. When she raised her eyebrows, Jacko quirked one side of his mouth up.

"First month in the Navy," he said quietly, "and we're all raw recruits and most of us come from what a sociologist would call disadvantaged homes and what we called dumps, and we're sent into a mess hall with seats and a blackboard at one end. And this tiny little lady comes out, not a hundred pounds dripping wet, and she was scarier than the scariest Drill Instructor and believe me when I say that most DIs boiled straight up from hell. But even they were scared of Mrs. Billings. She gave us long talks, with diagrams on the blackboard."

Lauren stopped stirring the frozen split pea soup she'd made a month ago, in another life, and listened to him, fascinated.

He continued working, placing the napkins with mathematical precision, folding them carefully. You could shave with the crease. "Half of us barely knew how to use cutlery. Most of us held forks like spears. Mrs. Billings walked up and down the mess halls during meals for six weeks. We'd have a lesson in dining etiquette from informal to highly formal meals and then we'd have a practice meal. You didn't hold your cutlery right and you got whipped across the knuckles with a stick. Hard. I had some Catholic buddies and they said Mrs. Billings was meaner than any of the nuns they had as kids, and that was saying something. But she got the job done. By the end, any of us could have gone to dinner at the White House and not disgrace ourselves."

"And you learned," she said as he lay a dessert spoon horizontally above the plate, spoon ladle left, handle right.

"Oh, yeah." He shook his head. "I learned everything the Navy could teach me, from handling a fifty cal to eating soup."

She turned off the burner and brought the pot to the table. "Well, you're going to be able to show me your soup-eating skills right now. I hope you like split pea soup." She ladled some into his bowl. He didn't begin until she sat down, placed her napkin across her lap and started eating. Only then did he eat himself, delicately, without spilling a drop.

"Yeah, I do," he said. "I'm not fussy about food. I'll

eat most anything, and have. But this is delicious." He looked over at her. "Everything looks delicious."

She still had a lot of stuff in her freezer, certainly enough to offer Jacko a decent meal. The soup, a square of eggplant Parmesan, a baguette, a whole frozen cheesecake.

Lauren smiled, pleased. "Well, you saved me from a life on the run. A meal seems like a poor thanks."

He put his huge hand on hers. "Don't," he said, deep voice serious. "I keep telling you. Don't even think that way. You don't owe me anything."

Oh but she did. She turned to him, opened her mouth to argue, and he stopped her with a kiss. Soft, hard, soft again. Enough to make her senses swim. He pulled back and she opened her eyes with difficulty. Her eyelids felt heavy.

When he was so close like this it was as if he were this huge planet that exerted its own gravity and it messed with the neurons in her head like the moon did with the tides. He sat back, watching her closely, and she was sure she had turned beet red.

Because, well…that kiss had been pure sex. Her entire body lit up, pulsed hot.

He put his hand on hers again, her hand disappearing under his. He gave a gentle squeeze then let her hand go. "This is a great meal. But why don't we go out to dinner tomorrow night? I heard Suzanne talk about a new French restaurant. You look like the kind of chick that likes French."

Lauren sighed, smiled. "A restaurant. I haven't been out to a fancy restaurant in two years." She looked at him out of the corner of her eyes. "It would be like— like a date."

"It would. We could even go to the movies after. Eat popcorn. Hold hands. Maybe smooch. Make the experience complete."

"Sure." She handed him an extra-large slice of cheesecake. "There's a film on by that Danish director. The one who doesn't believe in special effects or fancy camerawork or artificial light. It's about a woman sliding into Alzheimer's. Three hours long."

"Okay," Jacko said equably. Nothing in his deep voice betrayed any kind of emotion.

"Or…we could go to the new Spider-Man movie," Lauren suggested.

Jacko's lips moved slightly. But she was beginning to crack the Jacko code—in any other man it would have been a grin. "That was another test. How'd I do, coach?"

She smiled sunnily at him. "It *was* a test. And you passed with flying colors. Congratulations."

The contours of his face changed. Became hard, almost grim. His eyes narrowed, the dark skin over his cheekbones becoming even darker, lips red with blood. He looked at her mouth, then met her eyes. There was a question there and there was only one possible answer.

"Yes," she breathed.

Afterward, she could never remember how they got to her bedroom. Floated there, possibly because one second they were in the kitchen eating cheesecake and the next they were in her dark bedroom, clothes flying.

She landed on her back and Jacko landed on top of her, his weight almost too heavy to bear. Almost. Because it was also so incredibly exciting having him on top of her. It was the perfect position for her to touch him all over. Her hands could roam over his back, over those amazingly hard muscles that were like an anatomy chart. She could trace each one. Trapezius, deltoids, lats… Fitting over each other perfectly. Perfect, everything about him was perfect.

Everything about him was overwhelming. He was kissing her deeply, mouth moving over hers, tongue tasting her mouth, and she could lose herself in his kisses alone. He left her mouth and moved to her neck, which was, she had been astonished to discover, a huge erogenous zone for her. She'd had no idea.

When he kissed it, with that double whammy of soft lips and slightly abrasive beard, she shivered. Goose bumps rose along her arms.

"You like that," he murmured, and his voice was dark and enticing.

"Yeah," she breathed. "But then I like everything you do to me."

She could feel his smile against her throat. He nipped her lightly and she jumped, pleasure coursing through her like electricity. It seemed every time they made love she became more responsive, the feelings more intense.

At this rate, she'd be dead in a month.

There was never any awkwardness in the bed with them, ever. Everything he did to her seemed to be calculated to evoke maximum pleasure. And he seemed to enjoy every touch, every kiss of hers.

How many times had a man been rough, even unintentionally? Pinched her breast instead of stroking it. Sawing at her clitoris, holding her too tightly. There was absolutely nothing of that with Jacko, the strongest man she'd ever known. The strongest man she'd ever even seen.

He never hurt her, ever. His powerful hands seemed to know exactly how to touch her, better than she knew how to touch herself. She was like a book in a language he knew how to read.

His mouth drifted down to her breast and he did that perfectly, too. He never suckled too strongly, never bit her nipple hard. He licked her breast and she shivered. One big hand moved down, over her belly, cupping her mound. He didn't have to do anything—she understood. Her legs moved apart and there he was, hand touching her where her flesh was so sensitive. His touch was perfect here, too; so perfect her sheath wept with happiness.

That's what it felt like, anyway. She could feel moisture welling, her body reacting to him instinctively. He gave a long sigh against her breast when he felt her softening for him, becoming wetter.

He loved that and said so.

A finger was circling her flesh. His hands were rough, callused, but somehow he never hurt her. If anything, the calluses excited her, just that tiny touch of abrasion that was exciting.

"How are we doing down there, hmm?"

Lauren lifted her head slightly to look down at him. There was just enough light from the living room to see him. His eyes were closed, black lashes over high cheekbones, mouth on her breast.

His hand between her legs moved and he slid a finger inside her where she was supersensitive and she stiffened. The breath went out of her.

"We coming along?" he asked. He took her hand and curled it around his penis. "Because I sure am."

Lauren smiled and tightened her hand. He was huge, hard as steel, big engorged veins running up his penis. "Yes," she said, "you sure are. But you always seem to be in this state."

A rough rumble. Jacko chuckling. It was a charming sound that went straight to her sex. She contracted around his finger and he stopped chuckling. His finger entered more deeply and she contracted again, hard.

His penis pulsed, became somehow harder.

Jacko blew out a breath. He withdrew his finger, slid it back in, and she felt electric pleasure. Her fisted hand slid down to the root of his penis, back up. He was so aroused his hips moved with her hand. When he made a sound of helpless pleasure she did it again, and again.

His finger was sliding in and out of her now, thumb circling her clitoris. She contracted around him so hard her stomach muscles pulled and she moved straight into orgasm just as his penis enlarged even more around her hand and he started coming, too, in great pulses she could feel under her hand, jetting all over her stomach.

Her head tilted back against the pillow, all of her concentrated on his hand between her legs, inside her, stroking her as sparks of sensation so strong they were almost painful shot through her. He was stroking her harder, faster.

"Don't stop, honey. Ah, God…" His hips were moving fast and he groaned when she tightened her fist.

Lauren cried out, couldn't move, couldn't breathe, her body now completely out of her control. Her heart hammered and she felt close to blacking out. Jacko gave a shout, pulsed one more time and stilled. He was sprawling on her now, a complete deadweight, his heavy torso making her ribs creak.

Lauren lifted her hand, which weighed several tons, and caressed the back of his head. "God," she murmured. It was only foreplay and she was exhausted.

"Yeah," he answered. "Just as soon as I get some blood

back to my head we're going to do that again, only better."

Lauren smiled in the dark, remembering what Claire had said about her husband. "Any better than that and I'll pass out."

SLOWLY, HER SENSES returned. She became aware of the pinging on her bedroom window as the snow turned to sleet, loud in the deep quiet of the house. She pulled in a deep breath, the scent of Jacko mixed with her potpourri heady and exciting. By now his scent worked on her limbic system like pellets to a hamster. She felt lax, but energized, a crazy feeling, but good-crazy not awful-crazy. Actually, she felt good all over, joyful and hopeful all at once.

She turned her head slowly and watched Jacko sleep. He slept like he did everything—intensely. He was utterly still, fierce face slightly relaxed in repose. When he slept he looked younger, without that eternal vigilance. It occurred to her that maybe he was closer in age to her than she thought. He seemed like he'd lived a thousand lifetimes but that was because of the soldiering. When he woke up, she had to ask him how old he was.

When he woke up, she was going to ask him a lot of things, of this man she was unexpectedly going to be living with.

That was another thing. Living with Jacko. She barely knew him but the thought didn't scare her, not a bit. She lay there, staring at the darkness of the ceiling, turning that thought over and over in her mind.

Sharing her life with Jacko. Not being alone anymore, as she'd been these past two years. True, Suzanne and Allegra and Claire had simply pushed themselves into her life and she'd be eternally grateful that they never accepted no for an answer. Because of course she'd tried to push them away, gently, for their own sakes. Finding peace only when she closed the door of her little house behind her and she was on her own. Only it hadn't been peace, not really. It had only been emptiness, an emptiness that stretched out before her for her entire lifetime.

She'd been alone much more than the last two years though, she realized now. Maybe her entire life. Because she'd never felt like she did now, with Jacko by her side. He was like a rock. A sexy rock.

So much to look forward to. Coming home to Jacko, who had a strong, vibrant personality behind all that impassivity. Jacko who cared for her. Jacko who would accompany her anywhere, including to movies of ungodly boredom. She smiled at the thought of dragging him to that tedious Danish film. He'd sit through it with her, if that was what she wanted, and he'd pay attention, and he'd talk about it with her afterward.

That took courage.

A lot to look forward to. Someone to care for. Someone to care for her. Someone to have meals with, do things with, someone to share the cares of the day with.

She wasn't *alone* anymore. It was almost impossible to process. She'd been alone for so long. Most of her life, in fact.

From the living room came the sound of the opening bars of *The Four Seasons*. Her cell phone. She slipped out from under Jacko's heavy arm and out of bed, pulling on a dressing gown.

Closing the bedroom door quietly behind her, Lauren rushed to catch the phone.

"Hello?"

"Yes, this is Paul Andrews. May I speak with Ms. Lauren Dare?" The voice was a pleasant tenor, very Eastern Seaboard, very posh. A light tenor. The farthest thing from Jacko's Texas basso profundo possible.

"This is Lauren Dare. How did you get this number?" she asked suspiciously. Because she did not give it out easily. Perhaps ten people had the number.

"Ah—Suzanne Huntington gave it to me, I—I hope that is all right? I met with her this afternoon for a commission." The male voice suddenly quavered.

She took a deep breath. *Start as you mean to go on.* She'd just been handed her life back. Being paranoid and unpleasant would ruin her as surely as Jorge had tried to ruin her.

"Yes," she said, voice normal. "Of course. How may I help you?"

This must be Suzanne's three o'clock. The one who had looked at Jacko the way a shark looks at chum.

He must have been reassured that he hadn't been given the number of a crazy woman. "I am proceeding with a project together with Ms. Huntington—the decoration of the penthouse in the Sorenson Building. And I happened to see the show of your pictures of the homes decorated by Ms. Huntington, and I absolutely want to commission your work for the penthouse. I will have offices there and I want the artwork on the walls to be yours. I would have made an appointment tomorrow during normal office hours to begin the process but unfortunately I have been called to New York. An emergency. But I wanted to have a provisional agreement before leaving. My plane is departing later this evening, and I wonder if you could spare me ten minutes of your time. I assure you I am prepared to pay you handsomely for your work and would pay you a thousand dollars just to meet me now. What do you say?"

Wow. The penthouse of the Sorenson Building. Undoubtedly the priciest piece of real estate in Portland, in all of Oregon. Landing a commission to create illustrations, landing a *well-paying* commission...well.

Start as you mean to go on. She wanted, more than anything, a life. A successful life, doing work she enjoyed, living with Jacko. No more running, no more hiding her light under a bushel, keeping her head low.

She was free. And she had a new life to build.

"Certainly," she said crisply. "Where do you want to meet?"

"Where do you live?"

She forced herself not to hesitate. Suzanne had given him her number. Jacko was with her. It was crazy to think twice about it. "1124 Evergreen. It's near Warren Square—"

"I just put the address in my GPS, and it appears that I am not far from you. I could be there in fifteen minutes. So, may I come over? As I said, I will just take a few minutes of your time, which will be recompensed. Can you accept a check?"

"Yes, I can accept a check. And I look forward to our meeting."

Lauren had to hurry to make herself professionally presentable but before that, she had to let Felicity know she was okay. It had been on her mind a lot, that she hadn't contacted her virtual friend.

Taking her laptop out of its bag, she set up on the dining room table. In an instant she was diving into the depths of Tor.

Runner: Man, things are happening.

Felicity: Yeah, saw on the news. Your bad guy imploded, suicide by cop. What an idiot. We sure he's really dead?

Runner: Yeah.

Felicity: You sure he's not a Time Lord. Won't be coming back?

Runner: No. So I'm safe. Back in my house.

Felicity: With Captain America?

Lauren smiled. Jacko as Captain America. Well, why not? Except for the fact that he hadn't been encased in ice since World War II and didn't have a magic shield... yeah. The same.

Runner: Um, yeah.

Felicity: What's it feel like?

Runner: What does what feel like?

Felicity: Being safe. What does it feel like?

Runner: Good. Really good. Like someone has given me my life back.

Felicity: That must feel fantastic. Really...fantastic.

Runner: Will tell you all about it later. Bfn.

"Who was that on the phone?" a deep voice asked behind her.

Lauren whirled, heart in mouth. A very naked and very aroused Jacko was standing right behind her. As always he moved incredibly quietly.

"God!" She put a hand over her heart. "You have to learn to make some noise when you move, Jacko. You nearly gave me a heart attack." She waved a hand at him. "And, um, put some clothes on because *that* will definitely give me a heart attack."

"Who was it?" he repeated, going back into the bedroom.

"Dress fast. That was a client of Suzanne's. He has to leave unexpectedly but wanted to talk to me first, about a freelance assignment."

She entered the bedroom, went to her open suitcase and chose a soft turquoise sweater and black slacks. Perfectly respectable for someone who is in her own home.

Jacko was dressing, too, putting the clothes he'd been wearing back on. Lauren deliberately didn't look at him because, well…a naked Jacko was a sight, and seeing him cover up was a real shame.

He pulled up his jeans and she winced because he went commando. But he zipped up decisively without catching one hair, which showed real dexterity.

"How'd he get your number?" He pulled his long-sleeved black tee back on. Jacko never seemed to feel the cold.

Lauren applied fresh lipstick, combed her hair. Ideally she would have showered but there was no time. There'd be time after, though. Hmm. It was early evening. She had the makings of sandwiches and there were still a few beers in the fridge. Maybe they could watch TV once this man had left. Sandwiches on the coffee table, a nice action flick…

She hugged herself secretly. God, she thought that kind of thing had gone from her life forever. Such a simple thing really—watching TV on the couch with Jacko, laughing, munching. So simple, yet it seemed like heaven to her. Jacko would have some quirky take on the plot. He'd probably critique the weaponry.

"Lauren." Jacko's voice had gone deadly quiet.

"Hmm?"

"How'd this guy get your number?" He stood stock still in her bedroom, glaring fiercely at her.

"Oh, Suzanne gave it to him. What are you doing?"

He had his cell out, clicked a number on speed dial. "Checking." She could hear the voice mail message across the room. Instantly, Jacko dialed another number, probably John. Voice mail.

"Wait." Lauren laid a hand on his forearm. She could practically hear his muscles quivering. "They were going to some theater thing this evening. Suzanne designed the lobby of the theater. I remember John grumbling about going. I think he has a limit of one cultural event per month and *Inside/Out* was it, so he's pissed. But don't worry. Andrews had an appointment with Suzanne, and she knew she could give my number out."

Jacko's jaw muscles jumped as he sat down on the bed to put his boots back on.

Start as you mean to go on.

Lauren sat quietly on the bed beside him, a hand on his massive shoulder. Oh man, touching him was fantastic. It made her feel safe and excited all at once.

"Jacko." She stared at him as he kept his face stubbornly in profile, not looking at her. His vibe was strange.

Not anger. Could it be—did Jacko do anxiety? "I understand what you feel, believe me I do. But I need—I really, really need—to put this behind me and start living
a normal life. I love designing book covers but it's indoor
work. I really enjoyed creating those renderings of Suzanne's designs. I think it might be a lucrative sideline. I
think this man is going to offer me a contract. And more
might follow." She swallowed. The next words hurt, because they expressed a wish, and it had been two long
years in which she had never dared to think of anything
beyond survival. No desires allowed, just getting from
one day to the next. "I want this. Very much."

He'd finished lacing up his boots and his head hung
down as he stared at his knees. A heavy sigh. "Okay."
His deep voice was quiet.

Her doorbell rang. She sat and looked at him for a
long moment. He looked sideways at her without lifting his head.

"Doorbell."

"Yeah," she whispered.

"You should—you should get it."

A rush of joy pulsed through her. It was going to be
okay. "Yes. Yes, I will."

New Jacko followed her out her bedroom door. It was
going to take a while to train him not to be paranoid all
the time, just some of the time, but she was hopeful. She
texted Suzanne—*your three o'clock wants artwork*—and
sent it as she walked to the door.

Jacko had installed a video intercom for her. She saw
a perfectly innocuous man on the screen. Pale, looking
cold and anxious. Well, he said he had a plane to catch.

She switched on the speaker. "Yes?"

He turned eagerly to the speaker grill. "Ms. Dare?

My name is Paul Andrews? Suzanne Huntington gave me your name and cell phone number? I'm here to speak briefly about a commission?"

Each sentence was couched as a question. Face scrunched with anxiety.

Lauren swung wide the front door, Jacko right behind her. "How do you do, Mr.—" she began.

He stepped smartly into the room, took a gun out of his pocket, aimed at Jacko and shot twice. Jacko fell heavily to the ground.

Lauren stood still, too shocked to move.

The man pivoted to her. She saw the syringe too late. Something stabbed deeply and painfully into her neck and she simply switched off.

TWELVE

FREDERICK WONDERED WHETHER the thug was dead. Should he should bend down, touch two fingers to the side of the neck, find out? But he didn't want to touch the man, and he especially didn't want to get his shoes dirty with the blood spreading out from under this Morton Jackman.

It was imperative to get Anne Lowell out of the house and on their way to the airport. Time was pressing. It would be disastrous to be stuck all night at the airport with a kidnapping victim. Of course, Frederick would keep her under, but still. It was one thing to have a hidden briefcase, quite another to have an abducted woman on the plane. Plus, he'd promised his anonymous benefactor a living, breathing—but no one said anything about conscious—Anne Lowell by early tomorrow morning, and he had every intention of keeping his promise.

The man sounded like a good client. There might be more work coming from that quarter. A successful professional cultivates his clientele.

Frederick looked around, wondering what clues he was leaving. He hadn't touched the door and he was wearing latex gloves anyway. He'd made sure to keep his hands out of the reach of the intercom camera.

He had the gun and he had the syringe. Something white was in her hand. Cell phone. He nudged it away from her hand with his shoe and stamped on it heavily, repeatedly until nothing usable was left. If anyone was looking for her, there'd be no cell signal at all to follow. He'd used an untraceable cell to call her but better safe than sorry. He'd get rid of his cell and his shoes as fast as possible.

He bent down. Lifting a woman who was deadweight from the ground was not easy, even though Anne Lowell was slender. Though he hated to admit it, Frederick's knees were not what they once were. When he lifted the woman in his arms, he staggered. Carrying her in his arms as he would a child was not going to be feasible, not with the snow and ice outside. He shifted her torso, placing her over his shoulder in a fireman's lift.

Excellent. That worked.

Frederick stood unsteadily, looking down at the thug. The thug had dark skin, but was turning dusky pale from blood loss. His lips were turning white. If he wasn't dead, he would be soon.

Had the bullets gone clear through or were they still in Jackman's body? It didn't really make any difference. Even if they had gone through he didn't have time to look for them, and if they were still inside he definitely didn't have time to probe.

The gun had been "cold" anyway. Untraceable. He hadn't handled the bullets in any way; the gun was pre-loaded. He'd had an extra magazine, just in case. He hadn't expected a gun fight, which he knew he'd lose. He was a thinker not a shooter. He had to catch this Jackman totally by surprise—and he had.

All his meticulous planning had paid off. In one twenty-four-hour period, he'd discovered Anne Lowell's new identity, tracked her down, eliminated her protection and was bringing her back to his new employer.

Not bad. Not bad at all.

He'd probably have to sacrifice Paul Andrews and that was a pity. Eggs and omelets.

It had turned sleety outside. It was hard to walk in the icy snow with a full-grown woman on his shoulder. Hauling a woman over a shoulder in the open where anyone could see him was dangerous, but he took his time. A slip would be disastrous. And the weather was keeping everyone indoors. Not a car had passed since he'd parked at the curb.

He reached the rental, bent at the knees and put her in the front passenger seat. He'd thought of and discarded the idea of placing her lying down on the backseat. On the one hand, she'd be out of sight. On the other, if by some wild and disastrous chance he was pulled over, a passed-out woman buckled in next to him was easier to explain than an unconscious woman lying on the backseat. Plus, this way he could keep an eye on her. He wasn't entirely certain of the effects of these preloaded syringes. He'd been told that the range of unconsciousness went from an hour to three hours, but of course metabolisms differed. He'd keep another syringe handy, and if she showed signs of coming round, he'd simply jab her again.

He struggled to get her sitting in the passenger seat, but finally managed. The seat belt went around her shoulder and waist, plasticuffs around the wrists, and he stood, a bit winded, but happy with the results.

The seat belt held her tightly upright, head slumped forward. She looked like an attractive woman who'd been partying too much. Happened all the time.

Perfect.

Frederick got quietly into the rental and drove off, now happy for the heavy snowfall that had masked him walking out from Anne Lowell's house with her over his shoulder.

All in all, this was shaping up into a most satisfactory and remunerative job.

THE WORLD WAS pain. Every kind of pain there was. Sharp and dull. Piercing and throbbing. Pain everywhere, but concentrated in pounding pulses in his right shoulder.

Jacko tried to lift his head to look at his shoulder and while he was at it, try to figure out what the fuck was going on. But when he lifted the back of his head an inch, it was too much. His head thudded back to the floor and he blacked out.

The next time he came to, he was able to orient himself better. Lauren's house. Floor. Blood. His own. He tried to lift himself up on his elbow and blacked out again.

He swam back to consciousness. He was able to lift his hand enough to glance at his diver's watch to see it was 8:15 before blacking out again.

He came to fifteen minutes later, at 8:30. The floor felt tacky with blood. His. He had time and place and pain. But this time he realized Lauren was gone and the pain was nothing. His body screamed in protest as he lifted himself up on the elbow of the uninjured arm, came up on a knee, then up on shaking legs.

He nearly blacked out again but hung on grimly because *no Lauren* was infinitely worse than any pain his body could feel.

He'd spent a year in the most intense training in the world in which DIs screamed continuously that pain was weakness leaving the body. This didn't feel like that, though. This was pain *and* weakness. But if he'd learned one thing in training and in his eight years as a SEAL, it was that he was stronger than his body. When his body told him to quit, he didn't.

And if Lauren was missing, he couldn't.

Lauren.

He turned his head, seeking. It hurt. He ignored it. Blackness was at the edge of his vision but he scanned the room as fast as he could, looking for her. He was thorough but he knew she wasn't there. She was gone. The house had an unmistakably empty feel to it. Humans emanated some kind of vibration he was sensitive to. He was always point man going in because he could always tell if he was entering a space that was inhabited or not.

No Lauren. And the only blood was his.

Something on the floor. He bent to pick it up, nearly blacked out. He stood, swaying, for a full minute until blood could flow back to his head. He'd been wounded many times and knew that he was suffering from severe blood loss. But…fuck that. He didn't have time to get medical care, a transfusion. Because what he was holding was ….

Memory rushed back in. Lauren, carrying her cell, tapping in a text message as she walked to the door. What he held was shards of plastic, a lithium battery, a shattered chip. Someone had taken Lauren's cell phone and broken it. The white plastic had dark marks, some mud. Probably from a shoe.

The last few minutes before blacking out bloomed in his head. Lauren, answering the door. Jacko had been right behind her. She'd started to greet the man—tall, slender, dressed in expensive clothes, stylish black hat, the man he'd seen walking into the compound—and the man had pivoted without hesitation and fired at Jacko.

Getting rid of Lauren's protector first.

226 MIDNIGHT VENGEANCE

Even if Jacko'd had time to react, he couldn't have because his weapon had been back in the bedroom. He'd done that deliberately because he knew Lauren wanted this job, and knew she probably wouldn't get it if by her side was a glowering guy who looked like him, hand on sidearm.

Scare the shit out of her client.

Except that if Jacko had had his weapon, he'd have nailed the fucker for sure and Lauren would be exactly where she should be—by his side.

Instead of gone.

He could barely think. Spots danced in front of his eyes. He could block out the pain—no one could become a SEAL and not know how to block pain—but he was losing blood and he was fucking *weak*.

He stepped forward toward the front door, not knowing what he was doing, without any kind of a plan, just knowing that she must have gone out through that door with Hat Man, and so like a dumb animal he was going to follow. But his body betrayed him. His legs wouldn't hold him and he slipped to one knee. His head drooped forward, too heavy for his neck to support it. He watched as blood oozed out of his chest and dripped to the floor. Dripped, not spurted. Not arterial.

Dumbass. Of course. If it had been arterial blood he'd be dead by now. He shook his head sharply, trying to shake himself awake.

Took a deep breath. Could do it. No pulmonary atelectasis. Not lung shot. But deep tissue damage nonetheless.

Hat Man had killed Lauren's cell thinking she couldn't be tracked. But Jacko had a tactile memory of tracing the chain around her neck, feeling the silky softness of her skin beneath his fingers. He could follow her, but he couldn't do this alone.

He pulled out his own cell, punched a number.

"Yo. Jacko my man. 'Sup?" Metal's deep voice sounded reassuring. Jacko clung to it the way a mountaineer clings to a fissure in the rock.

"Shot," he gasped.

"Where?" Metal rapped out, all focus. Like Jacko he could react instantly to an emergency.

Where? Jacko could barely focus. "Lauren's…house."

An electronic beep and he could hear a vehicle start up. "No. Where were you shot?"

"Shoulder." He took in a painful breath. "Twice."

"Okay, I'm on my way—"

"No!" Jacko tried to shout but it came out more a low groan. "Not…here. Someone…took Lauren." Saying the words was more painful than his wounds. He sent the tracker code to Metal. "Sending tracker…coordinates. We…go…"

He stopped, wheezing, unable to say anything more. But he didn't need to.

"Got it. She's on Bleecker Avenue." Silence. "Are you thinking what I'm thinking?"

"Mmm." Bleecker led to Washington, which was then a straight shot up the freeway to the airport. If she got into the air, she was gone. The tracker had a radius of only ten miles. "Bad."

"Yeah. I'm on the other side of town—it'll take me some time. Weather's bad."

"Taking…bike."

"Negative," Metal said sharply. "You're wounded. I can make it faster than you."

"No." Through the haze, only one thing was crystal

clear, surer than death. He was going after Lauren. He was going after his woman. "Taking…bike."

He had his bike, as always, loaded in the back of his SUV. It would make faster time than the vehicle—he could take shortcuts. He was trying to map out a route in his head when Metal spoke again.

"Any crackling sounds when you breathe?"

He breathed in. It was hard to hear if his chest crackled over the sound of blood pounding in his head. "No," he said finally after a couple of breaths.

"No subcutaneous emphysema, didn't get your lung— that's good. How much blood have you lost?"

Jacko was staggering to the door, opened it, looked out in the snowy darkness toward his vehicle. It looked miles away. A continent away. "Some," he said.

"Jesus, Jacko. Don't do it. Let me go." Jacko could hear a tap. "I'm 8.7 miles away. Maybe I can make it."

Jacko was 5.2 miles away. But even if he'd been a thousand miles away there was no question what he had to do. "Going."

Jacko could hear a big gusty sigh. "Christ," was all Metal said. "I'll check in. Put your cell on the holder in the handlebars and switch on the audio in your helmet. I'll keep track of both of you. Weather's bad, Jacko."

Jacko stopped for a second, tilted his head to the sky. Massive snowflakes were falling, dulling sound, dropping visibility. He turned slowly to look behind him, at the slug-like tracks of his feet. He was shuffling. Not good.

"Yeah. Weather's…a bitch."

"It'll slow him down, too. Who's the fucker who took Lauren?"

"Can't…talk." Jacko was almost at the back of his

SUV. He reached it and leaned against the side of the vehicle for a long moment.

"Okay. Doesn't matter. Fucker's going down. I'm on the road—we'll meet where Lauren is and get her."

Jacko nodded, unable to speak, and tapped End Call. He pulled up the tracker app superimposed on a map of Portland. There she was on Bleecker. Almost six miles away. Getting farther away with every passing second. There was no way he would allow her to get to the ten-mile mark. No way he was going to lose her.

He pulled open the back of the SUV, pulled down the ramp.

Pulling his bike out and rolling it down to the ground was something he'd done thousands of times. He didn't even think about it. He wanted his bike on the ground, a little effort and then there it was, ready for him to ride.

Now? Now it could have been on Everest. On the fuck-ing *moon*. God, only one way to do this. The hard way. He reached out, grabbed the back tire and pulled as hard as he could. The bike came tumbling down, landing on its side.

If anyone else had dared to do that to his bike he'd have killed him.

He stood, panting, looking at his bike lying on its side like a wounded beast. Snow was already sticking to the deep red paint, red and white. Just like the ground at his feet. Red and white.

He was losing a lot of blood. His emergency aid kit was stowed neatly against the side. He opened it, pulled out a package of QuikClot, ripping it open with his teeth.

He kept his riding leathers neatly folded inside a gym bag. Wrestling the bag to the edge of the ramp, he pulled out his motorcycle jacket. It even had armor plates in the front in case he ever took a fall from the bike. Or got shot. Bit superfluous now.

The jacket was deliberately tight so there'd be no wind resistance. Hurt like a fucker to zip it up but he finally did it.

He checked his cell. Lauren was 7.7 miles away. In a little while she'd be lost to him. Portland airport was big. Hat Guy wouldn't put her on a commercial flight but he could have a private jet anywhere on the tarmac. Once she took off, Jacko would never find her.

No one to shoot at.

Speaking of which…he'd forgotten his weapon. Which was unheard of for a SEAL. A SEAL felt for his weapon first thing in the morning, last thing at night. Lucky thing Jacko believed in redundancy. He reached, wincing, for the gym bag again and pulled out his Beretta Pico with three magazines, because if it took a firefight to get Lauren back, so be it. He put the pistol and magazines in the jacket pocket and zipped the pocket closed. He had a shoulder holster but it wouldn't fit under the tight jacket. Full-face helmet and gloves and he was ready to go. Pulling his bike upright was merely a question of more pain.

Piece of cake.

The snow was coming in flurries mixed with ice so thick it pinged against his helmet. Soon, it would be hard for a car to make it over the streets, but not his bike. He pulled out his cell again and saw that Lauren was 9.1 miles away but the speed of the vehicle she was in had slowed.

That's right, you son of a bitch. Weather will slow you way down but not me.

He switched on his engine and felt the familiar power between his thighs. He was good on his bike, the movements familiar and smooth. He pulled out, pulled away, chest touching the tank, making his corners tight because he had a lot of ground to cover and not much time.

He kept his cell on a special holder on the handlebars, keeping Lauren's position and his position on the screen, with an overlay of a map of Portland. It shifted as the car made its way down Bleecker. Slowly. Well there was an app for that. Speed. Jacko was all about speed, especially on his bike. He'd topped 150 miles per hour on race tracks. Speed had always been his friend.

Except when he raced, he had full use of his body. He steered with the handlebars but with his body, too. And right now, his body wasn't very responsive. His right side hurt like a bitch. *Hurt* was the wrong word. It felt like someone was sticking red hot knives in him. He could ignore pain but he couldn't ignore the weakness. Without the full use of his right arm and hand, his steering was seriously compromised.

No matter. He'd have gone as fast as he could even if someone had lopped off his right arm, because with each gear change and increase in speed the space between the green dot that was him and the red dot that was Lauren decreased. Nothing else existed in his world but that red dot and watching while he raced to her, gaining on that fucker who'd kidnapped her.

He had to get to her, had to. He had to save her because the future without Lauren was this vast featureless emptiness he couldn't face. He'd never had a woman of his own, hadn't wanted one. But Lauren? Now that he had her he would never let her go. Couldn't. She gave his life color and warmth. A reason to come home. It felt like he'd just now discovered sex though he'd been fucking since he was thirteen. That wasn't what he had with

Lauren. What they had was something else completely. He'd found it only with her, and it would disappear out of his life forever if she died.

If she died, his entire life would be one long wait to die himself.

And he hadn't told her he loved her.

That was what burned most of all, the thought that if she died, she'd die not knowing what he felt. Bad enough that he'd wasted four fucking months circling her, scared shitless of her.

He wasn't going to lose her, not now, not when they had a life to build together.

The roads were icy but he knew exactly what he was doing. He knew exactly how to get to that red dot that could just as well have been his heart, beating out of his chest. He had maps in his head. He'd never been lost after seeing a map, even once. And since he'd been in Portland he'd crisscrossed it endless times. He cut through a city park, knowing exactly where the benches were, where the fountain was.

He crossed through backyards, knowing which had fences and which didn't.

With every passing minute, he drew closer. It was as if the red dot was standing still and he was an arrow that had been shot from a powerful bow.

Down two side streets the wrong way, jumping over a small meridian, going into a controlled slide, then upright again and shooting through a parking lot, sailing over a small ditch right onto Bleecker Street. It was almost empty. Good.

He checked the cell. They were separated by the width of a finger. If it weren't snowing, he'd be able to see the car. He increased his speed slightly, bent lower and...

there it was! Two red taillights, the fucker braking constantly.

He hadn't told Lauren he loved her. He was going to, as soon as he could.

But first—

Jacko understood cars and bikes and vectors. He knew exactly where to ram the car. If Lauren weren't in it, he'd ram the shithead right off the road, but he had Lauren so this would go more slowly than Jacko liked. Though the end result was never in doubt.

He'd lost a lot of blood. He was conscious because he narrowed his focus so tightly he was only aware of the back fender and the two red taillights looking like the eyes of Satan.

He kicked it up a gear and rammed the car from the right. The driver overreacted, braked heavily, started to spin. Fucker didn't know how to drive in the snow.

Jacko rammed the other side and felt the driver lose control, just a little. He turned right and came up against the passenger side window and there she was! Slumped against the window, face pale in the darkness. It was impossible to see whether she was conscious or not.

The pistol in his pocket felt heavy. Such an easy thing to take it out and shoot the driver point blank in the face. His fingers itched to do it.

But the driver had sped up, was fishtailing. Jacko couldn't be one hundred percent certain that his shot would hit the driver and not Lauren, and he wasn't going to shoot unless he had that certainty. Even if he came up on the driver's side and shot him in the head he couldn't be absolutely sure it wouldn't go through the son of a bitch's head and hit Lauren, too.

He was used to problems that could be solved with a

well-aimed shot but this wasn't one of them. He had to stop the driver with his bike. Jacko rammed him again and saw the driver flail, saw his hand slip on the gear stick.

Did Lauren have her eyes open? She wouldn't recognize him in his full-face helmet.

Hold on, Lauren, he thought. *I love you.*

LAUREN'S EYES FLUTTERED open briefly, then closed. She licked dry lips, tasted bitterness in her mouth. Her head leaned against something cold and hard. It hurt fiercely, as if someone had hammered nails into her skull. Shifting her head slightly hurt so much she thought she was going to throw up. She swallowed bile, knowing instinctively she couldn't throw up—it would be dangerous.

She didn't know where she was but a sense of menace was in the air, so powerful it penetrated even the fog in her brain.

She hurt all over but especially on the side of her neck, a deep pointed pain.

Eyes closed, she tried to take stock. A deep rumbling sound. A car. Someone next to her, close to her, cursing. A man. The car was starting and stopping and every time it stopped something tightened against her chest, across her waist. The seat belt. She was tied in to a car seat by a seat belt pulled way too tight. She flexed her hands slightly and discovered they were tied together with unbreakable plastic handcuffs.

Darkness behind her closed eyelids, interspersed with weak light. They were on a road with streetlights.

The sound of the engine rose when the vehicle took a tight corner. When the car turned, she shifted in the seat, rolling with the motion. She didn't try to resist but rolled loosely with it. For a second the car slid, tires no longer gripping the road. A vicious curse came from next to her. A male voice. Not Jacko.

Jacko!

Memory rushed in. Opening the door, Suzanne's client entering and, in a move so outrageous she didn't believe her eyes, pulling out a gun.

Shooting Jacko.

Jacko on the ground, lifeless. Then the man sticking her with a needle and then darkness. He'd killed Jacko and then drugged her. Where he punctured the skin it hurt, but it didn't hurt as much as the thought of Jacko, dead. She tightened her closed eyes, willing the tears back. Tears could be fatal.

Whoever had taken her obviously thought she was still out. She couldn't afford to cry. If the driver turned around and saw tears he'd know she was conscious.

Like a suddenly gravityless planet, she understood Jacko's importance in her life by its absence. She understood how much she looked forward to living with him, having him in her life. His massive quiet presence, that stoic face that never betrayed any emotion. Though she was starting to decode that face and understand the strong emotions beneath the impassive façade. She was starting to read him.

He'd surrounded her with loving care, and now he was dead.

Killed by the man driving the car.

Son of a bitch.

She was weak still, with no strength in her arms, brain still fuzzy with the effects of whatever it was he'd injected her with. She was helpless. Her only hope was to gather strength as quickly as she could, let the drug dissipate in her system, gain consciousness and then try to kill the sick bastard driving even if it cost her own life.

He was going down.

He wasn't going to kill Jacko and get away with it. Not while she could draw a breath. She was perfectly willing to die to bring him down, and she didn't care. The bastard had killed a magnificent man, *her* man, and he was going to pay.

So she played possum while trying to draw deep breaths, keeping it quiet. The fog in her head lifted slowly, dissipating unevenly like mist under the morning sun. Her hands and feet, the extremities, had been numb. Now feeling was coming back, more slowly to her hands, which were tightly bound. No matter. She could use her feet. If she had to destroy him with her teeth, she would. Nothing was going to stop her.

She flexed one hand slowly, then the other. Slowly pointed one toe then another. Took more deep breaths. Awareness grew stronger with each passing minute.

Slowly, imperceptibly, she opened her eyes a crack again, looked out the window. They were in the middle of a snowstorm. Small globes of light slowly pulsed in the sky. The streetlights, high overhead. The kind of streetlights on highways. The windshield wipers made a heavy sound as they tried to shift heavy masses of snow from the windshield.

The car slid again as they hit a patch of ice. Dark curses came from the driver. He had a light tenor. The voice of the man who'd called her up, who'd appeared at her door.

The man who'd killed Jacko.

Rage welled up inside her, an almost unstoppable wave of it, black and so bitter she thought she'd choke on it.

Hot and primitive. She wanted to slash his chest open, yank out his beating heart and slice it to shreds. Make him pay in pain and blood.

Make him suffer, make him...

A powerful thump came from behind the car. It fishtailed, the driver cursing as he fought the wheel. Another thump from the other side and the car started into a tailspin, straightened out at the last second.

Lauren kept her face averted, leaning against the cold windowpane. Through barely opened eyes she could see the faint reflection of the driver's face against the dark car windshield, lit by the dashboard lights. Lit from below, his face looked like that of a demon.

Maybe she didn't have to be so cautious. He never looked to his right toward her, not once. Right now she could probably shout and flail and he wouldn't pay her any attention. He was too busy trying to keep the car on the road. Another hard thump and he slammed his fist on the steering wheel in frustration as the car sideslipped again.

It was dark, the bright headlights throwing light ahead, sleety snow visible only in the cones of light. The wind was howling so strong it drove the snow sideways in frenzied flurries.

Another hard thump, from somewhere close to the passenger side door. The driver was screaming in frustration now. The car was barely in his control.

Her thought processes were so very slow, like walking through sludge. It took her a full minute to realize that someone was trying to get the driver to stop. Why? Were they under attack? Did this man have enemies who were trying to stop him?

The next thump was so close it could be felt through

the car door, the noise rising above the wind. She opened
her eyes again and saw...she opened her eyes wider. She
saw someone right outside her car window, so close she
could touch him if the window weren't closed. It was
a man, no question. Dressed in a biker jacket molded
around massive shoulders. The biker had a red helmet
and a dark visor. There was no way to know who he
was. Then the biker turned his head, looking straight
at her, and though she couldn't see him, her heart made
a wild leap in her chest because her heart knew before
her head did.

Jacko!

Jacko somehow come back from the dead, coming
to rescue her.

The driver turned his head to look at Jacko, face frozen in a snarl. He didn't even notice that Lauren was conscious. He only had eyes for Jacko, who was in his way.
Without warning, the man swerved the car to the right,
trying to bump Jacko off the road.

But somehow Jacko knew because he suddenly braked,
falling behind, the car swerving uselessly.

Oh God. Even knowing that Jacko was saving his own
life, she felt bereft. Seeing him on his bike, a massive
force of nature curved forward, huge gloved hands on
the handlebars, made her feel better. As if there could
be some hope after all.

Because this wasn't going to end well. A bike against
a car—death was riding right behind the biker.

There he was again, looking into the vehicle. He
seemed like an otherworldly creature, faceless, barely
human with the visor and jacket with plates set into it like
the carapace of a dinosaur. Some creature from the mists
of time. The big gloved hands moved on the handlebars

and the heavy bike slammed again into the door and the driver screamed with rage and frustration.

The biker disappeared. Lauren didn't dare swivel her head to see if she could catch a glimpse of him. Her heart gave a sharp punch in her chest. Had something happened to him, happened to Jacko? Had he crashed that big bike? Conditions on the road were horrible, the tires barely gaining traction, visibility down to a few feet. A car was heavier than a bike and this car was barely holding on to the road.

Was Jacko even now lying in a ditch, bleeding out? And—could that have really been Jacko or was she hallucinating, the drug making her see what her heart wanted to see? Jacko, alive and here with her.

Of course it wasn't Jacko. Now that the fog in her head was clearing, she distinctly remembered him being shot. Maybe twice. Things were fuzzy in her memory so she didn't remember exactly how many times he'd been shot, but that he'd been shot was beyond doubt.

Everything else was hazy but that image—it would stay with her for the rest of her days, however long she had left to live. The man pulling up his arm with a gun at the end of it, shooting Jacko. Jacko knocked off his feet, sprawled on his back, eyes closed, bleeding.

That was her last image of him before the man had plunged a needle into her neck.

So how could the rider be Jacko? The biker was someone who had to be after the driver, an enemy somehow. Had to be. It had nothing to do with her.

She heard tapping then the driver talking. The glow of a cell phone was reflected in the windshield. "Yes," the man said impatiently. "I know the weather is deteriorating. *When* are they closing down the airport? Shit.

Okay, I'm not far. I'll be there in about half an hour. Be ready to take off immediately."

Airport? Take off?

Oh God. He was taking her to a plane? A plane could fly anywhere. Doubtless he'd drug her again and she'd wake up who knew where? No one would know where she was. She'd be lost, friendless. At least in Portland she had Jacko's friends and colleagues. They'd look for her; they'd care. John Huntington has said she was "one of ours." Outside Portland…outside Portland she had literally no one in the world.

She had to escape before this terrible man put her on a plane. Her life was lost if she didn't. But she didn't have anything. Her hands were literally tied. How could she…

Another huge thump, the hardest yet, from the other side of the car, the driver's side. He almost lost control of the car. Lauren could smell him now—the tangy acrid sweat of fear. She heard him fumbling with his coat and saw him draw something out, a familiar shape in the reflection of the windshield.

A gun! He lifted the gun, driving one-handed. The gun was positioned across his chest, aiming out the window at the biker. Lauren finally turned her head, not caring if the driver caught on that she was awake.

She didn't give a damn because awareness flooded through her. The man on the motorcycle keeping pace with the car was Jacko and the driver was going to shoot him. There was no way Lauren was going to let that happen. She'd die first. She quietly unlatched her seat belt. The driver's arm lifted…

"No!" she screamed and launched herself at the driver. She used her body, her teeth and fists. She swung her tied fists at his face, straight at his nose, screaming at the top of her lungs. He lifted an arm, eyes so wide she could see the whites of them. He had a berserker where he thought he had a drugged woman. Screaming at the top of her lungs, she batted at him, trying to hurt him with every cell of her body. He shouted when she latched onto his ear with her teeth, snarling and tugging until she felt cartilage in her mouth coated with the salty taste of blood. The space was so small he couldn't defend himself against her as she writhed and swatted and crashed against him, bringing her tied hands up to his eyes, thumbs gouging.

The driver knocked her hard with his elbow and for a second she saw stars but her rage was stronger than the blow. With a wild primitive cry she launched herself against him again and the car slid, almost floated in a soundless free fall and then they left the road and tumbled, rolling over and over down a hill.

Lauren instinctively tried to brace herself but there was no possibility of it; it was like being a towel in the spinner, crashing helplessly against the ceiling, the dashboard, the door...

When they finally came to rest upside down she hung from the seat belt. A silence that felt like death and then blackness.

She came awake to the sound of a man cursing in a deep voice and metal tearing. The narrow beam of a flashlight illuminated the wreckage. Tears ran down her cheeks. She lifted a hand, saw something dark on the palm. Not tears. Blood.

And then her door was yanked open and the swirling snowstorm entered the car, the bitter cold hitting her like a wall. Something flashed—a knife?—and she was freed from the restraining straps of the seat belt and fell painfully, curled on the roof. A man was tugging at her arm, pulling her out, away from the car, over the frozen snow to a flat surface.

She could barely breathe, limbs paralyzed. She stared up at the night sky, snowflakes falling on her face.

An alien had rescued her, bigheaded, with scales on his chest and no face. She blinked against the snow.

"Lauren!" Something lifted and she saw Jacko. A pale Jacko, skin nearly bloodless and white, not the rich color she loved. Deep lines bracketed his mouth. He was breathing hard, wheezing. "Say something!"

It hurt but it had to be done. She lifted a trembling hand, touched his skin. It was him. Not an illusion. It was Jacko, a trembling wounded Jacko, but alive. Could she smile at him? She tried to but she couldn't control the muscles of her face.

"Talk to me!" His voice was deep but weak.

"Jacko." Her voice was weak, barely carrying over the wind.

"I love you," he whispered and closed his eyes, falling forward onto her, torso covering her, shielding her from the snow, from all bad things, even from death.

And that was how Metal found them—unconscious, Jacko protecting her even close to death.

EPILOGUE

Two weeks later

"THEY'RE _GORGEOUS_." LAUREN LIFTED a pair of red Louboutin stilettos—red!—by the ankle straps out of the box. In the past two years she'd become used to ballerinas and running shoes and it would probably take a little practice to walk on them, but who cared? They were beautiful and she was going to wear them every chance she got. They were sitting on her sofa and Jacko's arm was around her. If his stitches bothered him, he didn't show it.

"Glad you like them."

"Did you have help choosing them?" Because Lauren had some difficulties imagining Jacko in the upscale shoe store, pondering colors and style.

He winced.

"Not a good memory?" she smiled.

"I cheated. Suzanne bought them for me."

"Well, always go to the expert, right?" She was grateful. Jacko had fantastic qualities but probably good taste in shoes wasn't one of them. "Suzanne's taste is exquisite."

He breathed what felt like a sigh of relief.

Lauren stole a glance at him. "When I wear these I'll be taller than you are."

Jacko snorted. "In your dreams."

Yes, in her dreams. Even in her nosebleed shoes the

top of her head would barely reach his nose. Still, it was fun teasing him. "That made you smile."

The corner of his mouth lifted. "It did. 'Cause it was so preposterous."

Lauren laughed. Of all the things she thought might happen while living with Jacko, laughing often wasn't one of them. And yet… She found herself laughing several times a day. He had a wild, dry sense of humor that had totally escaped her notice while she was escaping a killer, before they'd nearly been killed. It was one of the many, many things about him she loved.

Like the fact that he would think to buy her red Louboutins. That earned him serious credit.

Jacko nudged the box with his knee. "You might want to look more carefully inside that box."

Lauren's eyes rounded. "There's something else?"

"Hmm." It was a noise she was familiar with. A sort of deep hum that made her diaphragm vibrate, and it could mean a million different things. In this case it meant *yes*.

The other thing she'd told him she wanted was a puppy but there definitely wasn't one in the box. Puppies and Louboutins didn't go together. She scrambled around, pulling out the tissue paper, frowning…and there they were.

"Jacko!" She held the tickets in her hand. The latest Cirque du Soleil show, in town for only a week. She'd heard they were impossible to find. "Did you have to shoot someone to get them? Because if you did, that is totally justified."

He gave a lazy half smile, watching her pleasure out of slitted eyes. Suddenly the smile stopped and he watched her carefully. A big hand fell on her shoulder. "You gonna be okay with it? Because I can always dig up the bodies and give the tickets back to their heirs."

She clutched the tickets to her chest. "No way!"

She still had some problems with being in large crowds but it was getting better. And, well, Cirque…

The trouble was over. She knew that intellectually. Everyone who could possibly want her dead was dead. Through lawyers she'd renounced the entire Guttierez estate and had no connection with any part of the criminal empire that was going to keep public prosecutors busy rubbing their hands with glee for the next decade.

So that was Jorge.

For Frederick Rydell it had all been about her mother's jewels. The man after her had confessed for a reduced sentence. He'd been hired to kidnap her so she could get her mother's jewels. There'd been more than she had imagined. Lauren had had the key to her mother's safe deposit box at a bank in Palm Beach. She refused to leave Jacko's side so she'd hired another lawyer and given him a proxy to open the box, together with a copy of the key.

Inside had been a fortune in historical jewels.

The jewels, assessed at forty million dollars, were slated for an auction organized by Sotheby's and she had already earmarked everything but one million dollars for art scholarships. The one million she was going to keep was for buying her house and establishing college funds for the three kids Jacko didn't know they were going to have.

He'd just have to deal.

So, really, no one at the moment wanted to kill her.

There was no reason for her to be afraid ever again, but the instincts she'd honed on the run were hard to shake. The first time they'd gone to the mall she'd started trembling and hyperventilating. Though she'd insisted she was fine, Jacko took her home. The second time she went she lasted half an hour before the shakes started. But two days ago, looking for a new couch, she completely forgot about her agoraphobia.

Through everything, Jacko had been a rock. He never said a word, just noticed when she started panicking, though she tried to hide it, and quietly took her home. She'd had a couple of nightmares and he held her and loved them away.

Every day she felt stronger. More like her old, pre-Jorge self.

She nestled her head against Jacko's left shoulder, careful to keep away from the slight swell of bandages on the right side of his chest. Luckily his chest was about an acre in size. He picked up her hand that was holding the tickets. "You want to go out to eat before the show?"

Lauren turned her head to kiss his chest. "There's a new Cuban restaurant not far from the theater. You okay with spicy?"

"Hmm," he said. But there was a gleam in his eye. "On a dare in Thailand I ate a curry that was sixteen million on the Scoville scale. Nothing can scare me again. I'm immune to chili peppers. The experience changed my DNA."

Lauren rolled her eyes. "You're lucky you still have taste buds. That's like an atom bomb."

"We trained for hot chili peppers in the SEALs," he said with a straight face. "So let's go to the Cuban—"

The refrain of "Who Let the Dogs Out?" sounded. Jacko dropped a kiss on her hair while picking up his cell. He got up and walked to the door. "Metal. Coming up the driveway. He's taking the staples out."

Lauren sighed. Jacko trusted Metal more than he trusted the hospital doctors. Said Metal had way more experience with gunshot wounds than any hospital doctor could ever have. Maybe so. Though Metal had such huge hands...not a surgeon's hands at all.

Metal walked into her living room, dressed in a tee and jean jacket though it was freezing cold outside. Like Jacko, he never seemed to feel the cold. He brought in energy and the metallic smell of snow with him and was carrying a doctor's medical case.

"Lauren." Metal bent low to kiss her cheek, cocked a thumb at Jacko. "So how's my patient? He been good? If you don't make a fuss when I take out your stitches I've got a lollipop with me."

Jacko shot him the bird and Metal laughed. He settled Jacko in the kitchen, washed his hands thoroughly with an antiseptic soap that smelled like a hospital, and snapped on latex gloves. "Show the nice lady your muscles, Jacko," Metal said as he brought out a big gauze square and started laying out instruments on it.

Jacko shrugged out of his shirt. Lauren took it from him, placing a hand on his shoulder. Touching him always thrilled her but she also wanted to reassure him. Not that he needed it. Jacko looked bored with the procedure. One thing she'd discovered while Jacko was in the hospital—he hated being sick. She knew he couldn't wait to get the stitches out.

Metal's hands were big but gentle as he carefully removed the bandage. He checked the bandage and grunted in satisfaction. The inside of the bandage was pristine white. No bleeding or even scabbing. Jacko had told Lauren that SEALs had special super-healing powers and she'd laughed. But he was healing remarkably well from two bullet wounds, so maybe SEALs really did have special powers.

Metal placed cotton in the grip of forceps, bathed the cotton with antiseptic and cleaned the wounds, both of which were closed with staples. Then he picked up a strange-looking set of curved scissors and started prying up the first staple. "Ouch," Lauren said in sympathy as Metal took the first staple out of Jacko's chest and dropped it into a stainless steel tray. Jacko himself would probably have his teeth pulled without benefit of anesthesia rather than make a sound. He didn't even wince.

Macho idiot.

She stretched to kiss his cheek. "That *ouch* was for you since you're not going to say it."

Jacko turned his head and his face was no longer impassive. She knew that look very well and it was always a precursor to blinding pleasure.

"Not now, kids," Metal said mildly as he dropped another staple into the tray.

Jacko'd almost died. Metal had found them in the nick of time. The doctors said that Jacko had lost nearly four liters of blood, almost incompatible with life. They started infusing him in the ambulance as they raced through the snowy streets.

The doctors had said that Jacko's chest muscles were so dense, it was almost as if he'd been wearing armor. That, and the fact that the bullet aimed at his heart ricocheted off a rib, had saved his life. Still, he'd been in surgery for three nail-biting hours.

The doctors had wanted to keep Lauren overnight but against medical advice she'd signed herself out and sat vigil in the hospital waiting room.

One by one all the members of ASI had come trickling into the waiting room where Lauren and Metal held vigil. Suzanne and John had arrived after Jacko had been in surgery for an hour. Suzanne had rushed to her and hugged her, and that was when Lauren had broken down. Douglas and Allegra, Claire and Bud and all the ASI operatives came. Lauren discovered just how beloved Jacko was.

Absolutely. He deserved love. He was brave and loyal and smart. She prayed every second he was in surgery that he'd come back to her.

When a deeply exhausted surgeon came in at three in the morning to say that Jacko would live, her legs gave out and only Metal's lightning reflexes kept her from crumpling to the floor.

Another staple fell with a clink into the tray. "Jesus," Metal grumbled. "Staples. What is this? 1999?"

Lauren looked at Jacko's chest, absolutely determined to do it clinically, totally ignoring how hot he looked shirtless. She bent to his chest and examined the scars closely. The doctors had done a really good job. No redness, no infection. Jacko's dark skin was clear. He looked exactly as he'd looked before only with scars.

She smiled at him. "Scars are kinda sexy."

He smiled back. The first couple of times he'd smiled at her she'd been startled. But he was smiling more and more lately. Looked good on him. "I get points, don't I?"

She stroked his arm on the uninjured side. "Absolutely. About a billion points. You saved my life. Doesn't get more heroic than that. You have my lifelong gratitude."

"Sounds good," Metal said, removing another staple. Jacko had ten of them. "Lifelong gratitude from a pretty lady who will bite a guy's ear off for you and who is also filthy rich. Pretty good deal."

"Not *that* rich," Lauren said. "Not any more."

"We're going to buy this house," she told Metal, looking at Jacko. "And then—"

Someone pounded on her front door.

Startled, Lauren looked at Jacko. "Another present?"

But Jacko and Metal were up with guns in hand. These days Jacko was never more than one step away from a gun. He even kept one on the bedside table on his side of the bed.

When they had kids, he was going to have to do something about that.

Metal beat Jacko to the door. They all looked at the security monitor. Lauren blinked. Outside on her porch was a very pretty blond woman, face pinched and sickly pale, cold sweat coating her face, looking up at the security camera. She was shaking.

Metal pushed the button to activate the speaker.

"Lauren?" The girl's voice was weak, slightly distorted by the speaker. "Runner?"

"Felicity!" Lauren rushed to the door, opened it. The woman stumbled over the threshold. Metal caught her before she could fall to the floor, laying her gently on her back.

Her entire left side was wet with blood. Metal was gently opening her coat and shirt underneath.

He probed carefully and looked up. "Knife wound and it's serious. We need to get her to a hospital. She's lost a lot of blood."

"No!" Felicity's voice was weak but fierce. She grabbed Metal's wrist with a bloodstained hand. She looked at Metal then at Lauren then back at Metal. "No hospital! *Please.* He's after me! He'll find me in a hospital! I just escaped from one and he—" She coughed, fresh blood welling from her side. "He was there!"

Lauren kneeled down, took her hand. It was cold. "Honey, we need to get you to a doctor."

Felicity's pretty face was scrunched with pain. "Please, please," she whispered. "He'll kill me."

Metal was examining the wound. "I can take care of her," he said. "At least stop the bleeding. There's a clinic I know where we can do X-rays, operate if necessary, completely off the grid."

He turned to Felicity. To her credit, she didn't recoil at Metal's face and size. He looked terrifying if you couldn't see the kindness in him. However terrifying he looked, though, the guy after Felicity must have been even more terrifying because she didn't flinch.

"Yes, yes. Keep me off the grid." Her hand tightened on Metal's wrist and he turned his hand to hold hers. "Please." Her voice was barely audible. A shudder ran through her and her eyes closed, then opened with effort.

"You're safe," he said, deep voice reassuring.

"That—that sounds nice. Not true, but nice."

"It's true," Metal said gently, gesturing urgently to Jacko to bring his medic kit.

Felicity looked at Lauren, tried to smile. "Nice to meet you, finally." She wheezed, coughed. "You know, I've always wanted to say this." She looked at Lauren, one hand clutching Metal's hand so tightly the knuckles were white, the other reaching out. "Help me, Obi-Wan Kenobi. You're my only hope."

And then she fainted.

* * * * *